For R.
He knows why.

## About the Author

Sue Barnard was born in North Wales but has spent most of her life in and around Manchester. She studied French and Italian at Durham University, and after graduating and getting married, she had a variety of office jobs interspersed with being a full-time parent. If she had her way, the phrase "non-working mother" would be banned from the English language. She follows the principle that an immaculate house is a sign of a wasted life. Hence, her house is chaotic to ensure that her life is very fulfilled.

More recently Sue studied Creative Writing with the Open University in the UK. In addition to doing work as a freelance copywriter, she is now a published and prize-winning poet. Her mind is sufficiently warped that she has been a question-setter for BBC Radio 4's Round Britain Quiz – a phase of her life which caused one of her sons to describe her as "professionally weird." She is also very interested in family history. Her own background defies description; she'd write a book about it if she thought anyone would believe her. She now lives in Cheshire with her husband and a large collection of unfinished scribblings.

Sue joined the editorial team of Crooked Cat Publishing in 2013. The Ghostly Father is her first novel.

# Acknowledgements

I remain eternally grateful to Laurence and Steph Patterson of Crooked Cat Publishing for believing in this story, and to my editor Simon Marshall-Jones for his invaluable input throughout the editorial process. Thanks too to all the Cats and Kittens for making me so welcome.

The book would never have happened without the help and support of my many writing buddies. These include the Manchester Crafty Writers Group and the Writing Asylum, friends on Facebook and Twitter, and my tutors and fellow-students from the Open University and the various workshops run by Calum Kerr and Sally Quilford. Special thanks are due to the following friends for their encouragement and inspiration: Sister Jean Mary CHN, Father Andrew Cole, Liz Foy, Liz Ponti, Susan Rampling, Sophia Roberts, Kay Sluterbeck, David & Susan Stratton, and Tom Williams.

Meanwhile, my sons Nick and Chris, and my wonderful husband Bob, have put up with the creation of this book – without complaint and with a certain morbid curiosity. Thanks, all of you.

Finally I must acknowledge my debt to a certain Mr William Shakespeare, who first gave me the idea for this story. For what I have done, and for what I am about to do, I hope he can forgive me.

Sue Barnard
February 2014

# The Ghostly
Father

*Where there is hatred, let me sow love*
*(from The Prayer of Saint Francis of Assisi)*

For what I have done, and for what I am about to do, may Almighty God have mercy upon me.

And I have much for which I need to seek forgiveness. During my lifetime I have concealed the truth, encouraged disobedience, plotted abduction, coveted another man's wife, and helped a convicted killer to escape justice.

This, for a man of God, is quite an impressive catalogue of misdemeanours.

And now I stand on the point of committing another...

*What, in the name of all that is holy, does one give someone for their hundredth birthday?*

*By the time anyone has reached that particular milestone along the rocky road of life, they will already have been there, done that, and dirtied the T-shirt, many times over. And chances are pretty high that if by this stage they haven't already got it, then they almost certainly don't want it.*

*And it's even more difficult when the centenarian is male. Ladies (of any age) will always appreciate a piece of jewellery, a box of chocolates, a romantic novel, or even simply a bunch of flowers. But men? All the traditionally testosterone-related gifts (power tools, porno mags, anything car-related...), or even a half-decent bottle of single malt, would only be appropriate if the recipient were in a position to make full use of them. To give something of that nature to someone who has spent the past seven years languishing in a nursing home – and who, into the bargain, is paralysed from the waist down and is on prescribed medication which means that anything alcoholic is completely off-limits – would be not only highly inappropriate, but also tactless in the extreme.*

*It's quite heartbreaking to see what happens when someone's body finds that its shelf-life has extended way beyond its "Best Before" date. I still can't come to any sensible conclusion whether it's a good thing or not that at 99 Not Out, Grandpa is still mentally as sharp as a tack. Okay, it's good that one can still hold a reasonable conversation with him (for most of the time, at any rate) – but the price he pays is that he remains fully aware of the pathetic state to which his poor physical self has now been sadly reduced.*

*For the past few years, Grandpa had been content to celebrate his birthday with simply a visit from the family and an excuse to be taken out in his wheelchair for a pub lunch. But this birthday, somehow, needed something extra. After racking my brains for ages and still coming up with no sensible ideas, I finally plucked up the courage to ask him, straight out, if there was anything special that he would like as a birthday present.*

*His answer knocked me sideways:*

7

"You've done Italian, haven't you?"

"Yes, why?" (I wondered if he was finally beginning to lose it, but I thought it was probably better to humour him.)

"Go and open that drawer over there – no, not that one, the one next to it – yes, that's right. Now, get the package from the back."

I cautiously rummaged around in the drawer and finally located what he wanted – a hefty bundle, about the size of a telephone directory – and fished it out. It was a clear plastic bag which contained something wrapped in old faded cloth – so old and faded, in fact, that it was impossible to tell what colour it might have been originally – and tied round with a shabby frayed ribbon.

"Is this it?"

"Yes, that's it. Now, open it up."

"But it's terribly old…"

"Yes," Grandpa beamed. "It's even older than me." (He had, thank Heavens, still managed to hold on to his sense of humour.)

I laid the plastic bag on the table, slid out the contents, undid the ribbon and unfolded the cloth. Where it had been more protected from the light, it showed some signs of having once been red.

The contents of the package were finally revealed to be a thick leather-bound book.

"What's this?"

"That's what I'd like you to find out."

I nervously opened the book. Its yellowing pages were covered in neat handwriting, all written in a language which I recognised as Italian.

"I've no idea how old this is," Grandpa went on, "but it was given to me by my grandfather, who said that he'd first been given it by his grandfather. Goodness knows how much further back it goes. But there's always been some rumour in the family that it has something to do with one of our ancestors."

For as long as I'd been able to remember, Grandpa had always been fanatical about family history. He'd had boxes and boxes of old letters, wills, certificates, photographs and goodness knows what else, card index boxes crammed with handwritten records, and family trees carefully drawn on the plain backs of rolls of wallpaper. And he'd done all this using the old, laborious methods (writing letters, visiting records offices, spending ages wandering around graveyards and peering at faded inscriptions, and occasionally even paying researchers), in the bad old days before the advent of the World Wide Web. Now that most searches can be done by the click of a mouse, and the delivery of the results is limited merely by the speed of one's internet connection, it's pretty hard to imagine.

I've never really been that interested in the subject myself, in the same way that I'd never really been that struck on History as a subject in school. What's the point, I often wondered, of Learning About Dead People? I'd only done History at all because the only alternative was Geography – a subject at which I was, and had always been, and still am, absolutely hopeless. It was a wonder that I ever found my way home from school each day. Even now, I can still manage to get lost on my way to my own front door.

With regard to family history, I do remember that my brother became very excited when Grandpa had once suggested that we might actually have a pirate as an ancestor. Our Kid was thrilled at the prospect of being descended from Bartholomew Roberts – better known as Black Bart, the scourge of the Spanish Main. But then, Roberts isn't exactly an uncommon surname for a family which had originated in Wales. Any story associated with that name would be pretty difficult to prove – but then, as Grandpa pointed out, equally difficult to disprove. Maybe it's the uncertainty of it all which keeps these kinds of legends alive.

Bizarrely, I'd always found it far more interesting Learning About People Who Had Never Even Existed In The First Place. Fictional characters somehow seemed far more fascinating than real ones. Sydney Carton was a much more romantic figure than Robespierre or Danton. I'd always preferred Phileas Fogg to Francis Drake, or Vasco Da Gama, or Ferdinand Magellan. Oliver Twist and Nancy had tugged at my heartstrings far more strongly than any of Doctor Barnardo's orphans, or Thomas Coram's foundlings, or William Ewart Gladstone's fallen women, had ever done. Even in cases where fact and fiction merged, the story of Julius Caesar as told in the history books couldn't hold a candle to the version as recounted by Shakespeare.

I was particularly thrilled when, at the age of eleven, I discovered that I shared my name with one of Shakespeare's most famous and best-loved heroines. And I can still recall how heartbroken I had been when, on studying the play at secondary school, I finally found out what happened to her.

I snapped out of my daydream as I realised that Grandpa was speaking again.

"I know there's some Italian blood somewhere in our ancestry," he was saying. "This book has been carefully treasured for so long, and I've always wondered what's in it. And I know you did Italian – so, can you translate this into English for me for my birthday present? Please?"

I gulped.

"Grandpa, it must be decades since I did any serious Italian. I haven't been to Italy for years. I reckon that if push came to shove I could still order a meal and blag my way into a museum, but—"

"Go on, give it a go – and make an old man very happy! I have great faith in you."

I was quite touched by his confidence, and secretly I must admit that I was pleased to have found something which he actually wanted for his birthday. But even so...

"Okay, Grandpa, I'll do my best. But please, don't expect miracles."

Grandpa beamed again.

"From you, my dear Juliet, I shall expect nothing less!"

I forced a smile back at him.

"The impossible I can usually manage fairly quickly, Grandpa. Miracles, on the other hand, might take a bit longer."

"You've got just over four weeks!"

Oh cripes, I thought, as I carefully packed the book into my bag – what on earth have I taken on?

\*\*\*

Later that afternoon I dug out my Italian dictionary, which hadn't seen active service since my long-forgotten days as a student. I gingerly removed Grandpa's mysterious family heirloom from its wrapping, polished my glasses, and squinted at the ancient script.

The handwriting, despite its age, proved to be surprisingly easy to decipher.

For what I have done, and for what I am about to do, may Almighty God have mercy upon me.

And I have much for which I need to seek forgiveness. During my lifetime I have concealed the truth, encouraged disobedience, plotted abduction, coveted another man's wife, and helped a convicted killer to escape justice.

This, for a man of God, is quite an impressive catalogue of misdemeanours.

And now I stand on the point of committing another.

*Hmm, I thought. Maybe this might turn out to be rather interesting after all. Who on earth was this man – and what could he possibly have done?*

*I powered up the laptop, settled myself at my desk, and resolved to find out…*

\*\*\*

*The manuscript went on:*

Although I am not what many would describe as an old man, I know nonetheless that my end is not far away. Despite the herbs and medicines with which I have kept myself – and others – well and healthy for so long, there are some afflictions against which even these remedies remain powerless.

For many years I have been haunted by the burden of a secret which, not once but twice, I made a solemn promise I would never reveal. But I have lived a lie for far too long – and I cannot allow the truth to die with me. So now, in my final days, I must (God forgive me) break that promise and set this story down. I do this not only for my own peace of mind, but also in the hope that it will, in the fullness of time, be read by the one person who needs – and deserves – to know the truth, but to whom, during my lifetime, I could never tell that truth face to face. And I hope and pray that after reading this tale, the reader may understand that all along I acted with the very best of intentions, and may be able to look upon me with understanding and compassion.

\*\*\*

In order that the story which I am about to relate might be better understood, I must first describe a little of the events which preceded it and the circumstances surrounding it. And to that end, I need to commence with myself.

The person to whom I principally address this narrative first knew me by another name, but I began life as Sebastiano Lorenzo Matteo Giovanni Battista Da Porto. I was the second son of a wealthy Venetian Count, and my boyhood home was a grand palazzo on the outskirts of that fine and beautiful city. I have fond childhood memories of my father Antonio; he was firm but also just and loving, and always dealt fairly with me and my brother Filippo, who was my senior by three years. Filippo and I were reared by our nurse, as our mother had died in the act of bringing me into the world.

I had always known that as the second son I would never inherit the family title and fortune, but this did not trouble me, for I had always believed that with a modest financial backing from my father I would be able to make my own way in the world. My burning desire was to become a physician. But when, on my seventeenth birthday, I ventured to discuss this with my father, he declared that I was to enter the Franciscan Order. When I asked him why, his response was to berate me for my insolence, and threaten to disinherit me if I did not obey him.

I was utterly amazed. Whilst I had always believed in God and had endeavoured to keep the faith, the idea of my becoming a monk had never been further from my thoughts. But far worse was the shock of my father's demeanour. This man was as a stranger to me. He was not the father whom I had always known, respected and loved.

But what could I do? I could become a penniless outcast, with no home, no family and no livelihood – or I could become a penniless monk, who, although bereft of possessions, would nonetheless have a roof over my head and some semblance of a purpose in life. So, realising that I had no alternative course, I reluctantly bowed to my father's command – although I did succeed in preserving some small vestige of my original dream. I persuaded my father to first allow me a little time to study medicine and herb-lore, by convincing him that I would want to be of some practical use to my fellow brothers, and perchance to their lay followers, once I had taken holy orders.

And so, for a twelvemonth, I became the apprentice, and later the assistant, to the local apothecary. This man had devoted his life to the study of plants, herbs and their medicinal uses, and he taught me well. From him I learned which herbs could do good, and which would do harm – and also how to tell apart those plants which to an untrained eye appear deceptively similar.

It was during this year that I first encountered Chiara.

*** 

Chiara was sixteen years old (less than a year younger than I), blue-eyed and golden-haired, with a smile so bright it could outshine the sunlight. She was the daughter of a successful and prosperous local merchant, who had already promised her in marriage to a nobleman from nearby Padua. Chiara and I loved each other at first glance. Up to that moment, I had foolishly believed myself to be immune from feminine charms – and as they would soon be forbidden to me in any case, I had not regarded this as a hindrance. But as soon as Chiara entered my life, she filled a need which, until then, I had not even realised existed. Although we were forced to meet only at night and in secret, I lived for every blissful moment spent in her company.

Although we both knew full well that our love had no future (already committed, as we both were, to different bonds), we both also knew that for that very reason, our few months of love were precious beyond measure. We conspired to cherish every moment we had together, then to cherish the memories of those moments once our time had come to an end. What we did not anticipate, in our youthful stupidity, was that shortly before that appointed time, Chiara should find herself to be carrying our child.

When she first told me, I feared that she might ask me to procure her a herbal remedy for her condition. I knew in principle that such things did exist; from time to time I had seen my employer discreetly dispense a mysterious concoction to the ladies of the night who came to him in distress, after having accidentally miscounted their days. But even if this had been possible, I had no idea of the effectiveness, or inherent danger, of such a desperate measure. On this subject, my employer maintained a firm silence.

But I had been reckoning without Chiara herself. True love had changed her from a mild-mannered and submissive daughter into a brave, strong-willed and resourceful young woman. She declared herself determined to keep the child, telling me firmly:

"This child will be born of our love, and will be the one part of you which I will be able to keep, after I have lost you to the church."

Chiara refused even to consider the option of surrendering the child to the *ruota dei trovatelli* (the "turning-wheel" where unwanted babies could be left, anonymously, at the Ospedale della Pietà orphanage). And the question of any dubious alternative remedy was never raised.

I held her close to me and gently asked if her betrothed might accept the child as being his.

She answered that even if her wedding date could be brought forward (which in itself would arouse deep suspicion), and even if she could subsequently convince her husband that the child had come before its time, she could now no longer countenance the idea of an arranged marriage with a man for whom she felt no affection. She declared that the only course of action would be for her to leave Venice before anyone knew of her condition. I reluctantly agreed, but insisted that first we should somehow contrive to legitimise our love, our union and our child.

I searched amongst my deceased mother's jewellery and eventually found a simple patterned ring, fashioned in silver, which would serve Chiara as a wedding ring. Three nights later we secretly entered the church, stood before the altar and exchanged our marriage vows. Having made those promises before God, we were satisfied that were married in his eyes, in our minds and in our hearts, even if not strictly according to the letter of the law.

\*\*\*

*A man of God who seems to think that he can write his own rules? Who IS he?*

\*\*\*

We had arranged that, on the day when I was to enter the friary, Chiara would flee from Venice and travel to Verona, there to present herself as the widow of a merchant adventurer who had perished at sea. Thus, she could preserve some aura of respectability – and even remarry if she so wished.

But this plan had one insurmountable flaw. It would not be possible for Chiara merely to disappear; her family and her betrothed

14

would search for her, and would not rest until they had found her. There was only one means of preventing this: they would have to be made to believe she was dead.

Even today, so many years later, I still marvel at the sacrifices which my darling was prepared to make – both for me and for our child.

The day we parted was a cold grey dawn, a bitter awakening after our last secret night together. We rode to the outskirts of the city, to the point where the Canale di Cannaregio joins the lagoon, and there we threw one of her cloaks and a pair of her shoes into the water. When, a few days later, they would be discovered, it would be presumed that she had drowned. As I held her in my arms for the last time, I sensed the movement of our child – the fruit of our brief period of happiness – the child I would never see – as it quickened within her. My tears mingled with hers as we kissed farewell. Then she mounted her horse, turned towards the causeway, and was gone.

I had heard people speak of heartache. But I had no idea, until that moment, that it could be physically painful.

\*\*\*

But I had little opportunity to grieve. Later that same day, I left my father's house and entered the Franciscan friary as a postulant.

Once the friary gates had swung closed behind me, I found myself standing next to another young man, who I divined was probably around my own age, or possibly a year or two older. His appearance suggested that he was every whit as bewildered and confused as I was. At the very least, I thought, I am not alone. I was about to introduce myself to him, when were approached by an elderly friar with a surprisingly kind face.

"Good morrow, gentlemen! Welcome to the friary. My name is Fra' Amadeo, and it is my task to take care of the new postulants. You two must be Sebastiano and Gianni – is that correct?"

We nodded. I stepped forward.

"I am Sebastiano."

"And I am Gianni," said the other.

Fra' Amadeo shook hands heartily with both of us and beckoned us to follow him. He led us into a small ante-room adjoining the cloister. In the centre was a large table, on which had been placed two plain brown robes.

"Those are your new postulant outfits," he said. "Please, change into them."

"What will happen to our ordinary clothes?" Gianni asked, less than a second before I was about to pose the same question.

"They are kept here, and given to the poor, as and when the poor need new clothes."

In awkward silence, Gianni and I both changed into the monastic attire. It seemed as though our worldly identities had been shed along with our worldly clothes, for once we were wearing the habits, we both looked exactly the same – apart from our build (mine tall and solid, his short and slight) and the colour of our hair (mine jet-black, his mid-brown).

My background, hitherto, had been privileged. Whatever Gianni's background might have been, I found that I neither knew nor cared – for suddenly I realised that now it did not matter. We were both at the same level, having been rendered thus by the monastic robes.

Fra' Amadeo beamed at us cheerfully.

"Come, my friends; there is someone you now need to meet!"

Sheep-like, we followed him into another office. This was slightly larger than the room in which we had changed, but in some indefinable way it was altogether a much more congenial place. Seated behind an oak desk was another friar, of indeterminate age. He had a thick shock of white hair, but his face, tanned and weatherbeaten though it was, showed very few wrinkles. As he rose to greet us I saw he was a tall man – around the same height as I – and also muscular, although not heavy. He stepped forward and smiled warmly as he extended his hand towards each of us in turn. His handshake was firm and strong.

"Welcome to the friary! You must be Sebastiano and Gianni. Which of you is which?"

We introduced ourselves as before.

"My name," the friar went on, "is Fra' Roberto. Officially my title here is the Father Superior, but I much prefer to be known, and addressed, simply as Fra' Roberto. I hope you will be happy here with us, Gianni and Sebastiano. Our aim is to serve God according to the doctrine of our founder, Saint Francis of Assisi."

He gestured towards a painting which hung on the wall to one side of his desk. It depicted the Saint, portrayed in a contemplative pose and surrounded by doves.

"I do not know," Fra' Roberto went on, "how much you already know about life in holy orders?"

We both shook our heads.

"Have you heard of the Rule of Saint Benedict?"

"Does that mean poverty, chastity and obedience?" I asked cautiously.

Fra' Roberto nodded.

"Yes, those three rules are the ones for which the cloister is best known – but there is much more to a monastic life than simply that. Saint Benedict also laid down rules concerning our daily worship, our diet, and our behaviour.

"But there are some orders which follow the Rule of Saint Benedict to an extent far beyond that which the Saint himself prescribed or intended. They fast rigorously, they purposely deprive themselves of sleep, and some even deliberately subject themselves to physical pain. I understand that they believe that by punishing the body, they are somehow improving the soul.

"For my part, I have never held that opinion – nor can I see any justification for it. God made the body as well as the soul, and I do not believe that He would wish us to subject it to wilful neglect or to unnecessary and gratuitous abuse. Nor do I believe that a happy soul can be housed in an unhappy body. If you are starving, or cold, or uncomfortable, or exhausted, you are not in a position to serve God fully or properly.

"So – poverty, chastity and obedience, yes. But unnecessary discomfort and chastisement, no."

I blinked in amazement. This cheerful, kind, friendly man, with his sensible and sympathetic demeanour, did not correspond at all with my imagined picture of a monastic.

"If you have any problems, of any kind," Fra' Roberto continued, "please do not hesitate to come to me to discuss them. Please regard me, from henceforth, as your spiritual director and guide. Here in the Order we have our own special name for this: the Ghostly Father.

"In the meantime, both of you, please take this to read, and take note of what it says. This is the prayer which is attributed to our founder. And this is the rule by which we in the Order of Saint

17

Francis aim to live our lives."

He handed each of us a piece of paper, on which was written:

*Lord, make me an instrument of Your peace. Where there is hatred, let me sow love; where there is injury, pardon; where there is doubt, faith; where there is despair, hope; where there is darkness, light; where there is sadness, joy.*

*O, Divine Master, grant that I may not so much seek to be consoled as to console; to be understood as to understand; to be loved as to love. For it is in giving that we receive; it is in pardoning that we are pardoned; it is in dying that we are born again to eternal life.*

My early days in the friary are not likely to be of great interest to anyone who reads this narrative, nor are they of any relevance to the story I must tell – so I will not spend time describing them in detail. Suffice it to say that after a short period as postulants, Gianni and I were formally admitted as novices for a period of twelve months. We were fully received into the Order as friars on the fourth day of October – the feast of Saint Francis of Assisi.

Whilst Gianni was able to keep his original name, I discovered that there was already in the friary a monk who bore the name of Fra' Sebastiano. Accordingly, Fra' Roberto asked me if I might like to choose another name by which I would be known after I had taken my vows.

Truth to say, I was not sorry to lose the name of Sebastiano Da Porto; it carried too many associations with an earlier life outside the cloister. Thankfully, I had plenty more names from which I could choose a suitable alternative.

And so it was that from that day forward, I became known simply as Fra' Lorenzo, of the Order of Saint Francis.

\*\*\*

I quickly learned that the Franciscans, unlike many of the stricter and more cloistered Orders, are much more closely associated with the community around them. Primarily because of my medicinal skills, I found that I was allowed even more contact with the outside world than was permitted to some of my brother friars. This was a blessing for me, for whilst I was able happily to accept the rules of St Francis of Assisi, I found that my nature was not naturally suited to the more conventional constraints of a monastic life. I took great pleasure in dealing with the people of the city who came to me with their ills, and I found it immensely satisfying to be able, at last, to follow my chosen profession.

As the friary's specialist in medicines I was also given charge of the herb garden, which was tended by myself and a few of the novices. There we grew the many herbs and plants which were needed for use in the dispensary.

This contented state of affairs continued for more than fifteen years. However, very little happened during that time which is of any great significance, save for one pivotal event which took place during my seventh year.

I had recently been allocated a new team of novices (my previous apprentices having been relieved of their additional duties in order to allow them time to prepare to take their final vows), and I had begun to train them as usual in the knowledge of our herbs and wild plants and the art of compounding basic beneficial mixtures. One night, one of the friars, in a state of great alarm, awoke me shortly after midnight to tell me that another of the brothers was very ill and needed urgent attention.

I rose from my bed and summoned one of my novices, a keen and intelligent boy named Pietro, to assist me. I discovered that the sick brother, Fra' Bartolomeo, was vomiting and had a high fever, and I despatched Pietro to the herb garden to gather quantities of fennel, chamomile, agrimony, herb Robert and golden feverfew.

Together we worked by flickering candlelight in our dispensary, frantically crushing, pounding, boiling and straining the herbs into a decoction which we rushed to Fra' Bartolomeo's bedside. We held up his head and carefully spooned the medicine into his mouth. He gasped and spluttered once or twice, then swallowed, sighed heavily and fell back upon his bed, apparently having sunk into a deep and peaceful slumber. Satisfied that our medicine had done its work, Pietro and I returned wearily to our beds.

I was shaken awake soon after dawn, to be told that Fra' Bartolomeo had been found dead.

I hurried back to the infirmary. Fra' Bartolomeo was lying, cold, still and lifeless, in the same pose as we had last seen him.

I was devastated. For the first time in my life, my medicinal skills had failed.

Fra' Roberto, mindful of my distress, beckoned me to his side and indicated that he wished to speak to me in private. Once we were alone, he gently explained that Fra' Bartolomeo's death was in no measure due to any supposed negligence on my part, and that although Fra' Bartolomeo was not an old man, nonetheless, if his affliction was of such severity that it would have been fatal in any case, then no medicine on earth could have saved him. Also mindful that I should not be left to brood on the matter, Fra' Roberto then asked me if I would take charge of the arrangements for the funeral.

I protested that this was a task with which I was totally unfamiliar, but Fra' Roberto simply smiled at me and said that that being the case, then this would be a good time to learn. He then summoned some bread and ham and a jug of ale to be brought to his office, insisting that I should first have some sustenance before commencing my task.

Although I had no appetite I forced down a little of the victuals, then spent the rest of the day in the chapel, studying and rehearsing the formula for the requiem Mass which would take place the following morning. Shortly before sunset, Fra' Bartolomeo's body was brought in and placed before the altar. Here it would remain overnight, in order that any friars who so wished might come and pray for the repose of his soul.

Briefly left alone with his corpse, I privately asked his forgiveness for having failed to save his life, then retired to my cell. Exhausted by my disturbed night and stressful day, I fell immediately into a deep and dreamless sleep.

Next morning I awoke with a heavy heart and made my way back to the chapel. By the hour of nine the whole of the Order were assembled, and as the hour struck I nervously began to recite the opening prayers of the requiem Mass.

We were almost at the end of the Credo, having reached the line "*Et exspecto resurrectionem mortuorum*," when the body on the bier stirred, stretched and opened its eyes.

\*\*\*

*Oh Heavens above. Not just Italian, but now Latin as well. It's even longer since I did any of that – and I don't even think I've got a Latin dictionary any more. Thank goodness for Google.*

*It seems that it means "And we look for the resurrection of the dead." How very appropriate…*

\*\*\*

It is difficult to describe the debacle which ensued. Several of the older friars fainted with the shock. Some of the younger novices screamed uncontrollably, and at least three of them rushed, weeping and retching, for the chapel door. I stood in the chancel, paralysed and robbed of the power of speech. Fra' Bartolomeo himself slowly eased himself up into a sitting position and looked around him. As his eyes and ears took in his surroundings, and as the full import of the exact circumstances became evident, he opened his mouth as if to cry out, but no sound would come.

Only Fra' Roberto, although momentarily nonplussed, succeeded in retaining his composure. He strode over to the bier, extended a hand to Fra' Bartolomeo and murmured something in his ear as he gently eased him to his feet. Beckoning to me to his side and signalling to me to support Fra' Bartolomeo's drooping form, he then turned towards the congregation and declared calmly:

"My fellow friars, please be at peace. There will be no requiem today."

He then pronounced a short benediction and dismissed the friars from the chapel, instructing them to return to their normal everyday tasks.

Back in the infirmary, I did my best to make Fra' Bartolomeo comfortable and sent to the refectory for some broth. As he sipped the warm, nourishing liquid the colour gradually returned to his pallid countenance, and he began to describe how, when gravely ill with the gastric fever, he had believed his final hour had come.

"We all believed your final hour had come, Bartolomeo."

I had failed to notice Fra' Roberto appearing at my side.

"But, praise God, you have been restored to us."

Smiling, he turned to me.

"Now, Lorenzo, you too should go and rest. I will sit with

Bartolomeo for a while. You are excused your obligations for the remainder of the day."

I thanked Fra' Roberto, took my leave of them, and trudged back to my cell. I do not even recall lying down, but my next conscious moment was hearing the friary clock chime the fourth hour of the afternoon. I shook myself awake, then made my way to the dispensary, whither I had not returned since before Fra' Bartolomeo's illness.

The ingredients for his medicine still lay, as Pietro and I had hastily left them, scattered across the table. I reached for a basin and began to sweep them into it, then stopped and peered more closely. Although now limp and wilted, the remains of the plants were still clearly recognisable. And with them, the reason for what had recently occurred.

What Pietro had gathered, in the dark and in his inexperienced haste, had been not the fennel and agrimony required to treat a disorder of the digestive system, but instead valerian and golden hop – both of them being plants which induce deep sleep. And in my turn, I – working by candlelight and in my confounded haste – had utterly failed to notice the distinction. Each of those herbs in isolation would have simply acted as a sleeping draught. But together, their combined action appeared to have caused Fra' Bartolomeo to sink into a profound trance – and, moreover, one which had deceived us all into believing he had died. But miraculously he had now returned to life, and was apparently cured of his affliction. I vowed to observe him closely over the coming few days to ensure that the accidentally-prepared draught bore him no evident ill-effects.

And, as far as I could ascertain, it did not. By the end of the following day Fra' Bartolomeo had risen from his sickbed, eaten supper in the refectory and attended Completorium, and after another day's repose he was able to return to his regular duties. Thereafter he continued well and healthy (within the usual limitations of advancing years), and the matter of his premature death was never raised again.

***

I was approaching the end of my seventeenth year at the friary when, one morning after Mass, Fra' Roberto sent for me. He told me that the Order was about to open a new friary in another city, and would need some experienced brothers to help to establish it. Whilst he would, he said, be sad to lose me from his flock here in Venice, he asked me if I might wish to be considered for this new venture.

I would, he said, hold a position of some authority in the new friary. As well as maintaining my present post as herbalist, healer and infirmarian, I would also be able to conduct baptisms, funerals and marriages, say Mass, hear confessions and pronounce absolution. These, theoretically, I already had the authority to perform, but (with the exception of the matter of Fra' Bartolomeo) there had hitherto been little or no call for me to do so.

I was taken aback by the question. Whilst my life as a friar was not the life I would have chosen for myself, my time at the friary had been a happy one, and I had never entertained the thought of leaving. I asked Fra' Roberto if I might have a little time to consider the matter. He happily concurred, and we agreed that we should meet again at the same time the following day.

As I made to leave, I asked him if he knew in which city the proposed new friary would be situated.

"Aye," he replied. "In Verona."

I froze where I stood; it was as though my heart had stopped.

Verona… Chiara…

Had my countenance – or my demeanour – betrayed me?

But Fra' Roberto made no sign of having noticed anything untoward. He merely smiled.

"Until tomorrow, Lorenzo."

I stumbled back to my cell, my mind in turmoil. To my dying day I will never know how I survived those ensuing four and twenty hours.

For the past seventeen years I had followed (though admittedly not always happily or willingly) the rules of poverty, obedience and chastity, and I had tried to banish all memories of my beloved Chiara from my mind. For the most part (by means of keeping myself wholly occupied throughout all my waking hours) I had succeeded – although from time to time I might stir from a deep slumber and half-envisage, in my semi-waking state, that she was once again lying by my side. On these occasions I was loth to open my eyes to the stark reality of my monastic cell. I knew that such thoughts were now forbidden to me, but I contrived to shrive myself by reciting the *Ave Maria* as soon as I had risen from my bed. I knew now that as a man of God I should agree to go wherever He sent me, but I also knew that by going to Verona, whither my darling wife had journeyed (to an unknown destiny) seventeen years earlier, I would be leading myself into almost unbearable temptation.

Would I be able to resist trying to ascertain what fate had befallen her? And if I were to encounter her again, what should I do?

Exhausted, I fell to my knees, and for the first time since I had taken the cowl, the prayer that emerged from my lips came not from a prescribed formula learned and recited by rote, but directly from my heart:

"Dear Lord, You, who have the steerage of my course, direct my sail. You have done this for a reason; as yet I know not what. Show me the way, and guide me and help me in whatever path you have chosen."

Next morning Fra' Roberto sought me out again, and asked me if I had come to a decision. I opened my mouth to answer, and my lips – as if of their own volition – formed the words:

"Yes, Fra' Roberto, I will go."

\*\*\*

It was a mere two months later that I, my dear friend Fra' Gianni, and a half-dozen other brothers, all took our leave of the Venetian friary and set out for – Heaven knew what. We all left with Fra' Roberto's blessing, and his promise that if, after a twelvemonth, any of us should find that our new positions in Verona were not to our liking, we could return to Venice with no loss of standing.

I reflected, not for the first time, that Fra Roberto's demeanour indicated a goodly measure of sympathy for the frailities of human nature – a sympathy not often found in one whose life is centred on spiritual rather than worldly issues. Did he, like myself, have some hidden history – a past life coloured with joy, or despair, or perchance both? I realised that during my time in the friary he had become not merely my ghostly sire, but also a replacement for the earthly father whom I had lost when I took the cowl.

Had Fra' Roberto, I wondered, known of the circumstances of my entering the Order? Had he divined that I was there by my father's decree rather than by my own choice? And if so, had he made it his especial business to ensure that I was not unhappy? Had his own past experiences – whatever they might have been – rendered him more sensitive to the needs of his flock?

I was well aware that I would probably never know the answers, but I resolved that in my new role as a ghostly father, I would endeavour to do the same for my own spiritual children. This might even help to atone – in my own mind at least – for what I had been unable to do for my own earthly child.

\*\*\*

Upon our arrival in Verona we made our way to the new friary. The sisters of the nearby Convent of the Poor Clares had been forewarned of our arrival, and had prepared our chapel with candles and incense, our cells with bedding, and our refectory with food and ale.

The next day, I made sure to visit the Convent in order to convey our thanks to the sisters for their kindness. I was conducted to the office of the Reverend Mother, a gentle and kindly lady of indeterminate age. She bade me welcome, and said that they were always pleased and honoured to take care of any visitors and newcomers – and it was a particular privilege to do so for members of an Order which, like their own, had its origins in Assisi. She then asked, if I were not pressed for time, if I might wish to join the sisters in their chapel, half-an-hour hence, for the office of Vesperae. During the interim, she told me a little about the city which was now my new home.

I knew very little about Verona save that it was, I believed, ruled by authority from Venice. It did, however, have its own governor, a young nobleman named Prince Bartolomeo Della Scala. But despite being well-respected by rich and poor alike, the Prince seemed unable to control the continuing civil unrest. Bloody and ugly street-brawls were, according to the Reverend Mother, regular occurrences. Although there had thus far been no fatalities, injuries from these sword-fights were commonplace – and the sisters were frequently called upon to tend the wounded.

Shocked though I was at her words, I told her of my medicinal skills and offered my services in this field. I then asked her if she knew the reasons behind the continuing violence.

Her response took me totally by surprise.

"It is, I understand, the ongoing result of an ancient feud between two powerful Verona households – the Montecchi and the Capuleti. The feud has now been in existence for so long that no-one – not even the members of the households themselves – can even recall how, when and why it began. But their hatred has now become an end in itself. Master fights master and servant fights servant in the city streets, with no need of prior provocation, and for no better purpose than that of keeping the quarrel alive. At our every act of worship we offer prayers for an end to the troubles and a reconciliation of the warring families – but thus far, sadly, we have seen no sign."

Holy Saint Francis, I thought – what kind of place is this, where neighbour takes up arms against neighbour? Aloud I said nothing, save a promise to the Reverend Mother that I would forewarn my fellow friars of these troubles and that we too would add our prayers to those of the sisters. I followed her into their chapel for Vesperae, then thanked her again for her hospitality, took my leave and returned to the friary.

\*\*\*

One of my first, and most pleasurable, tasks in the new friary was to establish the herb garden which would furnish the ingredients for my dispensary. We had procured a modest supply of living plants from the mature gardens of the friary in Venice, and these were now temporarily placed and tended in terracotta containers whilst the ground was made ready for their eventual planting.

It had originally been the intention to devote the cloister gardens to this purpose, but an exploration of the friary grounds revealed, to the rear of the refectory, a large area of undeveloped land. This, we concurred, would offer a far more suitable location, affording a good mix of light and shade (better to accommodate the varied needs of the herbs as they grew), together with a well in the corner, and also, adjoining the wall farthest from the friary, a small outbuilding – alongside which was a small separate entrance to the grounds. This building, it was decided, would become my cell and also the dispensary; it was conveniently situated so that any citizens who might need to call on my medicinal skills would be able to visit me there, without needing to disturb the usual day-to-day operations of the rest of the Order.

Once the ground had been thoroughly tilled and watered, I planted the herbs in their appointed places and carefully tended them over the ensuing weeks. I had also received a message from the Reverend Mother, saying that following some pruning and maintenance in their own gardens, the sisters had some plants which were surplus to their requirements, and these were at my disposal if I wished to take them. It was thus that I acquired a fine array of culinary herbs (basilicum, oreganum, persilium...) together with several well-established bushes of locally-grown lavandula.

The latter was a most versatile shrub. I had previously only encountered its fragrant flowers in their dried form, but I learned that it had many and varied uses. Its flowers (whether fresh or dried) could have a calming effect on the senses, keep the air fresh, deter unwelcome insects, and make an excellent agent in the laundering of clothing – even counteracting the unwelcome attentions of the clothes-moth. The distilled oil of the plant could act as a gentle yet powerful disinfectant (the sisters had often used it for cleansing the wounds of those injured in the street-brawls), whilst the living flowers were also favoured by bees to produce plentiful and flavoursome honey.

The sisters were well-versed in the keeping of bees, and offered us a few small wicker hives (each furnished with a queen and a small army of workers) to enable us to develop our own apiary. This task, being so closely associated with the upkeep of the gardens, also became my responsibility.

I soon became as fascinated by the workings of these industrious little creatures as I was already devoted to my herbs and medicines, and I resolved to investigate if honey – another gift from nature's bounty – might also have some beneficial or curative properties. I soon discovered that honey made an excellent salve for wounds and burns, treating them gently and swiftly but leaving little or no scar. And with some degree of experimentation I also ascertained that it produced a pale-gold, deliciously sweet wine. In the fullness of time we were able to sell some of the honey and the wine to the citizens of

Verona, thus helping to raise funds for our own essential needs at the friary.

But forgive me. In continuing to chronicle my love for all things natural, I fear I am moving away from the main purpose of this narrative.

***

The people of Verona, notwithstanding their own personal quarrels, were happy to welcome the Franciscan brothers as full members of their community.

Those members of the Montecchi household whom we encountered were genial people, who were friendly and welcoming to the friars. Conversely, the members of the House of Capuleti, devout though they were, appeared to be much more aloof. They were polite to the friars, but their civility went no further. Moreover, they took pains to orchestrate their visits to church so that they did not coincide with the times when the Montecchi were present. It appeared that both families had attended the friary church for many generations, since long before the feud had begun, and neither family had been willing to alter their place of worship. Thus, the pattern had emerged that the Montecchi would come to morning Mass, whist the Capuleti would attend in the evening.

How tragic, I thought, that even in the spiritual worship of their Creator, these two households (though so alike in dignity) could not find it in their hearts to put aside their worldly differences and tolerate each other's presence for one short hour each Sunday.

I have previously intimated that there were some aspects of the monastic life which did not come naturally to me, but although I might have had to struggle with them, I did (eventually) succeed in observing them. But here in Verona, for the first time, I encountered an obstacle which I found to be well-nigh insuperable.

As friars we had always known that we should aim to love and respect all our fellow human beings and to pass judgement upon none. Previously this had never presented me with much difficulty; whilst I might not necessarily like one or other particular individual, I could always manage to treat that person with a polite form of indifference. For me to take an active dislike to someone was extremely rare. To do so at first sight was, until this point, unheard of.

Nonetheless, there was one young man amongst the Capuleti for whom I could not, even in a professional capacity, form any degree of sympathy or affection. His name was Tebaldo, and he was – forgive me – a vain, priggish, loud-mouthed and self-centred trouble-maker.

Although he would come to Shrift, I never discerned any degree of remorse in his confessions, and I knew full well that as soon as he had served whatever penance I had prescribed, he would swagger back into the material world and return to committing the self-same sins all over again, with no vestige of conscience. It was no secret to anyone that whenever a brawl disturbed the peace of Verona's streets, Tebaldo would have had some involvement. Sooner or later, I feared, his arrogance and fiery temper would be the cause, or catalyst, of some great disaster.

But Tebaldo's pride, selfishness and ferocity were amply counterbalanced by the sweet disposition of his cousin (his junior by a few years) – a pretty, winsome girl called Giulietta. Although she came to Shrift twice-weekly, it seemed to me that she never had any need for confession or absolution. She was devout, sincere, modest and obedient.

Giulietta was accompanied on her visits to Shrift by her nurse, a kindly and good-natured widow named Agnese. From her I learned that Giulietta was the daughter of the Lord and Lady Capuleti, and had been the only child of theirs to have survived beyond infancy. Agnese herself had borne a daughter, whom she had named Susanna, but who had died before her first week of life had run its course. It was thus (having milk but no child of her own to feed) that she had become Giulietta's wet-nurse.

Privately recalling the loss of my own child, I could fully envisage Agnese's grief, and gently tendered my condolences. She thanked me, but said, with great fortitude that impressed me deeply, that Susanna was now with God. She had clearly been too good for this world.

***

As our friary became better-established our congregations grew, and we soon realised that our own resources alone would be insufficient to meet the liturgical needs of our increasing flock. After

29

discussing this matter at Chapter, the brothers agreed to issue a proclamation, inviting anyone who so wished to present themselves to be trained to assist at our acts of worship.

A few weeks later we received our first intake of trainees who were to be instructed to become servers at Mass. The intention was that they should receive sufficient training to enable them to perform their first liturgical duties at our High Mass on Easter Sunday. There were twelve pupils in total, all boys. Of these I was allocated three, whom I divined to be all aged between fifteen and eighteen.

These three young men were all good, diligent and devout learners. They were totally at ease in one another's company, despite being wildly different in personality. The first was a gentle, peace-loving youth, who seemed to have an unfailing talent for defusing any disagreements amongst his peers. The second, I soon discovered, was an intelligent, personable and sharp-witted joker. The third appeared to be a dreamy and brooding romantic – a quality I had never before seen in one so young. Their names were, respectively: Benvolio, Mercutio (who, it transpired, was a kinsman to Prince Bartolomeo Della Scala), and Romeo, the youngest of the House of Montecchi.

\*\*\*

*Oh ye gods, how on earth could I have failed to notice?*

*Two feuding households in the city of Verona… It had been staring me in the face all along.*

*The names in the manuscript were the Italian versions (Capuleti for Capulet, Montecchi for Montague, Giulietta for Juliet, Tebaldo for Tybalt) but the story was unmistakeable. So this monk whose memoir I was now reading – Fra' Lorenzo of the Order of Saint Francis – must be the character known in the story as Friar Lawrence.*

*I'd been pitched right into the middle of one of the world's greatest, most enduring – and most tragic – love stories.*

*And, of course, because (along with most of the civilised world) I already knew the story, I already knew the ending.*

*My heart sank. I wasn't sure I could go on with it.*

*Except, of course, that I had promised Grandpa.*

*And in spite of my misgivings, I was still intrigued to know what Friar Lawrence's great secret might be…*

"You are Fra' Lorenzo, I believe?"

"I am. How may I assist you?"

The woman sank to her knees.

"Bless me Father, for I have sinned. It has been one year since my last confession…"

The hour was approaching sunset on Easter Eve. The voice from the downcast face beneath the thick veil was low and gentle, scarcely breaking the silence of my cell.

"Before I hear your confession, My Lady, may I ask why it has been so long since your last time?"

"I come to Shrift and to Mass only at Easter, Father. And then only to please my husband. I do not share his devotion to the church."

There was a hint of sadness in the voice, but beyond that, something else – something which carried a suspicion of bitterness, or even anger.

"Do you wish to tell me why?"

She was silent for a moment, then said shakily,

"You would not understand."

*(Grant that I may never seek… to be understood, as to understand…)*

"Let me be the one to decide that," I answered gently.

She did not answer.

"But if you do not wish to tell me," I added, "I will not ask again."

She hesitated, wringing her hands within their silken gloves, her veiled head still bowed. Then she murmured something, speaking so quietly that I could barely discern the words.

"You will think badly of me."

"It is not for me to judge you…"

I waited. When she eventually broke her silence, her voice, though a little louder, still wavered.

"The church stole something from me. And since then, I have found it impossible to forgive them."

Although by now I was no stranger to the spiritual troubles of others, this was something completely new to me. I drew a deep breath before asking:

31

"What was it that you believe the church stole from you?"

She hesitated again, as if mustering her courage. Finally, without looking up, she answered,

"The man I loved."

I was dumbstruck. After what seemed like an age, I asked her (in what I hoped was a kindly tone),

"Do you not love your husband?"

"My husband is a good man, Father, and I am fond of him and I respect him. But I do not love him – not in the way I loved the other. But he was promised to the church, and thus he was lost to me."

"Do you know if this other man returned your affection?"

"Yes Father, he did. And he would have married me, had he not been foresworn to the church. I have never stopped loving him. And that is why I do not come to Mass. The church always makes me think of him, and of the happiness which we could have enjoyed together. And I find it hard to believe that God is love, if He punishes me thus for having loved."

Her voice suddenly became loud and bitter.

"But why am I telling you this? You are a monk. You will not understand that someone cannot love the church. And you would not understand about real love…"

By now she was openly sobbing, and reached into her reticule in search of a handkerchief. In doing so, she was obliged to remove the silken gloves.

I wanted to reassure her that I did indeed understand about love. I had begun to say,

"I have not always been a monk…"

But the words died on my lips as my gaze fell on her hand.

A simple patterned ring, fashioned in silver, adorned the third finger.

***

"Chiara…?"

She gasped.

"Fra' Lorenzo, how do you know…? I have not used that name these past seventeen years…"

"Chiara, look at me."

She raised her head and drew back her veil. Her clear blue eyes, still moist and red-rimmed with tears, widened as they met my own.

"It cannot be. I am dreaming. Sebastiano…?"

As I helped her to her feet and clasped her once again in my arms, I felt as though my heart would burst…

Over the following hour, as the small hand which wore my ring remained clasped tightly in my own, she told me of what had befallen her since she had ridden away from Venice on that cold grey dawn so many years earlier.

She had, as planned, made her way to Verona. On arrival she had sought food and shelter, and in so doing had found her way to the Convent of the Poor Clares. The Reverend Mother – that self-same Abbess who had welcomed the Franciscan friars to the city only a few months ago – had taken her in, readily believing her story that she was newly with child and recently widowed. She had given her name as Lucia, and by that name she had been known in Verona ever since.

Her husband, she explained, was a benefactor of the Convent. One of the sisters was an experienced midwife who had taken care of his first wife during her confinement, but even her skills had been insufficient to save a mother and child who had both bled to death during a breech delivery. Chiara, on hearing his story during one of his visits to the Convent to offer alms, had tendered her sympathy, which he had generously reciprocated on learning of her own (assumed) tragic circumstances. They had become close friends, and had married quietly with the Reverend Mother's blessing.

"We had both lost the one love of our own lives, and we readily accepted that we each would not attempt to supplant their memories." She indicated the silver ring. "And I knew that he would care for me and for the child I was to bear."

I forced myself to ask her the question which, until then, I had dared not pose:

"What became of our child?"

"A boy."

"Did he – survive…?"

A slow smile spread across her lovely face.

"You already know him. His name is Romeo."

\*\*\*

*Once again: oh ye gods.*

*I thought back to the events of the Romeo & Juliet story as I remembered them. I'd often wondered about Friar Lawrence – he'd always seemed to be a bit of a maverick; one who seemed prepared to bend the rules. What I'd so far learned about him from this memoir would certainly explain (if not excuse) why he'd behaved as he had.*

*So Romeo was his son. Suddenly it all began to fall into place.*

*Which made what was to follow all the more heartrending.*

*But I had to carry on…*

\*\*\*

"So your husband is…"

"Yes. The Lord Montecchi. And with no heir of his own, he has readily accepted Romeo as his son."

Her radiant smile was replaced by a sudden look of terror.

"Please, my love, promise me that you will never tell Romeo of this. He has known no other father."

I nodded silently.

Oh, how many times since then have I rued the moment I made that promise…

"What of the feud?"

She sighed.

"It pains me. I take no part in it; even my husband does not condone it. For our part we would be happy to let it rest. But the Capuleti seem to see things differently; it is always they who start the fights."

The ugly image of Tebaldo, rapier drawn and eyes fired with bloodlust, loomed menacingly into my mind. I shuddered. Involuntarily, I drew Chiara to me and held her close.

By now it was dusk, and she announced that she must leave, ere her prolonged absence should attract any undue attention. With a last kiss she promised to return the following week.

Only after she had left did I realise that I had never heard her confession.

\*\*\*

34

I rose on the morning of Easter Day as though the resurrection were my own.

My Chiara, the love of my life, was alive. And she still loved me. Moreover, she had told the anonymous Fra' Lorenzo of her love for her lost Sebastiano. A truth confided to a stranger is often proved to be of greater value than one spoken face to face.

And Romeo – the dreamy, blue-eyed youth (how could I have failed to recognise those blue eyes?) who had been my pupil these last few months – my own son! A son who had already, a hundred times over, addressed me as "Father." But a son whom I would never be able to acknowledge as my own flesh and blood; a son for whom I could only ever be, in every sense of the word, a ghostly father...

This reminded me that I must attend to my spiritual duties on this most holy of holy days.

I was grateful that I had, by now, celebrated Mass so many times that I could recite the prayers and perform the actions without having to apply my conscious mind to either. My eyes found themselves drawn constantly towards either the Lady Lucia Montecchi (sitting demure and veiled beside her husband in the nave) or one particular young man amongst the team of new servers at the altar. I hoped that (in the latter case at least) anyone who might have observed this attention would ascribe it to priestly concern for the new recruits who were performing their duties for the first time.

After the service, I summoned Benvolio, Mercutio and Romeo to my cell, and commended them all on having performed so excellently. Benvolio smiled graciously; Mercutio grinned cheekily, whilst Romeo's features lit up with that same slow smile which I had yesterday observed on his mother's countenance. Once again, I wondered how I could have not noticed the resemblance.

"Thank you, Father," he said gently.

I opened my mouth to respond; what emerged was,

"You did very well, my son."

The forbidden truth was too much to bear. I forced a smile as I dismissed them, then hurried back to my cell, barred the door, then broke down and sobbed like a child.

\*\*\*

The reserves of strength which had somehow carried me through the Easter Mass were, by now, exhausted. But I forced myself to remain occupied, and passed the rest of the day in tending the apiaries and the herb garden, both of which had been sadly neglected over the previous few days. The physical effort provided a fitting distraction from my mental and emotional turmoil. And I found it comforting to think that whatever might happen in the human world, plants and animals would always continue to go about their normal, uncomplicated business.

As I busied myself with propagating the lavandula bushes (it was my intention, longer term, to have sufficient to plant some in the garden of the cloister), their fresh scent worked its subtle magic on my troubled spirit. I did not attend evening Mass, but by the time for Completorium I was sufficiently relaxed and recovered to return to the chapel.

*Noctem quiétam, et finem perféctum concédat nobis Dóminus omnípotens…*

May the Lord Almighty grant us a quiet night and a perfect end…

As I allowed the gentle, peaceful chanting to flow over me, my gaze fell on the image of the founder of our Order: the compassionate and loving Francis of Assisi, whose portrait hung on the side-wall of the chapel. And in that moment, it was as though I heard his voice in my ear:

*"Be not troubled, Lorenzo; what is done cannot be undone. Love is also a gift from God. Would you wish your son unborn? If all were to take the vow of chastity, the human race would come to an end…"*

\*\*\*

The next seven days passed like seven years.
"Bless me, Father, for I have sinned…"
And this time, I did hear her confession.

\*\*\*

"What ails young Romeo?"

Mercutio sighed.

"He is in love again, Father. Or at least, he believes he is."

Benvolio nodded resignedly.

"He caught a glimpse of the lady when she was out walking in the city last week. Since then, he has thought and spoken of little else."

"Again? What do you mean by that?"

I must have appeared concerned, for Mercutio looked up at me and grinned.

"Please, Fra' Lorenzo, do not trouble yourself over this. You do not know Romeo as we do. He is always falling in love. Each time it happens, he behaves as though it were the first and only time. He is insufferable whilst he nurtures his latest infatuation. Thankfully it never lasts longer than a week, or two at most. He will soon be back to normal; you will see."

I fervently hoped that this good-natured buffoon was right. My son was in love. I had been in love myself. And I well knew what heartache it could bring...

\*\*\*

"What is her name this time?"

Two years had now elapsed, during which time Romeo had, as Mercutio and Benvolio had indicated, fallen in and out of love more times than I cared to remember. And, as they had also indicated, never did any of his one-sided affairs last for more than a week at a time.

"Rosaline, Father."

"And does she return your affection?"

"Alas, she has sworn to remain chaste. And I— "

"Then why do you persist in doting on her?"

"Doting? Father, I am not doting. I love her to distraction."

"If she does not love you in return, son, then your devotion is wasted."

Romeo turned angrily to face me.

"What do you know of love?"

*(Grant that I may never seek... so much to be understood as to understand...)*

"Much more than you might realise," I answered quietly.

"What? But you are a monk!"

"I was not always a monk, my son."

Romeo was startled. This possibility had clearly never entered his mind.

"Father," he asked cautiously, "have you ever been in love?"

"Yes, son, I have."

"What became of her?"

I hung my head, unable to meet his eyes.

"She married another."

(If you but knew, my son, I thought. If you but knew...)

I looked up to find Romeo studying me intently. It was almost as though he were seeing me for the very first time.

"So, was that the reason why you—"

His words were interrupted by a knock on the door. I opened it, to find one of the novices on the threshold.

"By your leave, Fra' Lorenzo, a letter has arrived for you."

The paper bore the seal of the friary in Venice. The hand was that of Fra' Roberto.

*Salve, Lorenzo.*

*I trust that this missive will find you in good health.*

*It is with deep distress that I must ask you to prepare yourself for some grave news. Your father, the Conte Antonio Da Porto, is seriously ill, and is not expected to survive for many more days. I visited him this forenoon, and he has asked me to summon you to his deathbed.*

*He is clearly troubled in his mind. When I tried to ascertain the reason, he would not tell me the details, but he indicated that there had been some quarrel, long ago, between himself and you. It seems that he wishes to make his peace with you before he leaves this world.*

*Please return to Venice at once. Lodgings will be made ready for you at the friary.*

*God speed you on your journey.*

*In D.no,*
*Fra' Roberto*

The letter was dated the previous day.

Until that moment I had no idea that my father was even still living. Almost two decades had passed since I had first entered the Order, but during that time I had heard no news of him or of my brother Filippo. To my shame, I had given little thought to either of them.

My countenance must have registered my shock, for when I looked up, young Romeo was regarding me with an expression of deep concern.

"What is the matter, Fra' Lorenzo?"

"Romeo, I am sorry, we must continue this discourse another time. It seems that I am going to have to go away for a few days. In the meantime, please take heed of what I have said."

Romeo looked at me steadily, though he made no promise to take any note of my advice.

"God-speed, my ghostly father," he murmured, then turned and left.

***

I hastened to find Fra' Gianni and showed him Fra' Roberto's letter.

"I am sorry, my friend, but I feel I must go."

"Of course you must."

Fra' Gianni handed back the paper to me. He seemed astonished that I should have even entertained the idea of acting to the contrary.

"I may be gone for some days; as yet I do not know how many."

Fra' Gianni laid a reassuring hand on my arm.

"Stay for as long as you have need. I will attend to the gardens and the apiaries."

He hesitated, then added slowly,

"Forgive me for asking, but – was there a quarrel?"

I paused, then nodded.

"There was, but by your leave I would rather not speak of it at this moment."

"Of course."

"What of my pupils?"

I was particularly concerned for Romeo, though I could neither admit to the fact, nor reveal the reason.

39

"They can survive without you for a few days. I will hear their confessions, should the need arise. Go now – take some food and drink with you, and the swiftest of our horses. If you leave within the hour, you should reach Venice by sundown."

\*\*\*

The scent of the salt air (cool, clear and fresh after the oppressive heat of Verona) greeted me like an old friend as I rode across the Venetian causeway. Nonetheless, it was with mixed emotions that I once again knocked on the door of the old friary. I recalled the first time I had done so, as a broken-hearted youth of eighteen, a mere few hours after I had bidden a tearful farewell to my darling Chiara and our unborn child. *Dei Gratia*, these two had (in one respect at least) been restored to me – but what fate was awaiting me now, at the deathbed of my estranged father?

Fra' Roberto greeted me cordially, though in view of the circumstances his face was sombre. He called for food and ale to be brought for me, insisting that I should have some sustenance after my journey. As I ate, he told me that my father had been taken ill only a few weeks earlier, but his condition had suddenly worsened, and it was at this juncture that he had begun asking for me. It was, I understood, the first time he had mentioned my name in almost twenty years.

On the road from Verona I had had plenty of time to ponder the reason for my father's sudden change of demeanour. I had come to no reasonable conclusion, and, truth to say, I was greatly worried by what I might find at the end of my journey. And this news did not, I am sorry to say, ease my troubled mind.

The simple repast over, Fra' Roberto asked gently,

"Are you ready, Lorenzo?"

I drew a deep breath and nodded.

"Come then. I will take you to your father."

\*\*\*

The strange emotion I had felt on returning to the friary was as nothing alongside that of returning to my childhood home. The hallway was unchanged from my last memory of it, even to the distinctive aroma which had always pervaded the wooden panelling and balustrades. As a child, I had always been fascinated by the mysterious scent. With the benefit of adult knowledge, I could now identify it as beeswax.

My father's chamber smelled faintly of thyme and rosemary. But mingled with those scents I detected another – the stench of death.

"Sebastiano – is that you?"

The voice was no more than a hoarse whisper, the face no more than a grey pelt stretched tautly over a gaunt skull, the eyes wide and bloodshot.

"I am here, Father."

Fra' Roberto motioned me to the chair which he had placed beside the bed. Then, tactful as always, he stepped aside, respectfully inclined his head, and discreetly withdrew.

My father stared at me.

"Sebastiano, please forgive me."

"Forgive you? For what, Father?"

"For what I forced upon you."

Breathing hard, he struggled to continue.

"I ordered you to go into the friary. I know that it was not what you desired."

I gasped. He had known, all along, it had not been my wish to take holy orders, and yet he had nonetheless insisted that I should…

Could I – dare I – now ask the question which had lain unanswered for nigh on two decades?

"Father – why did you do so?"

With difficulty, he raised himself up to the position of resting on his elbows, so that he was half-lying, half-sitting, the better to be able to look me in the face. His eyes were moist.

"It broke my heart, Sebastiano. But I had no choice. It is because you were the younger son. The patrimony has to pass, undivided, to the eldest male heir. It has been thus for many generations."

I was at a loss how to respond. I cast around in my mind for any memories of any of my father's relatives. I found that I could recall none.

"Father, was it also thus with you?"

"Aye. I had two brothers and one sister. All were predestined for

41

the cloister from the moment I was born."

"What became of them?"

His voice grew a little stronger.

"My brothers, like you, both entered the Order of Saint Francis here in Venice. It grieved me terribly, for I loved them dearly."

"What were their names?"

"The elder was named Bartolomeo. The younger, Giacomo."

(Bartolomeo…?)

"What became of them?"

"I believe they are now both dead." He spoke in a whisper.

"And your sister?"

A faraway look came into his eyes, and he smiled fondly as the memory returned.

"Her name was Caterina. She was the eldest of us; kind, gentle and loving to all her younger brothers. But although she was the first-born, she could not inherit because she was a woman. But neither could she marry. No suitor would countenance her, beautiful and good though she was, because the patrimony rule meant that there would be no provision for a dowry."

His voice faltered again; the injustice was clearly as painful for him to recollect as it was for me to hear.

"I was fifteen years old when she entered the Order of the Poor Clares. I never saw her again. Though I understand that she later became a Mother Superior in Verona." He fell back on to the pillow, struggling to regain his breath.

(Poor Clares…? Mother Superior…? Verona…?)

Eventually I found my own voice:

"Father, I believe I may have met her."

His eyes widened.

"Are you certain of that?"

I paused before answering carefully,

"As certain as I can ever be, Father."

Even if I am mistaken about this, I thought, this poor man will know no difference now. And if in his final hours it should bring him some comfort, what would it matter if I were wrong?

"What news do you have of her?"

"She fares well; she is indeed Mother Superior of the Poor Clares in Verona. And a sweeter, kinder lady would be difficult to find."

"I am glad." His face creased into a slow, sad smile. "Please, when you see her again, commend her brother to her. Tell her that I have always loved her."

I took hold of his thin, cold hand and pressed it lightly.

"I will, Father. I promise."

"Thank you. But now, there is something more I must tell you."

"What is that?"

"The rule of the patrimony, which I followed so blindly and so foolishly, has proved to be its own undoing."

"I am not sure I understand, Father."

He paused, as if mustering the courage to say something unutterably painful.

"It has ruined so many lives. Caterina's, Bartolomeo's, Giacomo's, yours... And also, in a manner of speaking, my own."

"Your own, Father? Why do you say that?"

"Because it has robbed me of my sister, my brothers, and one of my sons."

"But you have another son, Father."

I realised, with a shock, that this was the first time either of us had even alluded to Filippo. But this was instantly eclipsed by the shock of my father's response:

"Filippo is no longer my son."

I gasped.

"Why? What has happened? Is he dead?"

"Nay. Though perhaps it might have been better if he were."

(Holy Saint Francis, I thought – what was this?)

"Father, what do you mean? Where is he? What has he done? What has happened to make you say that?"

My father again laboured to raise himself on to his elbows. I rearranged his pillows to make him more comfortable, as he struggled to continue.

"For the patrimony to pass from father to son, the bloodline must

43

remain unbroken. I had foolishly assumed that Filippo would marry and have a son of his own. But I know now that that will never happen."

"Are you certain of that?"

"I am."

"Why?"

"Because…"

He faltered again – this time not for want of breath, but for want of the courage to continue.

"Because… Filippo… Filippo…"

"What is it, Father?" I encouraged him, gently – though I was sore afraid of what he might be about to say.

"Filippo... prefers men to women."

\*\*\*

*To use Friar Lawrence's own words: Holy Saint Francis!*

*First of all, he finds out that he has a son.*

*Next, he finds out that he was forced into holy orders by some outmoded and chauvinistic rule.*

*And now, he finds out that his brother is gay.*

*How much more can the poor man take?*

*And all this is before we've even begun to think about the tragedy to come…*

\*\*\*

My father had fallen back on to his bed, exhausted. I sat in stunned silence, still holding his thin, cold hand, as I tried to absorb the full import of what he had said.

"Father," I ventured, after what seemed like an eternity, "why are you telling me this?"

"Because, Sebastiano, I wanted you to learn of this from me, not from anyone else. And also because I need to prepare you for what is to come."

"For what is to come? What do you mean by that, Father?"

"I have issued instructions to the notary that the patrimony is to pass to you, not to Filippo."

Once again, I was dumbstruck. Eventually I heard myself ask, in a voice which sounded not a whit like my own,

"But I am a friar, Father – what can I do? I have taken vows of poverty, chastity and obedience. I cannot—"

He gently raised his hand to silence me.

"Worry not, Sebastiano. When Fra' Roberto told me that he had summoned you hither, I told him everything. He said that he can arrange for a special dispensation which will release you from your vows to the Order. You will be free to marry and continue the bloodline."

"But Father, I am over thirty years old—"

"You will find a way, my son. I have great faith in you."

The image of young Romeo – my father's grandson – swam before my eyes.

*If I could but tell you, Father,* I thought in anguish, *that your bloodline is already continuing…*

For the need of something to break the silence which had fallen, I cautiously asked,

"Where is Filippo now?"

"I have not seen him for over ten years."

My father's voice grew hard.

"I had asked him why he had not married. That was when he told me of his… his… preferences."

He spat out the word as though its very presence in his mouth left a vile taste.

"I told him he was no longer any son of mine. I believe he travelled south with his… his…" (again he struggled to complete the sentence) "his… paramour." This word was disgorged with even more venom than the last. "I heard that they went to Sorrento. But as to where they are now, I neither know nor care."

"Ten years, Father? Why did you not try to tell me of this ere now?"

He hesitated. Eventually he murmured,

"Because I was ashamed."

He lay back and closed his eyes. His thin cheeks were damp with tears. But whether these were shed in sorrow, in shame, or in anger, I could not tell.

I remained silent as I continued to hold his hand, though my mind was in turmoil.

How this poor man has suffered, I thought. For so long he has been enslaved to convention and tradition – at Heaven alone knows what cost. And, God forgive me, how I have misjudged him.

*(It is in pardoning that we are pardoned…)*

I was jolted out of my musings by a low murmur.

"Sebastiano…"

I looked up. My father had opened his eyes and was looking at me intently.

"Father?"

But he gave no response. The shallow breathing had ceased, the thin hand lay limp and lifeless, the moist, dark-rimmed eyes stared at me sightlessly. Trembling, I extended my hand towards his face to close them. But another hand stayed my own as a low voice spoke behind me:

"*In manus tuas, Domine, confidemus spiritum suum… Requiescat in pace…*"

Fra' Roberto had again appeared at my side. He gently closed my father's eyes, drew the coverlet over his face, and eased me to my feet.

"Come, Lorenzo. It is very late and you must rest. Come back to the friary; we will speak again tomorrow."

\*\*\*

"How much did he tell you?"

We had eaten a modest breakfast and were sitting on a bench in the cloister garden. Brightly-coloured butterflies, awoken by the morning sunshine, were flitting amongst the flowers around us.

"As much as I needed to hear," Fra' Roberto answered gently. "He explained why you had come to us originally—"

"Had you already realised?"

"I had suspected, although I was not totally certain. During my time in the Order I have seen many younger sons pass through our doors, and by no means all of them did so willingly. In many cases, their circumstances were much the same as yours – but unlike many of them, you were a good novice and you have been a good brother.

But for a first-born to take the cowl was extremely rare. The few who did so were the ones who did come of their own accord."

"What did my father say of his own first-born?"

"Enough for me to ascertain why he has acted in this way. It saddens me to think of it. But it is not our place to judge others…"

Not for the first time, I marvelled at the wisdom of this kindly man, and how fortunate I had been to have him as my spiritual mentor throughout my time as a friar. And, once again, I found myself wondering about his own past life.

I mustered the courage to enquire:

"Fra' Roberto, may I ask you: why did you enter the Order?"

He smiled wistfully.

"I was married, but my wife died in childbirth. After that, if I could not be an earthly father, then I knew I should become a ghostly one."

"I am sorry."

"Do not be sorry; we were happy for the short time we were together, and I will always be grateful for that."

I hesitated before answering,

"I too was once in love."

Fra' Roberto looked at me sympathetically.

"I am not surprised to hear that."

I looked up and met his gaze.

"Why?"

"I have observed that your understanding of human nature has always been far greater than that of most of your peers. That level of sympathy comes only to those who have had personal experience of it."

*(Grant that I may never seek… so much to be understood as to understand…)*

"Is that why you have always understood me so well?"

Fra' Roberto smiled.

"I expect so. Maybe in you I instinctively recognised a kindred spirit; another one who had loved and lost. When my wife was taken from me I knew I could never seek to replace her, so I then sought a life with a different purpose."

His talk of purpose reminded me of my own uncertain future.

"What will become of me now?"

"That is your choice, Lorenzo. You may have been forced into the Order, but no-one will force you out of it unless you wish to go."

I was stunned. For the first time in my life, I was free to choose my own path.

"And if I do choose to leave...?"

"Then we will make the necessary arrangements for you to be released. And whatever decision you make, be well assured that you will always have my blessing."

At my side a butterfly hovered between two of the flowers, as if trying to determine which one might have the better source of nectar.

"When must I decide?"

"Take as long as you need."

"Thank you." I hesitated, then added, "You have been much more of a father to me than my own has ever been. And I remain eternally grateful to you."

Fra' Roberto smiled.

"A ghostly father should complement an earthly one, Lorenzo. Not replace him."

\*\*\*

We rose from the bench and began to walk back towards the friary.

"May I ask – what became of Fra' Bartolomeo?"

"He passed away peacefully two years ago, shortly after you left for Verona."

"And – did he have a younger brother named Giacomo?"

Fra' Roberto nodded

"Giacomo had consumption, and lived for only a few years after he joined us." He looked at me curiously. "Why do you ask?"

"I believe they may both have been my uncles."

It was the first time in my life that I had ever seen Fra' Roberto appear surprised.

"How strange that I had not realised! Come, they are both buried here in the friary cemetery. I will show you their graves."

\*\*\*

The following day, Fra' Roberto conducted my father's requiem. But during this service, unlike that of his brother so many years earlier, there was no sudden and untimely resurrection of the dead.

My father was laid to rest in our family vault. As I was leaving the burial ground, I passed the tomb belonging to Chiara's family. It bore an inscription indicating that both her parents now lay within. There was also a much older inscription, erected in memory of *"our beloved daughter Chiara, whose body lies at sea and whose soul lies safe in the arms of our Lord."*

Fortunately, anyone who saw my tears would, I hope, presume they were for my father.

***

I remained in Venice for over a week, during which time I made a first attempt at sorting out my late father's affairs. Two days after my father's funeral I received a visit from the notary.

"My Lord…" he began.

I had not, until that moment, fully registered that I was now the next Conte Da Porto.

His next words were lost to me, eclipsed by my own torrent of thought. If I returned to Venice and accepted what was now my own, this would mean no more forced poverty or chastity – and any obedience could be to my own inclinations.

Then I thought of Chiara, and of young Romeo – both of whom would be lost to me for ever if I were to leave Verona.

I knew then that my decision would not be an easy one…

***

Back in Verona, the herb garden was flourishing and the honey in the hives was ready for harvesting. Fra' Gianni had done his work well.

"Good morrow, my friend! How was your visit to Venice?"

During my journey back, I had had plenty of time to consider how much I should reveal of what had happened. I had decided, finally, that for the moment I should say as little as possible – save one thing.

"My father is dead."

"I am sorry to hear that."

"Thank you, my friend. He had been ill for some time, and I am glad that he now has no more pain."

Fra' Gianni crossed himself reverentially.

"*Requiescat in pace*," he murmured.

"How are my pupils?"

Fra' Gianni sighed.

"Benvolio and Mercutio are both well – though I feel I could easily have a little too much of Mercutio's buffoonery!"

"I know what you mean. That boy regards everything as a joke. His bravado will be his undoing one day."


(How often is a true word spoken in jest, and how often does jest tempt Providence? And how many times, since then, have I wished that those words had remained unsaid…)


"And Romeo?"

Fra' Gianni's face grew serious.

"I am worried about him, Fra' Lorenzo. He is grown pale and thin, and he has the air of one who carries all the burdens of the world on his shoulders. His mother, too, is concerned for his welfare."

"What has she said to you?" I managed, with difficulty, to keep my voice steady.

"She said that he has taken to rising early and spending hours upon end wandering alone through the sycamore grove, out to the west of the city. He says little to his parents or his friends, save that he claims he will never be happy again."

I sighed.

"I think I know what may be troubling him; he told me a little of it before I left. I had hoped that the problem might have resolved itself during my absence, but it seems not. I will speak to him again. In the meantime—"

We were interrupted by a knock on the door. One of the novices stood on the threshold.

"Pardon me, Fra' Lorenzo, but someone wishes to speak to you."

I made my way to my cell, wondering who this visitor might be. My regular visitors were all known by name and would normally have been announced accordingly; however the novice who had delivered this message was new to the Order, and had not yet become familiar with the normal routine of the friary.

I opened the cell door expecting to see Benvolio, Mercutio, Romeo or Chiara – but instead, I was greeted by the Lady Giulietta. And she was alone.

"Good morrow, Father."

She dropped a discreet curtsey.

"Good morrow, daughter. Why are you not accompanied by Agnese?"

Giulietta smiled.

"I wished to speak to you alone, Father. And my parents have agreed that to come to Shrift I now no longer need a chaperone."

"Do you wish me to hear your confession?"

"Yes, Father, but first I need to talk to you."

"Why? Is something troubling you?"

Giulietta hesitated.

"I – am not sure how to tell you. It will seem as though I am being disloyal."

"Disloyal? To whom?"

"To – to – my cousin."

"Which cousin?"

"Tebaldo. Father, I know he is my own flesh and blood, and I know that I should love him and respect him, but his behaviour frightens me."

"What do you mean?"

(I already knew exactly what she meant, but I was most interested to hear her own perception of the situation.)

"He seems always to want to fight. And always against the Montecchi. He hates the very ground that they walk upon. During these past five days alone he has incited two vicious brawls in the city streets. Have you not heard?"

"Nay, I have been away from Verona and returned only yesterday evening. But please tell me more. Do you know why he hates the Montecchi so much?"

"If I knew that, perhaps I could understand more why he behaves as he does – though even then I doubt I could agree with his behaviour. But he hates simply for the sake of hating. It is as though it has become his sole purpose in life."

"What do you know of the cause of the feud?"

Giulietta relaxed a little.

"As much as anyone alive today knows of it – which is nothing at all. The feud has existed for so long that no-one living today can recall how it ever began. Truth to tell, Father, I believe that most of my family – save Tebaldo – would be happy to let matters rest. Tebaldo is the one person amongst us who seems determined to keep the feud alive. And I am afraid that one day he will be the cause of some great tragedy."

"I understand your concern, daughter – though why are you telling me of it?"

"Because I cannot tell anyone else. My father would simply not listen, and my mother will not hear a word spoken against her brother's son."

"Why do say your father would not listen?"

"He believes that women should not concern themselves with such matters."

(Did I detect a shadow of anger in her tone?)

"What about Agnese? Can you not talk to her?"

Giulietta sighed.

"She would not understand. And Tebaldo flatters her and flirts with her. She too would not believe any ill of him."

She sighed again.

"Thank you for listening, Father."

"It is what I am here to do, daughter. And do not trouble yourself that you have sounded, as you said earlier, disloyal." I thought of my father and Filippo, before adding cautiously, "Just because you are related to someone does not necessarily mean that you must always love that person unreservedly, and remain blind to whatever faults they might have."

She looked up in surprise.

"Truly, Father?"

"Truly, daughter. And conversely, there is no necessity to hate someone simply because you have been told to hate. Or" (again I thought of Tebaldo) "because you nurture a misguided belief in some ancient grudge."

Giulietta's face brightened.

"You are very wise, Father. But I wish Tebaldo could be made to see matters in this light."

"I will endeavour to speak to him next time he comes to Shrift – though I cannot promise you that he will take any heed of me."

"Thank you, Father. And now, please will you hear my confession?"

As on all previous occasions, Giulietta had very little to confess, and even less to absolve.

***

The following day was Saturday – the day when Chiara would come for her weekly visit. The Lord Montecchi, who usually came to Shrift on Thursdays, had once indicated to me his great pleasure that his wife was now willing to attend church more than just once a year.

"You have worked a minor miracle with the Lady Lucia, Fra' Lorenzo," he had said. "She now comes to Shrift and to Mass every week. What did you do to convince her?"

I chose my words carefully.

"I ascertained the reason for her original aversion to the church, which was that she blamed God for the loss of her first husband. And I was able to persuade her to see that she still has much to live for."

My answer was not untruthful, and yet the Lord Montecchi would remain none the wiser as to the true reason for his lady's sudden and unexplained change of heart.

Although Chiara was expected, her arrival, a quarter of an hour earlier than usual, nonetheless took me by surprise.

"I am sorry, but I could wait no longer. I have missed you terribly. What news from Venice?"

"Sit down. I have much to tell you."

She looked at me nervously as I took her hand.

"My love, it grieves me to be the one to be the bearer of sad news, but I must tell you: your mother and father are both dead."

She was silent. When she finally spoke, her voice was barely above a whisper.

"How long since?"

"Several years." I paused before adding, "They had erected a

53

memorial to you on the family tomb."

Chiara faltered.

"I will say a prayer for them. I have no doubt that they have said many for me…"

She tried, but failed, to fight back her tears. I took her in my arms as she sobbed, knowing full well that here in my cell was the only place in the whole of Verona where she would be able to show her grief.

When her tears were spent, she asked quietly,

"What else do you have to tell me? You said there was much."

"Nothing that cannot wait for a little longer. I will tell you next time—"

"No, please tell me now. It cannot be worse than what you have just told me."

"Very well. But please prepare yourself, my love – this is not what you will be expecting to hear…"

Her eyes widened as I told her of my father's deathbed confession: of the reason why I had originally been forced into the cloister, of my brother's homosexuality, of my father's complete change of mind about the patrimony, and of the decision which I was now being called upon to make.

"So – what will you do?"

"Fra' Roberto has said I may take as long as I need, but I cannot delay my decision for ever. But, truth to tell, I do not know what I should do. It is very tempting to leave Verona, with all its unrest, and return to Venice, take up my birthright and live out the rest of my days in comfort. But if I do so, I will never see you again. I must leave you here—"

"Must you?"

I blinked.

"What do you mean?"

"Take me with you."

"What? How can I ever do that? You are the Lady Montecchi, the wife of the head of one of the most powerful households in Verona. How can you simply disappear?"

"I do not need to, as you say, 'simply disappear.' I could say that my first husband, who was previously believed to have drowned, has now unexpectedly returned."

"But would the Lord Montecchi believe you?"

"Why should he not?"

"Will he not realise who I am?"

"He knows you as Fra' Lorenzo, but he knows of my first husband only by the name of Sebastiano. There is no reason why he should realise—"

"But would he not wish to meet your first husband?" I persisted. "And would he not recognise me?"

Chiara frowned.

"Ah. I had not thought of that..."

Then her face brightened.

"But there is another way."

"What is that?"

She looked at me conspiratorially.

"I have faked my death once before. Why should I not do so again?"

Holy Saint Francis, I prayed – what must I do?

And the Saint's answer came, as before:

*"If all were to take the vow of chastity, the human race would come to an end..."*

Our founder's words reminded me of our own son.

"But what would become of Romeo? We would either have to leave him here in Verona and allow him to believe that you are dead, or allow him to come with us to Venice – which would mean we must tell him the truth."

Chiara was silent; this had evidently not occurred to her.

Eventually she murmured,

"We will speak of this again. I must go. Farewell, My Lord..."

*My Lord.* How sweet those words sounded. And how sweet was the prospect of hearing her say them to me, every day, for the rest of our lives...

\*\*\*

I have no idea for how long, after she had left, I sat staring into space, my mind in as great a turmoil as the day when Fra' Roberto had first asked me to move to Verona. Then, as now, I was facing a decision which had the potential to change my whole life.

Then, my choices had been that I could remain safely in Venice, or venture to Verona to an unknown destiny.

Now, I faced another dilemma. I might return to Venice as the Conte Da Porto, and could at last proclaim my darling Chiara as my legal wife – but to do so would mean we would never see our son again. Or I could renounce my birthright and remain as a friar in Verona, where I would remain close to the two people I loved most in all the world – but would remain forever unable to acknowledge them.

And if I were to take that course, what then would become of the Da Porto patrimony? As the case now stood, there was a strong possibility that the title would die with me in any case.

And Chiara wished to fake her death – for a second time.

Back in Venice this had been very easy; who knows how many thousands of its citizens have miscarried at sea and have no known grave? But here in Verona, miles from the coast and where the only body of water was the River Adige, a presumed drowning was not an option. How could one convincingly fake a death without producing a cadaver? It would not even be possible to attempt to inter an empty coffin – for the burial custom in Verona, at least amongst the richest and most powerful families, was for the departed not to be placed in a casket, but to be arrayed in their finest garments and laid to rest, uncovered, on a bier in their family's mausoleum. I had never encountered this practice in Venice, and truth to say I found it somewhat distasteful.

And I was no closer to knowing what I must do.

Eventually I roused myself from my stupor, opened the door and wandered out into the herb garden. The calming scents of lavandula and lemon balm greeted me; I allowed them to embrace me as an old friend.

The lengthening shadows and the setting sun cast an eerie twilight over the garden. Many of the plants were now indistinguishable from one another, save by their scents. I thought idly of my early days with the apothecary back in Venice, and of how he had impressed upon me the importance of being able to tell them apart...

It came to me as a thunderbolt. Fra' Bartolomeo. The medicine...

I sank down on to the bench, suddenly feeling quite dizzy.

Could I re-create the draught which I had accidentally

administered to him – the sleeping draught which had deceived us all into believing he had died – and give it to Chiara? For a short while after taking it she would appear to be dead – and even Verona's peculiar burial customs could be made to work to our advantage. After her interment, I could secretly rescue her from the vault and spirit her away to Venice.

Provided, of course, that either of us could bring ourselves to leave Romeo here in Verona...

My musings were interrupted by the bell summoning me to Completorium.

*Noctem quiétam, et finem perféctum concédat nobis Dóminus omnípotens...*

May the Lord Almighty grant us a quiet night and a perfect end...

Whatever perfect end might lie in store, I did not envisage a quiet night. After the service I returned to my cell, lit a candle, picked up pen and paper, and racked my brains to recall exactly how I had created the medicine which I had inadvertently concocted more than a decade earlier.

\*\*\*

I slept fitfully that night, and was already wide awake when the nightingale's song gave way to that of the lark.

After early Mass I made my way to the Convent of the Poor Clares. I had not forgotten that I had a vital message to deliver – assuming, of course, that I was not mistaken about the identity of its intended recipient.

The Mother Superior welcomed me as before, although it had been some time since I had last seen her.

"Reverend Mother, I have something which I must ask you – something which relates to your time before you entered the Order."

"Very well, Fra' Lorenzo."

"First, may I ask – have you always lived here in Verona?"

She looked momentarily surprised, but responded,

"Nay, only these past thirty years. I was born and raised in Venice. As were you, I believe?"

"That is true. And – did you have any brothers or sisters?"

She sat very still before answering slowly,

"Aye, I had three brothers, all younger than myself. And I believe that my mother had also had another daughter, born a year after I was, but she had died at birth. I am not totally certain of that; it was something which was never spoken of at home. I know of it only because it was inadvertently mentioned once by my nurse when I was a child." She sighed. "I loved my brothers dearly. I often think of them, and pray that life has been good to them. I have had no news of any of them since I entered the Order."

"What were the names of your brothers?"

"The eldest was Antonio, the second Bartolomeo, and the youngest Giacomo. Why do you ask?"

"Before I answer that question, may I please ask you one more? Was your own name Caterina Da Porto?"

The deafening silence which met this question was response enough. And for the second time within four and twenty hours, I had to impart news which I knew would be shocking and almost certainly distressing. In what I hoped was a kindly tone, I said,

"Please, prepare yourself for what I have to tell you."

She remained motionless, save her lips, which moved in a silent prayer. Eventually she murmured,

"Very well, Fra' Lorenzo, I am ready."

"Antonio Da Porto – your brother – was my father."

Another deafening silence ensued. When she spoke again, her voice was trembling.

"It is strange, but when I first encountered you, it seemed to me that you reminded me of someone. At the time I could not understand why; now I know. Please tell me, what news of Antonio?"

She looked at me steadily and read the unspoken answer in my countenance.

"He is…?" She could not bring herself to say the word.

I nodded.

"I am sorry to be the one who has to tell you. But he asked me—"

She gasped.

"You have seen him?"

"Aye, not two weeks since. He summoned me to his deathbed. And he asked me to tell you that he has always loved you."

Her lower lip quivered and a solitary tear trickled down her cheek. She wiped it away with a corner of her veil.

"And what of Bartolomeo and Giacomo?"

"They became Franciscan friars, like myself. I am sorry, they too are both dead. Giacomo died quite young, of consumption—"

"He was never strong, even as a child," she said sadly. "And Bartolomeo?"

"He died two years ago." I hesitated. "I knew him in the friary in Venice, though at the time I knew not who he was."

Now it was my turn to wipe away a tear.

It was she who eventually broke the silence:

"What else did Antonio say to you?"

I was not sure how much more I dared repeat to her, but I began cautiously,

"He told me of the patrimony rule."

She looked up in surprise.

"What was that?"

"I am sorry – do you not know of it?"

"Nay."

"It was the reason why you, and Bartolomeo, and Giacomo, and indeed I, all entered holy orders."

She looked at me intently.

"I am not sure I fully understand what you are telling me."

"Forgive me; I myself only learned of this at my father's deathbed. It seems that it has been the rule in our family, for many generations, that the patrimony must pass undivided to the eldest son. For that reason – and that reason only – all other children, male or female, have been destined for the cloister."

Her troubled face suddenly cleared.

"So that would explain why the only dolls I was ever given were those which wore a nun's habit. Or why the only praise I ever received, as a child, was 'What a perfect Lady Abbess!' And why, as I grew older, I was never allowed any suitors."

"My father told me that the reason for that was because you would have had no dowry. The patrimony rule prevented it. It pained him to speak of it."

A faraway look came into her eyes – eerily similar to that which I had recently discerned on the face of my dying father.

"I have often wondered… And it is good to know that Antonio cared about me a little. Thank you for bringing me his message."

"I am sorry that in doing so I must also have had to bring you such sad tidings."

She turned again to look at me.

"May I now ask you a question?"

"By all means."

"If you are my brother's younger son, then why did he summon you from the friary to his deathbed? I presume he must have had an older son – so what became of him?"

This was the question I had been dreading most of all, for I had no idea how I should respond to it. But ere I could give her an answer, there was a knock on the door.

One of the sisters entered hurriedly.

"By your leave, Reverend Mother, Fra' Lorenzo – there has been more fighting in the streets. There are some wounded to be tended."

\*\*\*

As we hurried to the Convent's infirmary, my aunt (for that is how I found I now regarded her) advised me that during the past few weeks the violence had once again escalated. I recalled what Giulietta had intimated to me the previous day, and wondered if, once again, Tebaldo had been involved in this latest fray.

I was to learn the answer to this much sooner than I had anticipated, for amongst the walking wounded was none other than Benvolio.

As I inspected his injury (a long, but thankfully not deep, cut to his left upper arm), he told me what had occurred in the city that morning.

It appeared that two of the servants of the Capuleti household had by chance encountered some of those of the House of Montecchi in the marketplace. They had quarrelled, first with words and then with swords. Benvolio, mindful of the Prince's previous decrees forbidding fighting in the streets, had drawn his own sword and attempted to stop the assault.

It was then that Tebaldo had appeared, and had commented on Benvolio's drawn sword. Benvolio had replied that he had drawn only to keep the peace, and had asked for Tebaldo's assistance in parting the combatants.

Tebaldo had responded by sneering and drawing his own rapier, with the words:

"I hate peace. I hate all of the House of Montecchi. And I hate you. Have at you!"

And Benvolio, fearful for his own safety, had had no alternative than to use his sword to defend himself.

It had been Tebaldo who had wounded Benvolio. Why, I asked myself, was I not surprised to hear this?

The fighting had ceased only when the Prince himself had appeared and ordered the rebellious citizens to throw down their weapons. By this time, the Lords Capuleti and Montecchi had also arrived upon the scene. Their respective ladies had tried, with limited success, to prevent them from entering into the bloody fray themselves. The Prince had ordered the Lord Capuleti to return with him forthwith to the palace, and the Lord Montecchi to attend on him later in the day. Both were to be bound, on pain of death, to keep the peace.

"Fra' Lorenzo, I am so tired of all this." Benvolio winced as I cleaned his wound and applied a honey salve. "What will have to happen to make them stop fighting?"

What indeed, I wondered.

It was only after I had left the Convent that I remembered that I had not answered my aunt's question about what had become of my elder brother. But perhaps, on reflection, it was better that she should not know.

\*\*\*

As Benvolio and I made our way back to the friary we encountered Mercutio, who had only just risen from his bed and hence had avoided any involvement in the fray. In his usual jovial manner, he jested about his disappointment at having missed the excitement.

But of Romeo there was no sign.

"Where is Romeo?" I asked cautiously. "Was he involved in the fighting?"

Benvolio sighed.

"Nay, Father. He always avoids the fights in any case, but of late he has taken to rising early and spending long hours walking in the sycamore grove out to the west. I went for a walk earlier today – long before the fray broke forth – and saw him in the distance. I made to go and speak with him, but he saw me approaching and ran away ere I could reach him. I believe he may still be there now."

"Do you know what is the matter with him?"

"What is ever the matter with Romeo, Fra' Lorenzo?" retorted Mercutio, with the weary air of one who has trodden this same path many times before. "He is in love again."

"With whom?"

"Rosaline. Still. This time, it has lasted far longer than any of the others. A full two weeks!"

"And what of the lady?"

Benvolio sighed.

"It seems that she will have none of him."

I paused to recollect. In view of what I now knew of Romeo's current state of mind, it now seemed that one of the best courses of action would be for him to be taken as far away as possible from Verona, and from the object of his unrequited affection. But (aside from the problem of how Chiara and I could do so without revealing to him the truth about his parentage) I feared that if he were forced to live without his love, he might easily be tempted to take matters into his own hands – with Heaven alone knew what consequence.

But Mercutio was speaking again.

"Fear not, Father. If love plays roughly with Romeo, then Romeo must play roughly with love. We will cure him of it!"

"You seem very confident, son. How do you propose to do that?"

"By showing him that there are far lovelier ladies than Rosaline!"

Mercutio grinned.

"I and my brother are this evening invited as guests to a banquet. We will attend as masquers, and Benvolio and Romeo will accompany us in disguise."

Benvolio smiled and nodded agreement.

"And we will demonstrate to our lovelorn friend that there are many more fair ladies who are far more worthy of his affection!"

I fervently hoped they would succeed. It might not present a solution to my own dilemma, but it might, at the very least, help my son.

Back at my cell, I retrieved the piece of paper from the previous evening, picked up a basket and wandered out into the herb garden. Valerian, golden hop, mandragora, lavandula, chamomile, poppy – all prescribed remedies for those for whom sleep is elusive. I gathered a little of each, together with some of the other herbs which I recalled having used in the original medicine, returned to my cell and set to work.

For the remainder of the day I chopped, crushed, boiled and distilled the herbs, in varying quantities, strengths and combinations. At last, by sunset, I was cautiously optimistic that I had at last re-created a fair quantity of the trance-inducing draught which could bring about the borrowed likeness of death. I decanted it into a few small vials, secreted them in a hidden corner of my cell, and betook myself to the chapel for Completorium.

And on this occasion, I did have a quiet night.

***

*It was now looking as though the manuscript had caught up with the beginning of the main story. I paused briefly to dig out my elderly and battered copy of* Romeo & Juliet. *Yes, there it was – a bloody brawl in the streets, Romeo brooding over Rosaline, and the plans for the three friends to gatecrash the party at the Capulet mansion.*

*Oh Friar Lawrence – if you only knew what was about to happen, I very much doubt that you would have had a quiet night…*

***

The following morning I rose early, shortly after sunrise, and began to harvest the honey from the beehives.

"Good morrow, Father!"

I looked up in surprise, and beheld none other than young Romeo. He was attired in festive garments, his hair was tousled and his eyes rimmed with shadows. But he appeared brighter and more animated than I had seen him for many a long week.

I laid aside my pail.

"Good morrow, son! Why are you risen so early? Are you unwell? Or worried?"

63

He grinned, but did not answer.

"Otherwise, is it that you are not risen very early, but out of bed very late? Tell me, son – am I correct in saying that you did not even see your bed last night?"

"That is true, Father. I did not. But I had a much sweeter rest—"

"Heaven forgive you, son! Were you with Rosaline last night?"

"With Rosaline?" Romeo looked genuinely surprised at the question. "Nay, Father. I have forgotten that name, and all the trouble which it brought to me."

Praise Heaven, I thought. Benvolio and Mercutio have clearly done their work well!

"That is good, son. And I am mightily pleased to hear it. But tell me – where were you last night? And why have you come here so early this morning?"

"I was feasting with my enemy."

"What?"

"And at that same feast I was wounded by my enemy, but I too wounded in return. And both I and my enemy now need your assistance."

His drift was lost on me. I shook my head in exasperation.

"Son, I am sorry, I do not understand you. You are talking in riddles; please explain what you mean. Who is this enemy of which you speak, and why do you both need my assistance?"

I looked at him steadily.

"Have you been fighting?"

He turned to face me, his blue eyes ablaze with passion despite their having been so long deprived of sleep.

"Nay, Father, the very opposite. Not fighting, but loving."

Oh no, I thought. Heaven preserve us; he is in love again. How many levels of heartache will this one bring?

"Loving whom, my son?" I ventured to ask.

His reply came as a thunderbolt:

"The fair Giulietta."

Eventually I found my voice.

"Holy Saint Francis! How has this come about? Not four and twenty hours ago you had eyes for none but Rosaline – and now it is as though she had never existed! How many bitter tears have you shed in vain for her? Clearly you did not love her as you had believed – and

I am right glad that you have now realised that – but how do you know that this new love of yours will fare any better? You have loved before and it has all come to naught. And what a choice you have made on whom to bestow your affection now! The Lady Giulietta, the daughter of the House of Capuleti, your family's sworn enemies! Son, you rush from one unattainable ideal to another!"

"Father, how often have you chided me for loving Rosaline?"

"I did not chide you for loving her, son, but for wasting your affection on one who did not love you in return."

"I know now that I was foolish in doting on her as I did. But my new love is not unattainable. Giulietta does love me in return. And we wish to marry. It is for this reason that we need your help. Please, agree to marry us. Today."

My first thought on hearing this passionate outpouring was that my son had finally taken all leave of his senses. But on looking at him again, I discerned in his demeanour something which had been sorely lacking with all of his previous affairs of the heart. He now looked vital, warm, sincere, and (for the first time since I could remember) fully alive. I racked my brains to recall where I had seen that look elsewhere. It came to me in a flash: it was the look I had seen on the face of his mother, on the day when I had first met her.

Perhaps it was this recollection which convinced me that this time, Romeo was not now harbouring another mere boyish fantasy, but had genuinely met the love of his life. His mother and I had experienced this same instantaneous passion – a passion which was still as strong today as it had been on the day we had met, and after twenty years of nigh-impossible adversity and obstacles. If the parents could love thus, then it would naturally follow that their son was equally capable of it.

And what of Giulietta? She had always been a good and sensible girl, often displaying a level of wisdom far beyond her tender years. If she did indeed love Romeo as much as he loved her, this contract would not be something she had entered into lightly or trivially. A love which was capable of transcending the barriers of the two households' ancient grudge must indeed be very strong.

This thought in turn led to another: could the marriage of these two young people eventually bring about the reconciliation of their warring families? Could this be the one good, lasting thing I could procure in strife-torn Verona, before I departed for ever…?

*(Where there is hatred, let me sow love…)*

"Please, Father?"

Romeo's voice interrupted my idealistic musings. He was still looking at me beseechingly. I forced what I hoped was a sensible-sounding response.

"Pray tell me, son, how has all this come about? And so suddenly?"

"I will tell you anon. But first, please, will you consent to marry us?"

I smiled at him and nodded.

"Aye, I will assist you. And I hope that your marriage, and your happiness, will at last bring an end to the strife between your two households."

"Today?"

"Today. Here. This very afternoon."

Romeo leapt up in glee.

"Thank you! I must go and send a message to her. I will be back anon."

He was already through the door when I called after him,

"Take care, son…"

But I doubt he would have heard me.

I wandered back into the herb garden in an attempt to collect my thoughts. The honey harvest would have to wait. I now had much to attend to in the meantime.

\*\*\*

The last clandestine marriage ceremony I had attended had been my own. Recalling the chill of the dark and gloomy church in which Chiara and I had secretly pledged our vows, I resolved to make our son's wedding a little more festive. To perform the marriage in the friary chapel would incur too great a risk of discovery, so as I awaited the return of the eager bridegroom I created a makeshift altar in my cell, adorned with candles and a few flowers gathered from the friary garden.

Romeo was back at my cell within the hour.

"Well, son, you promised you would tell me what happened."

He hesitated for a moment, then nodded.

"Yesterday morning I arose early and went for a long walk in the sycamore grove. I was thinking of Rosaline."

He shrugged and shook his head, before continuing:

"I had just arrived back in the city when I encountered Benvolio and Mercutio. Benvolio's arm was bandaged—"

"Aye, son, this I know. It was I who dressed it. Your friend had been caught up in a fray in the street. Though thankfully he was not badly hurt."

"As we talked, a man approached me with a paper and asked me if I could read. He, it seemed, could not. The paper bore a list of names of people whom the man had been asked to seek out. They were all to be invited to a feast that evening at the house of his master, the Lord Capuleti. Amongst them were Mercutio and his brother Valentino."

"Mercutio knew already of this intended feast; he told me of it himself yesterday ere he encountered you. Though he did not say where it was to be," I added quietly.

"The man said to Benvolio and myself that if we were not of the House of Montecchi, we too would be welcome to come and take wine with them." Romeo grinned. "Clearly he did not recognise us!"

"Clearly not!" I grinned also. "What then?"

"After the Lord Capuleti's man had left us, Benvolio said that we should all go as masquers to the feast – and there he would demonstrate to me that my fair swan was no more than an ugly crow! I naturally did not believe him, but I agreed to go, because elsewhere on the list was the name of my very own Rosaline – the Lord Capuleti's niece. I wished to go to the feast simply to be able to gaze upon her."

"It seems that you had no wish to be cured of her."

"Nay, Father, that is true. But I must own that, ere we arrived at the house of the Capuleti, I had felt as though something strange was about to happen. I tried to warn my friends of my foreboding, but Mercutio simply made light of it."

"In what way, son?"

"He said I must have been visited by Queen Mab. The fairies' midwife, he called her. He said she invades lovers' minds whilst they sleep."

Romeo shook his head, then continued:

"It was as though he thought I had imagined it all. He does not understand. It can only be that he himself has never loved a woman."

I too had discerned that Mercutio, unlike Benvolio, had never shown any interest in the fairer sex. Indeed, I had sometimes wondered if his preferences, like those of my own estranged brother, might possibly lie in a different direction. But this was hardly an appropriate moment to give voice to this thought...

"But then," Romeo continued, "we put on our masks and went into the house. The Lord Capuleti himself bade us welcome! Mercutio and Benvolio quickly vanished into the crowd. I, meantimes, concealed myself in a corner and kept watch, looking to catch a glimpse of Rosaline."

He paused and shook his head again, as if to dislodge the thought from his mind.

"It was then that I saw Giulietta. She was dancing with someone who I believe is a kinsman of Mercutio."

"Did you know, when you first saw her, who she was?"

"Not by name, Father, but I knew straight away that she was to be my lady and my love."

"Just as you had thought with Rosaline?"

Romeo looked at me indignantly.

"Nay, Father! When I saw Giulietta I realised that I had truly never loved any other."

"And this, ere you had even spoken to the lady?"

Romeo sighed.

"You would not understand..."

I made as if to protest, but Romeo continued apace.

"When the measure ended, I took care to observe where she went. I followed her and we – we – conversed."

He paused, and smiled to himself at the recollection. I wondered what else they had done that he was not willing to tell me.

"Then we were interrupted by a lady who told her that her mother wished to speak with her. I asked the lady who her mother was, and she told me that she was the lady of the house, and that she herself had nursed the daughter with whom I had recently been talking."

He paused and sighed again.

"It was only then I learned that my love was the daughter of my family's sworn enemy."

"Did you speak to her again?"

"Not immediately. Benvolio and Mercutio found me again and said we must leave; it seemed that despite our masks Tebaldo had recognised us, and would fain have made trouble. But once we were outside in the street I knew I would have to go back and find Giulietta again, so I hid in the shadows. They called out for me but I stayed hidden, and eventually they left without me."

"What then? Did you go back into the house?"

"Nay. I climbed over the wall and found myself in the orchard. There was a window above me, open but lit from within. As I watched, she appeared."

"Giulietta?"

"Aye, it was the window of her chamber."

"Did she see you?"

"Nay, it was dark and I was concealed by the trees. I wanted to speak to her, but then she began to speak aloud to herself."

His blue eyes shone.

"It was then that I knew, for certain, that she loved me as I love her."

"How so?"

"Unaware that I could hear her, she asked aloud why I was named Romeo, and declared that it was only my name which was her enemy, and that if I were called by any other name than Montecchi she would still love me for what I am."

"Truly, son?"

"Truly, Father. I wished to answer her, but at first I did not dare believe what I was hearing. But then she said that if I loved her, she would renounce the name of Capuleti. I called out to her and said that I would take her at her word."

"Did that not alarm her, when you called out?"

"When I first spoke it surprised her, but when she recognised my voice she welcomed me gladly. She came down into the orchard so that we could talk more discreetly, as she was afraid lest her kinsmen should find me there."

"And rightly so, son – if they had found you…"

I shivered, unable to bear the thought of what might have befallen Romeo, had Tebaldo discovered him.

"But it was dark and I knew they could not see me. Indeed, it was so dark that I could scarcely see her."

69

He chuckled.

"She said that she was glad that it was dark, else I might see her blushing because of what I had heard her say. But she could not wish the words unsaid, for they were true nonetheless."

What a change was here, I thought. Gone was the dreamy, brooding, idealistic and romantic boy I had always known. Never before had I seen Romeo so animated, so talkative, so alive. I was about to speak, but Romeo began again:

"And it was then that she asked me if I truly loved her and wished to marry her."

I gasped.

"What? It was she, not you, who first spoke of marriage?"

If this were true, then I knew this love must be genuine. Whilst Romeo, idealistic and romantic as he was, might well propose marriage on a whim, the sensible and practical Giulietta certainly would not.

"Aye, Father. She said that she would send a messenger to me this morning, so that I could send her word of where and when we should wed."

He paused to catch his breath.

"Forgive me, Father, that was why I had to leave you so suddenly earlier."

"Did you meet with this messenger? Who was it?"

So much now depended on this venture that I was worried lest this messenger might not be trustworthy.

"I did. Her nurse. She promised me that my Giulietta will be here this afternoon."

I sighed with relief. Giulietta's messenger was none other than the discreet and dependable Agnese.

"Does anyone else know of this plan?"

Romeo hesitated.

"Only my servant, Balthasar. I – had to tell him. He is to meet with the nurse to deliver a rope ladder, which I will need later for—"

This, however, was a detail which I had no need to hear.

"And how will your Giulietta devise a means to come hither today?" I asked quickly.

"She will tell her parents that she is coming to Shrift."

I sighed again, though this time with sympathetic fatigue. Romeo's energy had, by proxy, left me exhausted.

***

The friary clock struck the hour of four.

"May it please Heaven to smile upon this happy union."

"Amen to that, Father!"

Romeo was pacing around my cell in great agitation.

"But just to be able to call her my wife is sufficient."

I shuddered. Had I been too hasty in agreeing to perform this marriage?

He loves too strongly, and too soon, I thought. Could he fall out of love just as swiftly and as violently? Heaven forfend…

"Son, even the sweetest things can lose their appeal if taken to excess."

I gestured towards the half-filled pots of honey on the table.

"So do not wear out your love too quickly. It will last longer, and be stronger, if you love in moderation."

There came a faint tapping at the door. Romeo froze.

"Come in!" I called.

The door opened and Giulietta entered.

As she bade me good afternoon, Romeo crossed the room in two strides, clasped her tightly in his arms and kissed her passionately – a kiss which she returned with equal fervour. If I had previously harboured any doubts about the strength of their feelings for each other, now I saw them together these doubts were utterly dispelled. Each totally absorbed in the other, it was as though they had already forgotten that I was even there.

I coughed gently to attract their attention, and beckoned them towards the improvised altar. As one they knelt down before it, their faces radiant, their fingers still interlaced.

I opened my breviary:

"*Ego conjugo vos in matrimonium, in nomine Patris, Filii et Spiritus Sancti…*"

Their vows exchanged, and one of Giulietta's own rings blessed and employed as a wedding ring, the newly-made husband and wife left my cell and reluctantly went their separate ways until they would meet again at nightfall. I watched them go, and murmured a silent prayer for their happiness.

Had I but known what was to befall them ere that very same day was over, I would have said many, many more...

***

As I finished harvesting the honey, I turned my thoughts again to my own situation. If Romeo now had a good and valid reason to remain in Verona, the thought of leaving him here was now much less difficult to contemplate.

On returning to my cell I picked up paper and quill, and began to compose my letter to Fra' Roberto.

*Salve, Fra' Roberto.*

*Once again, may I thank you for your kindness to me, both throughout my time as a friar in Venice and more recently at the time of my father's passing.*

*Since returning to Verona I have spent much time in considering the decision which I must make, and I have—*

I was interrupted by a sudden and frantic hammering at the door. I rose from my seat to answer it, but before I had taken a single step, the door crashed open and Romeo burst in. He was shaking violently, there was a look of abject terror in his wild blue eyes, his pale skin was hot and clammy, and his clothes were torn and bloodstained.

"Father, you must help me! Hide me, I beg of you!"

Holy Saint Francis, I thought, what has befallen him?

"Son, what has happened?"

His breathing was so laboured that he could barely form the words. Eventually, he gasped,

"Mercutio is dead. And I have killed a man."

"What?"

"Please, Father, let me hide here. I will be put to death if I am found."

My first thought was that he must be delirious, but I forced myself to remain calm. I took him by the shoulders and faced him.

"Please, son, tell me what happened."

But his strength had given out. He gave no answer, but crumpled to the floor, still shaking.

I quickly mixed him a calming draught and knelt down beside him, gently supporting him as he drank it.

As the draught took effect his violent trembling gradually slowed, and his breathing became more controlled. Eventually he managed to gasp,

"Father, please go and find out what the Prince has decreed for me."

I was loth to leave him alone in this state, but I was sure that if, as he claimed, he genuinely feared for his life, then he would not stir from the cell. I passed him the remainder of the sedative draught, waited until he had drunk it, then told him to rest until I returned. I cautiously left the cell, locked the door behind me, and made my worried way into the city.

*  *  *

As I approached the centre I became aware of sounds of screaming and wailing. Nervously I followed the noise, and soon found myself on the edge of a large frenzied crowd gathered outside the palace of Prince Bartolomeo Della Scala.

Whatever had happened here, it had clearly been no mere ordinary street-brawl.

I eased my way round the edge of the baying crowd, with mounting fear of what I would find at the front of it. As I drew level with the front row, I gasped as I recognised the figures of the Lord and Lady Capuleti (and, standing behind them, Agnese), on the one side, and on the other the Lord Montecchi and Benvolio, together with a young man whom I recognised as Valentino, the brother of Mercutio. Panic-stricken, I looked around frantically for Chiara, but of her there was apparently no sign. For the first time ever, her absence came as a blessed relief.

What I saw next made my blood run cold.

Lying on the ground, between the front of the crowd and the steps of the Prince's palace, were the bodies of two young men. Both were heavily bloodstained, both totally motionless. And as I peered at their

73

lifeless faces, I realised – to my utter horror – that I recognised both of them.

The cadaver nearest to me was, as Romeo had intimated, that of Mercutio.

Oh dear God, I thought.

The other corpse, over which the Lady Capuleti was wailing hysterically, was that of Tebaldo.

Even today, ever so many years later, I am ashamed to own that my first thought, on seeing this sorry spectacle, was one which was totally unworthy of any human being, let alone of a man of God. My unparalleled grief at the death of Mercutio was mingled with a curious and guilty notion of sheer relief, brought about by the thought that the evil Tebaldo was now incapable of causing any further harm.

How naïf of me, I now realise, to have reasoned thus. I was soon to discover that even in death, Tebaldo still had the power to ruin the lives of the living.

The Prince had, by now, appeared on the steps of the palace. On catching sight of the body of Mercutio, he ran towards it as if in disbelief, bent over it, then straightened up and stared at the crowd, his tearful eyes ablaze with a mixture of grief and anger.

"This is my beloved kinsman," he declared. "Why is he lying dead at my feet?"

Benvolio stepped nervously forward.

"Sir…" he began, then faltered.

The Prince looked at him kindly.

"Please tell me, Benvolio – how did this bloody fray come about? Who began it?"

Benvolio, emboldened by the Prince's encouragement, spoke again.

"It was begun by Tebaldo."

Benvolio gestured towards Tebaldo's corpse. The Lady Capuleti began to screech as if to contradict Benvolio's words, but her protest was swiftly and silently quelled by a single gesture from the Prince.

Benvolio continued,

"Sir, it is my understanding that Tebaldo appeared to hold some unaccustomed grudge against Romeo, and I believe that he had even sent a letter to Romeo challenging him to a duel. But I do not know the cause of this quarrel."

He paused, as if mustering the courage to continue; clearly what he was about to relate was painful for him to recall.

"Sir, not two hours ago, I and your kinsman Mercutio were walking together through the main square, when Tebaldo and some of the other Capuleti approached us. Mercutio seemed unconcerned, but for myself I was worried, for I well knew that Tebaldo might pick a quarrel with us—"

The Lady Capuleti again screeched in protest. And again, the Prince silenced her with an angry gesture.

"Benvolio, pray continue."

He fixed the Lady Capuleti with a commanding stare, defying her to interrupt again.

Benvolio glanced uneasily towards the Capuleti, then spoke afresh.

"Tebaldo said to Mercutio: 'You consort with Romeo.' He made it sound as though this were a heinous crime."

(In Tebaldo's eyes, I thought, anyone even remotely connected with the Montecchi was a heinous criminal...)

"Mercutio still appeared unconcerned by Tebaldo's provocation; he even made light of it, although I feared that by doing so he might provoke Tebaldo even further. Mindful of your own decree, Sir, I tried to suggest to them that they should not be quarrelling in a public place. But then Romeo himself appeared, and Tebaldo bade Mercutio a curt farewell, turned away from him and approached Romeo."

"What did Mercutio do then?" the Prince asked.

"He and I both stood aside, but we stayed close by." Benvolio shuddered. "Truth to say, Sir, we were afeared for my cousin's safety."

"Go on."

"Tebaldo drew his sword, strode up to Romeo and said to him, 'Romeo, you are a villain.'"

The Prince was visibly shocked.

"And how did Romeo respond?"

"He answered with great politeness: 'Tebaldo, I will take no note of such an unfriendly greeting. But I am no villain, and I see that you do not know me properly. Farewell.' Then he bowed and turned away as if to leave."

"Was Tebaldo satisfied with this?"

"Nay, Sir. He insisted that Romeo had deeply offended him, and

75

called upon him to fight. But Romeo still would not be drawn. He turned back and replied, 'Tebaldo, I say again: I have no quarrel with you. Please be content with that.' And again he turned to leave."

As I listened to Benvolio's report, I wondered what Romeo (who had always taken such great pains to avoid becoming involved in the families' longstanding feud) could possibly have done to have caused such purported offence to Tebaldo. I could think of nothing, save that Romeo had infiltrated the feast at the house of the Capuleti the previous evening. Romeo had himself said that Tebaldo had apparently recognised the interlopers; would this alone have been sufficient to provoke Tebaldo into sending Romeo a letter challenging him to a duel? I realised instantly that I had already answered my own question, almost before I had finished asking it.

The Prince was speaking again.

"So how did Mercutio become involved?"

"Tebaldo still would not put away his sword, and began to follow Romeo as he walked away. It was then that Mercutio, seemingly afraid that Tebaldo would do Romeo harm, drew his own sword and placed himself between them, as if ready to act in Romeo's defence."

"Was Mercutio not afraid for his own safety?" The Prince's words gave voice to my own thoughts.

"I know not, Sir. But truth to say, I do not think that Mercutio intended to fight with Tebaldo; it is my belief that he wished only to deter him from attacking Romeo."

The Prince nodded.

"'Twas ever thus," he said sadly. "My kinsman was well-known for his loyalty and his bravery."

(And for his bravado, I added mentally – recalling my own earlier foreboding that this bravado might prove to be the youth's undoing.)

"What then?"

"Tebaldo turned on Mercutio, Sir—"

The Lady Capuleti again screeched.

"Prince, this man does not speak truly. He is the nephew of the Lord Montecchi. His testimony is biased in their favour."

The Prince spun round to face her.

"Madam," he thundered, "Were you present here when these

events were taking place?"

The Lady Capuleti reluctantly shook her head.

"In that case, Madam, you cannot relate what you did not witness. Hold your peace."

He turned back to Benvolio and motioned him to continue.

"Sir, Tebaldo and Mercutio fought hard. Romeo shouted to them that after the last civil brawls, you had declared that fighting in the streets was strictly forbidden. He and I both attempted to separate them."

Benvolio hesitated, shuddered, then added,

"Romeo somehow succeeded in placing himself between the two of them, and forced their swords downwards, which seemed to distract Mercutio for a moment. Then Tebaldo thrust his own sword upwards under Romeo's arm, and Mercutio, caught off his guard, was hurt."

"Do you believe that Tebaldo intended to cause Mercutio harm?"

Benvolio again glanced nervously at the Capuleti, before murmuring,

"That I cannot tell, Sir. But I do know that he wished harm to Romeo – indeed, it may be that his sword-thrust was intended for Romeo rather than for Mercutio."

The Prince considered this for a moment, then nodded.

Benvolio continued:

"As Mercutio fell to the ground, Tebaldo then put away his sword and walked away. Mercutio called to us 'Fetch me a surgeon. I am hurt.' We could see that he was bleeding, but we could not tell straight away how badly he was injured. He stood up, turned to Romeo and asked him why he had come between them. Before Romeo could answer, Mercutio suddenly said that he felt faint, and asked me to help him indoors. It was only when he leaned on me and we saw the depth of his injury that we realised he was mortally wounded." Benvolio shuddered. "His last words were to curse the feud between the two households, for having brought about his own end."

"A cursed feud indeed," said the Prince under his breath, as he gazed again at Mercutio's lifeless body. Wiping away a tear, he addressed Benvolio again:

"What happened next?"

"Romeo appeared to be unable to take in what had happened. He bent over Mercutio and muttered something, but I could not hear what he said. Then suddenly he jumped up and looked round. I turned to see what he was looking at, and saw that Tebaldo was coming back towards us, with his sword drawn." Benvolio shuddered again. "I told Romeo to leave before there was any more trouble or bloodshed, but before I could stop him, he had drawn his own sword."

"Did you try to separate them?"

"Aye, Sir, but Tebaldo pushed me aside. As he turned back to face Romeo, he appeared to run on to Romeo's sword."

The Lady Capuleti screamed.

"Prince, I say again, he is lying!"

The Prince rounded on her.

"And I say again, Madam, that you cannot gainsay Benvolio's testimony if you did not see with your own eyes what occurred here! Benvolio may be of the House of Montecchi, but that does not in itself mean that he is an unreliable witness."

He turned to address the crowd.

"Does anyone here have any evidence which will confirm, or refute, the story which Benvolio has told me?"

The silence which followed spoke volumes.

"Very well," said the Prince, staring at the Lady Capuleti, "as Benvolio was the only witness, we must accept his account as being the truth."

The Lady Capuleti glowered, but said nothing.

The Prince went on:

"Whatever the initial intention of these two fights might have been, their conclusion remains the same. My kinsman here was slain by Tebaldo. Tebaldo, in his turn, was slain by Romeo."

The Lady Capuleti broke her silence.

"And for that, Romeo must die!" she screeched.

The Lord Montecchi now spoke for the first time.

"Noble Prince, your kinsman Mercutio died at the hands of Tebaldo. Should Tebaldo not then have been put to death for that crime, regardless of what my son might have done thereafter?"

I had never before heard the Lord Montecchi say the words "my son". This unexpected utterance made me catch my breath.

The Prince did not answer immediately. He stared down at the two bodies which lay on the ground before him. Eventually he declared:

"Tebaldo slew Mercutio; Romeo slew Tebaldo. For that offence, Romeo is herewith banished from Verona."

A gasp went round the crowd. The Lady Capuleti made as if to protest again, but was silenced by a gesture from her husband.

"Take these bodies away."

The Prince was now beckoning to two of his servants, who at his instruction hoisted Mercutio's body on to a stretcher and carried it through the gates into the Prince's palace. Valentino followed it, his eyes moist, his shoulders drooping, and his hands visibly shaking. As the crowd slowly dispersed, two other men (whom I recognised as being servants of the Capuleti) began to bear the body of Tebaldo back towards their house.

I caught Agnese's eye as she turned to follow them. For a moment she held my questioning gaze, then she nodded imperceptibly before turning away. I was thus reassured on one point – that she would be the one who would impart these dreadful tidings to Giulietta.

The Lord Montecchi and Benvolio would have the task of informing Chiara. I must own that I did not envy them.

It but remained for me to do the same to Romeo.

***

As I turned, with a heavy heart, back towards the friary, I began to rehearse in my mind how I might break the news to my son that he must now leave Verona – and with it, his beloved wife of only a few short hours. My train of thought was suddenly halted by a restraining hand on my arm and an unfamiliar voice in my ear.

"Fra' Lorenzo?"

I looked up to see a young man, simply dressed in dark doublet and hose.

"Aye?"

"Fra' Lorenzo, my name is Paolo. I am a servant of Prince Bartolomeo Della Scala."

"Good afternoon, Paolo. What do you wish with me?"

"By your leave, Fra' Lorenzo, the Prince would like to speak to you in private. Please, will you come back with me to the palace?"

This question, unexpected though it had been, was one which clearly precluded any answer in the negative. Curious (and slightly nervous), I turned and followed Paolo back across the square. The palace guards had evidently been forewarned of my arrival, for they offered no challenge as Paolo accompanied me through the gates.

Once inside, I found myself inside a large and bright atrium. Paolo escorted me through a side door into a small but comfortable ante-room.

"Pray be seated, Fra' Lorenzo. I will inform the Prince you are here."

I seated myself on a chair covered in soft crimson velvet. As I waited, I cautiously took stock of my surroundings. The Prince's furnishings appeared to be surprisingly modest in design; of good quality, but elegant rather than opulent. If by a man's possessions shall ye know him, I thought, the Prince displays much good taste and good sense.

"Fra' Lorenzo?"

The door opened; Paolo had returned with the Prince. I rose from my seat as Paolo bowed and withdrew.

"Sir." I inclined my head. "You sent for me?"

"Aye, Fra' Lorenzo. Please, sit down."

He motioned me back to my chair, settling himself in another.

It was the first time I had seen the Prince at close quarters. I was somewhat surprised to note that he appeared to be no more than my own age.

"There are two reasons why I wish to speak with you." He hesitated. "You… knew my kinsman well, I believe?"

"Aye, Sir. He was one of my pupils. Please may I offer you my condolences on your sad loss."

"Thank you. May I ask you, then, would you please conduct his requiem?"

I was taken aback at this request, but responded:

"It would be an honour, Sir."

"Thank you."

"When do you wish it to take place, Sir?"

"Tomorrow afternoon, please. Paolo will assist you with the arrangements."

"Thank you."

I relaxed a little. This would be the first time I had conducted a requiem for a nobleman; any such assistance would be very welcome.

"You said there were two reasons you wished to speak with me, Sir?" I ventured to ask after a moment's silence.

The Prince's face became more serious.

"I saw you standing at the edge of the crowd just now. Tell me, could you hear what Benvolio was saying?"

"I could, Sir, very clearly."

"Do you know the youth at all well?"

"Very well indeed. He, like your kinsman Mercutio, is another of my pupils."

"Do you feel that he was speaking the truth about what happened here today?"

I was surprised to think that the Prince could entertain the idea that Benvolio might have been lying, but then I realised that he did not know Benvolio nearly as well as I did.

"I do, Sir. Benvolio is a good, truthful and peace-loving youth. His testimony can certainly be trusted."

The Prince relaxed.

"I am glad to hear you say so. I was afraid that he might, as the Lady Capuleti suggested, have biased his account in order to show his friend and his cousin in a more favourable light. Though if what I have elsewhere heard concerning Tebaldo is correct," he added gravely, "that does not seem to be very likely."

"Sir, my own experience of Tebaldo, limited though it has been, has shown him to display an unhealthy tendency towards violence. I can well believe that he would have started a fight simply for its own sake. Indeed, I am of the opinion that it was he who has been the principal force in keeping the feud alive."

"A feud which has cost me dearly," the Prince said bitterly.

"It has cost Verona dearly, Sir."

The Prince looked up and sighed.

"Aye, Fra' Lorenzo, you are right. But it is only now, now that this feud has affected me personally, that I realise just how futile it has been. And how I should have done more to control it."

"Sir, you have done much; indeed, as much as you have been able. But sadly, there are some who believe that the rules do not apply to them."

"Do you mean Tebaldo?"

"Aye, Sir."

81

The Prince nodded.

"And as the Lord Montecchi has said, he should in any case have paid the prescribed penalty for my kinsman's murder."

I finally summoned up the courage to ask:

"What of Romeo, then?"

The Prince considered for a moment, before answering:

"It is my belief that it was Tebaldo's deliberate intention to kill, even if Mercutio had not been his intended victim. As for Romeo – you know him too, do you not?"

I nodded.

"He also is one of my pupils."

"Do you consider him to be capable of such action?"

I drew a deep breath. Here, at last, was the opportunity to speak in my son's defence.

"Nay, Sir, not a whit. He has, until today, always taken great pains to avoid becoming involved in the feud."

"Why do you think he became involved in the fight today?"

"I know not, Sir, though I believe he was probably acting in his own defence." I tried, but failed, to suppress a shudder as I added, "If he had not done so, then Tebaldo would doubtless have killed him too."

The Prince nodded again.

"I am relieved to hear you say this. It confirms my faith in the decision I was forced to make."

"What do you mean by that, Sir?" His words intrigued me.

"I agree with the Lord Montecchi that following Mercutio's murder, Tebaldo should have been put to death according to the law. In that respect, Romeo (whether he killed Tebaldo deliberately or by accident) was merely carrying out that sentence." He paused. "But that, sadly, does not alter the fact that Romeo caused the death of Tebaldo. And whilst I am unwilling to condemn Romeo to death, I could not appear to be showing lenience to someone who is, in the eyes of some, nonetheless a convicted killer. Do you mark me?"

"I do, Sir."

"It is partly for that reason that I have sentenced him to exile from Verona. But it is not the only reason."

"Why else, then?" I was by now even more intrigued.

"For his own safety."

I gasped.

"His safety, Sir?"

"Aye. If he were to remain here in Verona, I fear that the Capuleti would attempt to take the law into their own hands. And that is a risk which I am not prepared to take."

I was silent as I considered this. The Prince was clearly a wiser, fairer and more just man than I had previously credited. Eventually, emboldened by this new knowledge, I ventured to ask:

"Will Romeo's exile be for life, Sir?"

"I will reserve judgement on that for the moment," the Prince answered. "But I ask you, please, Fra' Lorenzo, to tell no-one of this conversation."

"Sir, you may be assured of my utmost discretion." I indicated my monastic habit.

The Prince smiled and nodded.

"Thank you, Fra' Lorenzo."

He stood up, signalling that the interview was now at an end.

"Have you time to speak with Paolo now about the arrangements for the requiem?"

"Of course, Sir."

Anxious though I was to return to tend to Romeo, this was a matter which could not easily be postponed.

"Very well. And afterwards, he will escort you back to the friary."

\*\*\*

It was almost dusk when I finally unlocked the door to my cell. Lying on the ground inside the door, evidently having been pushed beneath it during my absence, was a letter, addressed to me in an unfamiliar hand. As I bent to pick it up, Romeo, who had been lying on my bed dozing, leapt up. His blue eyes stared into mine in undisguised terror.

"Fra' Lorenzo, what did the Prince say? Am I a dead man?"

I tossed the unopened letter down on to the table as I answered him:

"Nay, son. The Prince has been merciful. You are not to be put to death, but he has sentenced you to exile from Verona."

I do not know what kind of reaction I had been expecting him to give, but his response took me totally by surprise. Far from showing relief, he broke out into a high-pitched, bestial howl.

"No! Do not say exile! I would rather be put to death than sent into exile!"

I took him by the shoulders and looked at him steadily.

"Son, you know not what you say! Do you not understand? Instead of death you have life!"

"What does life hold for me if I am banished from Verona?"

"The world is large, son – you may go anywhere you wish."

"My world is here, and here only."

He broke away from me and slumped into a chair.

"Here, in Verona, with my Giulietta. My love. My wife! Do you not see that?" His voice trembled and he began to sob uncontrollably. "I cannot live without her."

After years of nursing my son through his many and various infatuations, I was well aware that he had inherited both my own and his mother's enormous capacity to love. And I did not doubt that without his beloved Giulietta, he would indeed regard his life as holding no purpose. Truth to say, the prospect of what he might do, if forced to live without her, terrified me.

I drew up another chair and sat beside him.

"Romeo, listen to me—"

"Why should I listen to you?" he snapped. "What do you know of what I am suffering? You are a friar. What do you know of love? What do you know of the real world? If you were as young as I am, and as much in love, and married only for a few hours, and then found yourself forced to leave your wife – then I might listen to you. But you would not understand…"

Oh my son, I thought, if you but knew the truth…

"Romeo," I said wearily, "as I have told you before, I do understand. And perhaps rather more than you can imagine. It may surprise you, but I was not always a friar. I did not emerge from my mother's womb wearing this monastic habit. I have lived in the real world, and I was once as young as you. And do you not remember that I told you that I too was once—"

A hammering at the door cut my words short.

"Romeo, hide yourself!" I hissed.

He did not move.

84

"Who's there?" I called.

The hammering came again.

"Who's there?"

I approached the door, frantically gesturing to Romeo to hide ere I opened it. He hauled himself up from the chair and slid to the floor behind my bed.

A woman's low voice answered.

"Please let me in, Fra' Lorenzo. I have come from the Lady Giulietta."

I eased the door open a crack, and peered out into the darkness beyond.

"Agnese?"

"Aye, Fra' Lorenzo, it is I. Please, may I come in?"

I opened the door a little further to admit her, then closed it swiftly as she entered. She was flushed and out of breath, having evidently come hither in great haste.

"Please, Fra' Lorenzo, tell me – do you know where Romeo is?"

I nodded, and gestured towards the crumpled, shuddering heap on the ground.

Agnese gazed at him for a moment, then turned back to me.

"It is just the same with her."

She crossed the room and knelt down beside Romeo.

"Stand up! If you have any backbone, then for Giulietta's sake, stand up!"

At the mention of his wife's name, Romeo raised his tearful eyes and gazed pitifully into Agnese's face.

"Tell me, Agnese, how is my lady?" he asked pathetically. "What does she think of her lord now?"

Agnese helped him to his feet.

"Sir, she is not well. She refuses to leave her chamber. She is very shaken, and just lies on her bed weeping. Sometimes she cries 'Tebaldo', then other times she calls 'Romeo'—"

Romeo howled hysterically.

"Ah, my name is still her enemy!"

He spun round towards me, his anguished eyes blazing.

"Father, tell me, whereabouts in this cursed body of mine does my name live? Tell me, so I may cut it out!"

And ere we could prevent him, he had drawn his dagger and made

85

as if to turn it upon himself.

As one, Agnese and I leapt towards him. I succeeded in staying his arm; she grasped the dagger, wrenched it out of his grasp and tossed it aside. Defeated, he slumped to the floor again, sobbing bitterly.

"Romeo, get up!"

I knelt down, seized him by the shoulders and forced him to sit up.

"Romeo, tell me, are you a man? I am beginning to doubt it! It is true that you look like a man, but you are crying like a woman, and you are baying like a wild animal! Merciful Heaven, I had credited you with more sense! What pain would your dear wife suffer if you did such violence upon yourself?"

He said nothing, but this shaft had evidently found its mark, for his sobs gradually subsided.

"Romeo, listen to me. Consider this: your lady Giulietta, whom you love with all your heart, loves you in return. Is that not a blessing? Tebaldo, who killed Mercutio, would almost certainly have killed you too. But instead, he is the one who is now dead, not you. Is that not a blessing? The Prince, who should have condemned you to death, has instead commuted your sentence to exile. Is that not also a blessing? Do you not see how fortunate you are? So why are you behaving like a spoiled, ungrateful child?"

In the corner of my eye I could see Agnese nodding her agreement. Romeo still said nothing, but slowly raised his head and wiped away his tears.

"Go, son. Go to your wife now. She needs you every bit as much as you need her."

His tearful face broke into a faint smile.

"Truly, father?"

I nodded.

"Truly, son. But be mindful of the Watch. If you cannot leave the city before the gates are locked tonight, then you must disguise yourself and leave at daybreak."

"Where shall I go?"

"Go to Mantua. It is not far, but you will be safe there. I will find your servant and send word to you. Stay there until we can arrange for you to return to Verona."

Romeo gasped.

"You believe I will be able to return?"

"I doubt it not, son. In the fullness of time, we will petition the Prince to pardon you. And then, perchance, we will be able to announce your marriage properly."

I turned to Agnese.

"Go on ahead, and tell Giulietta that Romeo will be with her anon. Tell the rest of the household that she is in mourning for her cousin and that she wishes to be left alone with her grief."

Agnese nodded.

"Fra' Lorenzo, you are very wise."

She turned to Romeo, who by now had struggled to his feet.

"I will go and tell my lady that her lord is coming to comfort her."

"Thank you."

Agnese made her way to the door, then turned back and fumbled in her reticule.

"Sir, my lady bade me give you this. Make haste now, for it is already very late."

As the door clicked closed behind her, Romeo stared at the small object in his palm. It was the ring which had served, only a few hours earlier, as Giulietta's wedding ring.

"I am much comforted by this," he murmured.

I handed him a cloak.

"Go now, son. Go to her. But remember: you must be gone by daybreak. I cannot answer for what will happen if you are discovered in Verona thereafter."

I shuddered involuntarily at the prospect. Thankfully Romeo, absorbed in donning the cloak and strapping on his dagger, appeared not to have noticed.

"Thank you, my ghostly father."

And with those words, he was gone.

***

I was on the point of retiring to bed when I remembered the letter, still lying unopened on the table.

In the faint candlelight I could not distinguish the insignia of the seal. I picked up a knife from the table, cautiously eased the paper open and squinted at the unfamiliar handwriting inside.

*Fra' Lorenzo,*

*It is with great sorrow that I must inform you that our dearly beloved nephew Tebaldo was today most brutally murdered.*

*I understand that you were our nephew's ghostly confessor. Would you consent, therefore, to conduct his requiem?*

It was signed by the Lord Capuleti.

I read the letter for a second time. Clearly the Lord Capuleti, when he had written it, had not been aware that I was already party to this news.

In life, Tebaldo had been my nemesis – the one person to whom I could not, even as a man of God, feel any degree of compassion. And (may God forgive me for saying this) I still could not bring myself to feel any degree of sorrow at his death.

On reading the words *most brutally murdered*, I bit back the curse which sprang unbidden to my lips, even though there was none present to hear it.

I dropped the letter as though it had burned my fingers.

Regardless of my personal interest in this sorry affair, how could I possibly conduct a requiem for one who was himself a brutal murderer? One who had already slain my beloved pupil, and who would just as happily have slain my own son?

I opened the window of my cell and peered out. The friary was, for the most part, swathed in darkness, but a light still burned in the chapel. I picked up the Lord Capuleti's note and made my way across the cloister.

Inside the chapel, Fra' Gianni was finishing tidying the altar after Completorium. He looked up as I entered.

"Good e'en, Fra' Lorenzo. You were not at Completorium?"

"Nay, Fra' Gianni. I had other spiritual matters which required my attention."

Fra' Gianni nodded sagely. He knew better than to ask any further questions.

"But please, I must ask for your assistance."

I passed him the Lord Capuleti's letter. He read it and whistled under his breath.

"Is this what happened in the city this afternoon?"

I nodded.

"Tebaldo killed Mercutio, then was himself killed in another brawl with young Romeo. Benvolio, who witnessed the fight, said that he believes that Tebaldo's death was an accident. Though it seems the Capuleti appear to think otherwise."

Fra' Gianni was silent for a moment as he read the letter again.

"And what assistance do you ask from me?"

I drew a deep breath before answering.

"Fra' Gianni, I knew this young man and I am sorry to say that I have always found his conduct to be utterly despicable. I do not feel able to conduct his requiem myself, as I feel it would be hypocritical of me to do so. Would you be able to take this service in my stead?"

Fra' Gianni smiled.

"I did not know Tebaldo personally, but I see no reason why that should prevent me from conducting his requiem." He glanced at the letter again. "The Lord Capuleti does not say when he wishes the requiem to take place, but please convey to him that I will be happy to assist him."

I sighed with relief.

"Thank you, my friend. I will write to the Lord Capuleti tonight. I am most grateful to you."

We bade each other goodnight. As I walked back across the cloister, I thought how fortunate Fra' Gianni had been in not being personally acquainted with Tebaldo in life. There were some circumstances in which ignorance was a clear advantage.

Back in my cell, I picked up quill and paper, then composed a carefully-worded response:

*My Lord Capuleti,*
*I received your letter this evening. Please accept my condolences on your loss.*

*I have discussed the matter of your nephew's requiem with one of my fellow friars, Fra' Gianni. If, due to a conflict of commitment, I find that I will not be able to conduct the service myself, please be assured that Fra' Gianni will be happy to assist you.*

*In D.no,*
*Fra' Lorenzo*

As to the nature of my "conflict of commitment," what the Lord

Capuleti did not know could have no power to offend him.

***

After a fitful night, I rose early and handed the letter to one of the novices, who set off straightaway to deliver it to the house of the Capuleti. I returned by way of the chapel and murmured a prayer that Romeo would have made a safe escape from the city. I feared that the only news I would hear of him would be news which I had no wish to hear, so I fervently hoped, with the very best of intentions, that I would hear nothing further about my son until such time as I would be able to contact him myself.

But in the meantime, there still remained the matter of how Chiara would react to this latest development. It would only be a matter of time before I would have to face this particular dilemma. And she, of course, still knew nothing about our son's clandestine marriage.

On returning to my cell I was astonished to find that I had a visitor.

"Good morrow, Fra' Lorenzo."

My visitor was a well-dressed and well-spoken young man. I had a vague recollection that I had seen him somewhere before, but I was at a loss to recall where or why.

"Good morrow, Sir."

I hesitated, unsure of how to continue.

"Forgive me, Sir, but I am afraid I do not recognise you."

The young man smiled at me pleasantly.

"Forgiveness is not necessary, Fra' Lorenzo. Our paths have not crossed before, so there is no reason why you should know me. Allow me to introduce myself. My name is Count Paris; I am a kinsman to Prince Bartolomeo Della Scala."

"Sir, I am honoured to meet you. You are also, then, a kinsman of Mercutio?"

I could now see that he bore a striking resemblance to Mercutio's brother Valentino. Could this be why I thought his face seemed familiar?

"Aye." His face fell.

"Sir, I knew Mercutio very well. I too feel great sorrow at his tragic death."

90

"Thank you, Fra' Lorenzo." He sighed, then his face brightened slightly. "But it is not for that reason that I am come to speak with you."

"Indeed? How, then, may I assist you?"

And why, I added mentally, have you come to visit me so early in the morning?

"Fra' Lorenzo, I am about to be married. And I am come to ask you if you will consent to performing the ceremony."

(Holy Saint Francis, I thought. Not four and twenty hours ago, Romeo had appeared in this very same spot and had asked me the very same question!)

"When do you envisage the marriage will take place, Sir?" I answered cautiously.

"On Thursday."

I jumped in surprise.

"Thursday next week?" I ventured, deliberately misinterpreting his reply.

"Nay, Fra' Lorenzo, this coming Thursday. The day after tomorrow."

"Forgive me, Sir, but that is very soon."

(Slightly less hasty than Romeo's wedding, I mused, but hasty nonetheless.)

"It is what my bride's father has decreed."

"Do you yourself agree, Sir, that it should be so soon?"

Count Paris smiled.

"I raise no objection."

"And what of your bride? Is she also happy to marry in such haste?"

As I uttered these words the thought came to me that the couple might be marrying in such haste, as Chiara and I had done, for reasons of premature procreativity. But the Count's face immediately grew sombre.

"I know not, Fra' Lorenzo," he murmured, unable to meet my gaze.

"I beg your pardon, Sir?"

The Count eventually raised his head.

"The marriage has been arranged by my bride's father on her behalf."

"And she knows nothing of it?"

The Count hesitated before replying:

"I am told that she has been informed of it."

"Whether or not she has been informed of it, does not her consent also play a part in this? I must own, Sir, that I feel uneasy at conducting a marriage which has been arranged in such haste, and without the willing consent of both bridegroom and bride."

A faint look of desperation crossed the Count's face.

"Believe me, Fra' Lorenzo, I love her dearly."

I nodded.

"I have no doubt that you do, Sir. But be that as it may, why then have you not wooed the lady ere now?"

The Count's face fell.

"Because she is in mourning."

My blood ran cold at these words, though I forced myself to continue:

"In mourning? For whom?"

"For her cousin."

After what felt like an eternity, I heard myself ask:

"So your bride is…?"

(Though I feared I knew the answer even before the words were out.)

"Aye, the fair Lady Giulietta."

O Merciful Heaven, I screamed inwardly.

In a voice which I barely recognised as my own, I croaked:

"Do you really believe, Sir, that it would be appropriate to marry this lady when you have not courted her, when you do not know her own feelings, and moreover when her cousin's corpse is still barely cold?"

The Count turned to face me.

"Fra' Lorenzo, I would willingly have courted her ere now. I approached her father two days ago and asked his permission to press my suit with her."

Two days ago, I thought – that would have been the day when Giulietta had first encountered Romeo.

"And what was the Lord Capuleti's reply?"

"At first he said that she was too young, and that I should wait another two years before she would be ready for marriage. I reminded him that some ladies in Verona, younger than Giulietta, are already married with children, but he would not be swayed by that." The Count paused. "But he then conceded that I should at the very least meet with his daughter and try to win her affection. A ball was being held at his house that same evening, and he invited me to join the guests."

"And did you meet with the lady, as her father had intended?"

"Aye, I danced with her, and conversed with her. But then she disappeared from the ballroom, and I did not see her again for the remainder of the evening..."

This struck a chord in my mind. Had not Romeo said that when he had first caught sight of Giulietta, she had been dancing with a kinsman of Mercutio?

"... and I have not spoken to her again since then."

"Why not?" I asked carefully.

The Count sighed heavily.

"Because since her cousin's death she has confined herself to her chamber and refuses to see, or speak to, anyone. And a household in mourning is not a place to speak of love."

"So why are you coming to me now, asking me to conduct a marriage ceremony, in two days' time, between yourself and a lady whom you have not courted, and who moreover is clearly in a state of great distress?"

"Because her father arranged this with me late last night. I would fain have spoken with her then and there, but she would not come down from her chamber."

I froze as I absorbed the full import of his words, and swiftly turned away lest my face should betray my horror. Even as Giulietta's marriage to Romeo was being secretly consummated, another marriage was, without her knowledge, being decided for her.

I drew a deep breath as I turned back to face the Count.

"Forgive me, Sir, but I am not sure that I fully understand your drift. You tell me that the Lord Capuleti first told you, not two days

93

since, that he considered that his daughter was far too young to be a bride, and that there was plenty of time for you to earn her affection. Yet now, scarcely more than four and twenty hours later, he is promising her to you in marriage – a marriage which he himself has deemed will take place two days from now – and this despite neither of you knowing the lady's own mind?"

The Count considered for a moment before answering:

"It is I who must ask you to forgive me, Fra' Lorenzo. I have clearly not explained matters properly to you."

"Pray, continue, Sir."

"The Lord Capuleti is greatly afeared that Giulietta's immense sorrow for the death of her cousin is unhealthy; indeed, perhaps even dangerous. I believe he may even fear that in the worst excesses of her grief she may do herself harm. He prescribes this swift marriage in the cause of her own well-being, with the intention of rendering her happy again."

"I think I can comprehend the sentiment behind the Lord Capuleti's reasoning," I replied, choosing my words very carefully. "But I have no doubt that Giulietta's grief is occasioned by a true and profound love for the person whom she has lost. A hasty arranged marriage will, I fear, do little to alleviate that."

"I well know that I can never hope to replace him in her affection…" the Count demurred.

(No, Sir, I thought, indeed you cannot.)

"… and I would not wish to try. But I do love her, and I will do my utmost to comfort her now, sustain her as her grief abates, and, in the fullness of time, make her happy."

I was at a loss how to respond to this. The Count was clearly very sincere, and I did not doubt that he was genuinely fond of Giulietta. But none of this altered the fact that even if Giulietta returned his affections, her hand (and her heart) were already contracted elsewhere.

I was saved the necessity to think of a spoken reply, for at this point there came a faint knock on my cell door.

"By your leave, Sir?"

"Of course, Fra' Lorenzo."

I called to bid the visitor to come in.

94

The door creaked open to reveal Giulietta herself. Her face was veiled, evidently to conceal from view the fact that she had been weeping. As she entered my cell I could see that she was visibly trembling, but on catching sight of the Count, she froze as if rooted to the spot.

The Count, presumably ascribing her subdued manner to her prolonged grief for the death of her cousin, appeared to be mercifully unaware of anything untoward in her demeanour. He ran towards her, took hold of her hand and raised it to his lips.

"Giulietta! Well-met, my lady. And soon to be my wife."

Giulietta bowed her head, as if in reverence.

"Sir, that may be, when I am able to become your wife."

The Count smiled.

"Not 'may be', my dear, but 'must be'. And you shall become my wife on Thursday morning."

Giulietta slowly raised her head.

"That which must be, shall be," she murmured.

What an intelligent and quick-thinking young woman, I thought. She speaks the truth, and yet the Count is so cleverly deceived!

"Indeed so," I added. "Of that there can be no doubt."

To lay further stress on this point, I crossed myself ostentatiously. Giulietta, momentarily catching my eye, seized the opportunity to withdraw her hand from the Count's grasp as she did likewise.

The Count, after a moment's hesitation, clumsily followed suit. Unseen by him, Giulietta wiped her hand within the folds of her cloak, as if to purge it of his touch.

He turned to her again.

"Giulietta, are you come here to make confession to Fra' Lorenzo?"

What an impertinent question for him to ask her, I thought. Though thankfully, he could not possibly have divined whatever other reason she might now have for coming to see me. I, however, knew exactly what cause had brought her hither.

"Sir," Giulietta replied, "if I were to answer that question, I should be making confession to you."

The Count seemed unperturbed.

"If you love me, Giulietta, pray do not conceal that knowledge from this holy friar."

"I will not conceal from you, Sir, the knowledge that I love my ghostly father."

"I am sure, also, that you will tell him that you love me."

Giulietta bowed her head in seeming modesty, before murmuring:

"Sir, if I do love you, it will mean more if I were to say so to my ghostly father in private, than to say so here to you face to face."

He smiled again, evidently quietly confident. Emboldened by this apparent encouragement, he turned towards her and carefully raised her veil. Her pretty face was pale and drawn, and her eyes red-rimmed and bloodshot.

"You poor soul; you have abused your face terribly with your tears."

"I think not, Sir; my tears have done little to worsen something which was already very bad."

"Do not slander yourself, my dear."

"It is not slander, Sir, it is the truth."

"But—"

As the Count began to speak again Giulietta turned to me, acting as though she had not heard him.

"Fra' Lorenzo, do you have the time to see me now, or shall I come back to you later this afternoon?"

"Daughter, I have as much time as you need to attend you in your time of such great sorrow."

I turned to the Count.

"By your leave, Sir, we must ask you to grant us time alone."

Far from being offended by this request (as I had feared he might be), the Count seemed delighted that his future wife appeared to be so demure and devout.

"Heaven forfend that I should stand in the way of true devotion."

He made a low bow.

"Giulietta, on Thursday morning I will come and bring you to church. Until then, farewell."

After a moment's hesitation, he planted a chaste kiss on her pale and unresponsive lips. What a difference, I thought, from the kiss which I had seen her receive, and return, less than four and twenty hours ago in this very same room.

She stood very still as she waited until the door had clicked closed behind him, then dragged the back of her hand across her lips as if to eradicate the sensation and the memory of his invasion. Then –

exactly as her husband had done last night – she turned to me, crumpled to her knees and sobbed pitifully.

"Come, Fra' Lorenzo, and weep with me! I am beyond hope and beyond help."

"Daughter, I already know of your trouble. The Count had come to ask me to conduct your marriage on Thursday."

"Father," she wailed, "please do not tell me that you know about this, unless you can also tell me how I can prevent it from happening! If even you, the wisest of all people, cannot provide me with a way out of this, then, God help me, I will provide my own."

As she spoke, a wild look came into her tearful eyes and she drew her dagger from its sheath.

"Giulietta! You do not know what you are doing!"

"Father, I know all too well what I am doing – and I pray that God will understand why I am doing it, and will look mercifully upon me when I come to face him. Was it not God who arranged that Romeo and I should meet and fall in love? He joined our hearts; you joined our hands in holy marriage. And before this hand of mine will ever be given in marriage to another, then it will use this knife to hasten my departure from this cruel world. If you cannot help me, then rather than betray my Romeo I will willingly die, here and now."

And I truly believed that she would. How could I have ever doubted how much she loved my son?

"Tell me, dear daughter – why does your father insist on this marriage taking place so soon?"

"I know not, Fra' Lorenzo. He says only that if I do not consent to the marriage, then he will disown me."

"And what says your mother?"

Giulietta sighed.

"My mother says that she will have nothing more to do with me unless I obey my father."

This was spoken without bitterness, but nonetheless in such a dejected tone that it left me in no doubt that Giulietta had never fully expected to receive any support from that quarter.

"It surprises me not," she added. "My mother was herself married very young. Ere she had even reached my own age, she had already given birth to me."

"And what of Agnese?"

This time, there was a reaction – and one which astounded me every bit as much as its origin had clearly astounded Giulietta.

"Agnese said that I should marry the Count."

She spat out the words as though they burned her tongue in the uttering.

"What?" I was aghast.

"Aye. She said that as my husband was banished – and hence was as good as dead – it was probably better that I should agree to this second marriage." Giulietta looked up pitifully. "You, Fra' Lorenzo, are my only hope. All others have abandoned me."

Her last word ended in another shuddering sob.

Dear God, I thought. What, in Heaven's name, can I do to help this poor creature?

"Giulietta," I asked gently, "Romeo has told me that he cannot live without you. Have you not considered how he would fare if you were to carry out this threat to slay yourself?"

Her sobs quietened as she considered this. Eventually she murmured:

"I have no doubt that he would wish to follow me to the grave."

She shuddered.

"Is that not a reason, then, for you to stay alive?"

"I would gladly stay alive for my Romeo's sake," she answered forlornly. "But I would rather die than betray him and be forced to live without his presence. And that is what I would suffer if I consent to marry Count Paris. How else can I prevent that, save as a corpse?"

A corpse…?

Or, perchance, the likeness of a corpse…?

The sleeping potion…?

Oh, what a blind fool I have been…

"Giulietta," I knelt down beside her. "I believe I know of a solution. It is a desperate measure, but a desperate cause calls for desperate action. It will be difficult, but if it works it will save you from this second marriage, and will restore you to your Romeo."

She looked up, her dark eyes suddenly shining with hope.

"You told me just now that you would rather die than marry Count Paris—"

"And I spoke truly."

"I doubt it not. But if you have the strength of will to slay yourself, then would you also be strong enough to use something like death to find a way out of this catastrophe? If you are brave enough for that, then I believe I can help you."

Her eyes flashed.

"Fra' Lorenzo, I would gladly take refuge in an ancient charnel-house, or hide in a newly-dug grave with a stinking corpse, if by doing so I might stay true and faithful to my dear lord."

"Very well."

I raised her to her feet and settled her on a chair, then retrieved one of the vials of the sleeping draught from its hiding place.

"Here, then, is the plan. Go home, and tell your father that you came to me this morning to make confession after having disobeyed him. Tell him that I have instructed you to beg his pardon, and that you will consent to marry Count Paris."

She looked shocked, but said nothing.

"Pretend to concur with all the arrangements for the wedding. It is planned for the day after tomorrow. But when you go to bed tomorrow night, take this vial of potion and drink it all."

"What is this potion, father?"

"It is a sleeping draught, but it will send you into a deep trance. You will become cold and pale, and your breathing and your pulse will cease, for a little over thirty hours. During that time, to all who behold you, you will appear to be dead. And when Count Paris comes on Thursday morning to bring you to church, that is how he will find you."

Her face brightened.

"What will happen to me thereafter?"

"You will be dressed in your finest robes, and brought to church – not for your wedding, but for your requiem. I will ensure that it takes place on that very same day. Then you will be laid to rest in your family's vault."

"And at the end of that thirty hours?"

"You will wake, as if from a pleasant sleep."

"Inside the vault?" She shuddered.

I nodded.

"But please, do not be afraid. True, it will be cold and dark inside the vault, but mark you: those who already lie there will be in no state to do you harm."

99

She considered.

"But how will I escape from thence?" she murmured.

"Whilst you sleep, I will send a letter to Romeo and tell him of our plan. He will return here in secret, and he and I will be at your side when you awaken. Then, you will be able to flee with him back to Mantua."

For the first time since she had entered my cell, Giulietta smiled.

"Do you have courage enough for this venture?"

"I have, my ghostly father. Give me the potion."

"Go then. Be strong."

"Love will give me the strength to see this accomplished. Farewell…"

***

After Giulietta had left, I slumped back onto my bed, utterly exhausted by the maelstrom of the past four and twenty hours. I knew nothing further until I heard the friary clock striking the hour of noon.

I wandered across to the chapel for the midday office and took my place in the pew alongside Fra' Gianni. He gave me a surreptitious sidelong glance which immediately took stock of my troubled state. As we filed out of the chapel when the office had ended, he laid an enquiring hand upon my arm.

"Fra' Lorenzo, what is the matter? Is there anything I can do to help you?"

"There is much that is the matter, but I fear there is but little that I am able to tell you."

Fra' Gianni raised his eyebrows.

"The secret of the confessional?"

"Aye, in part. But there is one thing which perchance you can do to help."

"Name it, my friend."

"Will you be able to ride to Mantua tomorrow, to deliver a letter to young Romeo?"

"Romeo Montecchi, who was lately sent into exile? Is that where he has gone?"

"Aye, the same. I am still his ghostly father; I wish him to know that he remains in my thoughts and in my prayers in his time of trial. And I must also inform him of another urgent matter…"

Fra' Gianni nodded and smiled.

"Gladly, my friend. But I cannot go tomorrow, for that is when the Lord Capuleti has asked me to conduct Tebaldo's requiem. But if you can give me the letter within the hour, I can take it thither this afternoon."

Glancing at the clock, I calculated that I would have just sufficient time to write the letter before I would need to leave for Mercutio's requiem. I hurried back to my cell, locked the door and took up my quill.

*Romeo,*

*I trust that you made a safe journey to Mantua.*

*I have some vital news which I must impart to you forthwith. Please read this letter carefully and take good note of its content – much hinges upon the action you must take.*

*Your lady Giulietta now finds that, without her knowledge or consent, she has been promised in marriage by her father to the Count Paris (a kinsman of Mercutio and the Prince). The wedding has been arranged for Thursday, which is the day after tomorrow. She came to me this morning in deep distress, and begged for my assistance in helping her to escape from this second marriage.*

*We have devised a plan whereby tomorrow night she will drink a potion which will, for a short time, send her into a profound and seemingly lifeless trance. The Count, and her family, will be deceived into believing that she has died.*

*On Thursday she will be laid to rest in her family vault, where she will remain until she wakens early on Friday morning.*

*Please return in secret to Verona on Thursday night, and make your way to my cell. I will conceal you there; we will go to the vault together in time to be at your lady's side when she wakes.*

*Thereafter, she will return with you to Mantua.*

*The friar who brings you this letter is a trusted friend. Please send me word, by him, that you will meet with me here on Thursday night.*

*God speed you on your journey.*

*In D.No,*
*Fra' Lorenzo*

When I took the letter to Fra' Gianni's cell he was not there, so I left it on the table. Then I turned my attention to the other matter which was weighing most heavily on my mind: the requiem for my dear murdered pupil.

I will not dwell on the matter of Mercutio's funeral; I will say only that it was the most harrowing experience of my life up to that point.

***

When at last I trudged back to my cell through the late afternoon heat, I was met, once again, by the Count Paris.

"Fra' Lorenzo!" He greeted me most cheerfully. His blissful mood was clearly at great variance with my own heavy heart.

"Sir," I wearily returned his greeting, but not his smile. "How may I assist you?"

"Fra' Lorenzo, the date of my wedding has been brought forward! The Lady Giulietta and I are to be married tomorrow morning!"

How fortunate, I thought, that my face was concealed in shadow. Heaven alone knew what degree of horror it would have displayed, had the Count been able to see it.

"Tomorrow morning, Sir? Why so, rather than Thursday?"

"The Lord Capuleti has decreed it."

"And – what says the lady herself?"

"He tells me that she has consented."

Then she needs must drink the potion this very night, I thought. But she is a strong and resourceful girl; she will do what she must do.

I drew a deep breath and turned to face the Count.

"Very well, Sir, I will come to the Capuleti mansion tomorrow morning to conduct you and the lady Giulietta to church."

But not for a wedding, I added mentally. Instead you will be following her cortège.

The Count beamed.

"A thousand thanks, Fra' Lorenzo. Until tomorrow, then."

"Until tomorrow, Sir."

Poor innocent lovesick pawn, I thought. In spite of everything, I could not help but feel sorry for him.

***

As we left Completorium, Fra' Gianni hastened to my side.

"Fra' Lorenzo, a thousand pardons. I was unable to deliver your letter this afternoon."

"What?"

"Just after I left you after midday office, I received a message saying that Tebaldo's requiem would have to be held today rather than tomorrow. It seems that the Lord Capuleti has arranged for his daughter to be married tomorrow, so the requiem needed to be brought forward to this afternoon."

As indeed it would. What family would ever hold a funeral and a wedding on the same day? Why had this not occurred to me when the Count Paris told me of the change of arrangements for the wedding? What a fool I was, not to have thought of this...

"So I will take the letter to Mantua tomorrow. Will that suffice?"

"Yes, thank you, my friend," I answered wearily, my mind already heavy for want of sleep. "Goodnight."

In years to come, I would many times look back on this discourse – and curse the momentary inattention brought about by my mental stupor...

\*\*\*

The following morning (Wednesday) I rose at my usual hour and made my way to the Capuleti mansion. As I approached, I forced myself into the frame of mind which would be expected of me: until I was told otherwise, I was attending upon the household in order to celebrate a wedding. And I would need to remain mindful of that fact.

Accordingly, I delivered a long, loud and hard knock on the door of the mansion, and flashed a broad smile at the servant who opened it to admit me. The stricken faces and wailing sounds which greeted me when I entered the hall were sufficient to tell me all I needed to know; that I would indeed be conducting a requiem, not a marriage.

But until I had been officially informed, I must remember that I knew nothing.

"Where is the Lord Capuleti?" I announced cheerfully. "Is the bride ready to come to church?"

The servant's lower lip trembled. He muttered something which I did not hear, then turned away. He had gone two or three steps ere he

103

remembered his manners, whereupon he turned back and bowed half-heartedly to me before resuming his errand.

A few minutes later he returned, followed by the Lord Capuleti.

The master of the house was still clad in his nightshirt; his hair was tangled and matted, and somewhere along the way he appeared to have lost one of his slippers. Were it not for his ashen countenance, he would have cut a comical figure.

"My Lord," I greeted him cheerfully. "I am sorry – am I come too early?"

"Nay, Fra' Lorenzo," he answered flatly. "On the contrary, I fear you are come far too late."

"Too late? Too late for what? Forgive me, My Lord, but I am sorry; I do not understand you. Is the bride not ready to come to church?"

I am ashamed to admit that, in spite of everything, I was rather enjoying this little charade. After all the anguish to which the Lord Capuleti had subjected young Giulietta yesterday, did he not merit some form of retribution?

"My father Capuleti, what ails you?"

I had failed to notice that the Count Paris had appeared at my side.

"Indeed, My Lord," I added. "Pray tell, please – what is wrong?"

The Lord Capuleti slumped into a chair, slowly shook his tousled head and supported it in his hands. When he looked up again, his eyes were streaming.

"Fra' Lorenzo, Count Paris – there will be no wedding today."

The Count froze. I affected an expression of shock and disbelief.

As one man, the two of us asked:

"Why not?"

The Lord Capuleti rose unsteadily from the chair and turned to address the Count.

"Son, your bride has already been claimed by another."

I caught my breath. Did Giulietta's father know after all about her secret marriage to Romeo? But thankfully, neither the Lord Capuleti nor Count Paris appeared to be paying any attention to me. And if they had done, I hoped they would simply believe that my reaction was occasioned by the same shock as their own.

"Who then?" The Count's voice was barely audible.

"Death."

I breathed again. But again, my reaction was masked by that of the

Count, who let out a pitiful and agonised wail.

"My lady is dead?"

"Aye. Death, not you, is now my son-in-law."

The Count sank into the chair lately vacated by the Lord Capuleti. He too put his head into his hands.

"By your leave, Sir," I addressed the Lord Capuleti, "may I see her?"

The Lord Capuleti paused, then nodded and motioned us to follow him.

Giulietta's chamber was a pitiful sight. The bridal clothes were arranged ready for her to put on, and a garland of flowers and a bunch of rosemary lay on a table. Slumped in a chair to one side of the bed was the Lady Capuleti, to the other side Agnese. Both were still in their nightclothes; both were sobbing uncontrollably.

The curtains around the bed were drawn. I approached the bed cautiously, took hold of one of the hangings and turned questioningly to the Lord Capuleti.

"May I, Sir?"

He gave another dejected nod.

I drew back the curtain to reveal Giulietta, cold, pale and stiff. The potion had done its work well.

"I have waited so long for this day," murmured the Count brokenly. "And now that it is come, what a sight it brings me."

Again, I could not help but feel a twinge of pity for this poor fellow.

The Lady Capuleti rose from her chair and approached the bed.

"O my child!" she howled. "My only child!"

She flung herself down on to the bed alongside Giulietta and clung to her lifeless form, sobbing hysterically. The Lord Capuleti and Count Paris both attempted, in vain, to calm her.

I took advantage of this new distraction to look surreptitiously around for the vial. Giulietta was lying on her side with her right arm stretched out, and her hand, with fingers extended, overhung the edge of the bed. I calculated (correctly) that the vial would be somewhere on the floor beneath. I knelt down, crossing myself as if to say a prayer, and carefully retrieved it.

Agnese, meanwhile, was still sitting shuddering in the other chair. As I arose from my knees, she looked up at me.

"O Fra' Lorenzo, what a lamentable day is this! What a curse is come upon me, that I should be the one to find her dead!"

So Agnese had been the one who had discovered Giulietta couched in the likeness of death. If, as the girl herself had told me the day before, Agnese had indeed told her that she should abandon her husband and marry the Count, I could not help wondering if the nurse felt that she was now paying the price for such a betrayal.

And yet, she was withal a good woman. It grieved me to think that she, like the Count, must through no fault of their own be amongst those to suffer. But sadly, I found that I could feel no such sympathy with the parents who had jockeyed with their daughter's happiness – and with it, that of my own son (whose very life they would fain have forfeited).

I adopted a pose of reverential silence for a minute or two whilst the weeping and wailing continued, then eventually decided I needed to assume the voice of reason.

"My Lord, My Lady, My Lord Count, Madam," I began (the last word being addressed to Agnese). "Please, calm yourselves. I am as distraught as all of you at what has happened here today, but I fear that the answer does not lie in your protracted weeping. Consider this, I beg you: Giulietta's earthly body may have died – and no amount of your tears can restore her to earthly life – but her immortal soul now rests in Heaven. Consider how much better placed she is now, safe from the cares and strife of this cruel world. Are you not happy for her?"

They gave no answer.

"Come," I continued. "Let us not delay this sad business further. Array this fair corpse in her finest robes and bring her to church."

The Lord Capuleti looked wearily up.

"Aye, Fra' Lorenzo. We had thought to bring her to church for her wedding…"

His voice cracked and he turned away hastily.

"My Lord," I answered gently, "Go and prepare yourself. You too, My Lady." I turned towards the Count. "Sir, will you follow with them?"

The Count nodded.

I gestured to Agnese, who trudged across to the bed and helped the prostrate Lady Capuleti to her feet. The latter cast another pitiful glance at Giulietta, then murmured brokenly,

"First my nephew, now my daughter. There is a curse upon this house."

I shuddered as I recalled Benvolio's report of Mercutio's dying words. He had cursed both houses for having brought about his own end.

Both. What curse might well yet befall the other house…?

"The Heavens have indeed frowned upon you," I answered carefully. "Pray God that there will be no more misfortune…"

*** 

Within a little over an hour, the cortège was ready to depart. Giulietta was arrayed in her wedding dress with the garland of flowers on her head, and her bier was strewn with rosemary and lavandula. I thought, in passing, that these fragrant herbs would at the very least make her awakening in the vault a little less unpleasant.

Mentally rehearsing how I might conduct the service, I led the way from the Capuleti mansion to the church nearby. Mercutio's requiem had taken place in the Prince's private chapel, and he had been laid to rest in the family vault within the precincts of the palace. But this funeral was a much more public affair; the citizens of Verona stopped in their tracks and crossed themselves solemnly as the cortège passed through the streets. Giulietta was carried on the bier by four of the strongest of the Capuleti's serving men. Behind them followed a lone drummer beating a mournful tattoo. After him came the Lord and Lady Capuleti, then the Count Paris and Agnese; thereafter the remainder of the household – all clad in sombre black (a stark contrast with the shimmering white apparel worn by the corpse), all weeping silently.

Once inside the church they took their places in the pews, for the second time within four and twenty hours.

*"Requiescat in pace, in nomine Patris, Filii et Spiritus Sancti…"*

From the church it was but a short distance (the length of the churchyard) to the Capuleti family tomb, the key to which was held in the sacristy. I lit a flambard and unlocked the tomb's heavy iron gates, which creaked open for the second time in as many days, and

107

Giulietta was carried down a short flight of stone steps into the crypt below.

The flickering light of my flambard cast a pattern of eerie shadows about the vaulted interior. As Giulietta was being placed on a vacant bier, adjacent to the one where the body of Tebaldo was already lying, I cast a surreptitious glance around. All those interred therein, save Tebaldo, were already reduced to mere bones and dust. I recalled Giulietta's desperate words of the previous morning, when she had told me that she would happily take refuge in a charnel-house or a newly-dug grave. It now transpired that she would have to do both.

Giulietta was covered with a fine layer of muslin, and the sprigs of rosemary and lavandula were strewn over her.

"*Et exspecto resurrectionem mortuorum…*"
We look for the resurrection of the dead…

In anticipation of the resurrection of this particular dead, I realised that I might well need some plausible pretext to return to the vault. Accordingly, before leaving, I secretly dropped my rosary on to the ground by Giulietta's resting place.

When I returned to the friary there was no sign of Fra' Gianni. I presumed that he must have set off for Mantua at first light. It was only then that I realised what I had failed to realise when I had spoken to him last night: that what was written in my letter to Romeo was now incorrect. I had told him that he should return to Verona on Thursday night – but I had written the letter ere I knew that the marriage ceremony had been brought forward by one day. And by my cursed lack of attention I had not updated the contents before dispatching it.

However, all was not lost. I would merely need to return to the vault alone in time for when Giulietta would awaken. She would no doubt berate me for the fact that her Romeo was not also there to greet her, but I could nonetheless keep her hidden at my cell until such time as Romeo arrived.

\*\*\*

*I had to keep reminding myself that Friar Lawrence had lived through these events as they had actually happened. Even if he was recording them afterwards with the benefit of hindsight, at this stage he still had no notion of what was to follow.*

*And on the face of it, it did indeed seem like a good plan. He presumably had no idea, as everyone who came afterwards has always known, that in a matter of only a few hours it was all going to go so horribly wrong.*

*Knowing what was to come, I could hardly bear to carry on. I poured myself an industrial-sized glass of Chianti and forced myself to continue...*

\*\*\*

Returning to my cell, I pushed open the door – to behold the one person who, ever since the catastrophic events of Monday afternoon, I am ashamed to say I had been dreading to encounter.

Almost before the door had clicked closed behind me, Chiara – all caution forgotten – had thrown herself into my arms.

"My darling," she sobbed against my shoulder. "I cannot bear it!"

"Hush, my sweet." I stroked her hair through her veil.

Please God, I prayed, help me to find the right words.

In the end it was she who broke the silence.

"Do you know what happened?"

"I know only what I have heard from Benvolio. Have you spoken to him yourself?"

She nodded.

"He came back with my husband on Monday afternoon, after the – the..."

Her voice cracked, unable to form whatever word was sticking in her throat. Eventually she drew a deep breath and spoke again.

"Benvolio told me that one of the Capuleti had fought with Mercutio and killed him..."

"Tebaldo."

"Aye, Tebaldo." She spat out the name almost as though its very presence in her mouth were sufficient to choke her.

"...and that he had then turned on Romeo. And that Romeo had to fight for his life."

I nodded.

"I have no doubt that if Romeo had not fought and won, he too

109

would have been slain."

"But then the Lady Capuleti protested to the Prince that Romeo should be put to death."

"Aye, my love, she did. But your husband pleaded that Tebaldo should have been put to death for killing Mercutio. It would appear that the Prince evidently agreed with him on that matter."

"Why, then, did the Prince sentence Romeo to exile? Why not just pardon him?"

I remembered my promise to the Prince – that I would tell no-one of our conversation. But nonetheless, Chiara still needed, and deserved, an answer.

"I believe, my love, that he felt that he could not do that – however much he might have wished to. Consider this: if the Prince had pardoned someone who had caused the death of another, some might accuse him of partiality. As it stood, he took into account the circumstances – including, I expect, the plea of self-defence – and pronounced a sentence which he no doubt felt was more appropriate."

She was silent as she considered this. Eventually she murmured,

"Do you know where Romeo is now?"

I replied, with complete honesty,

"No, my love, I do not."

She looked up.

"Can you find out?"

I hesitated, and turned away from her for fear that my face might betray my thoughts.

How much could I tell her? I had to remind myself that she still knew nothing of Romeo and Giulietta's marriage. I had no idea how, in her parlous state, she might react to the news of that. And so much depended on the escape plan that I dared not risk compromising it at this stage.

"I can try," I replied eventually. "I could send word to the friaries in other cities and ask if he has been sighted anywhere about. Though I know not what good it would do—"

"It would, at the very least, tell us that he is still alive," she interrupted, a faint note of desperation creeping into her voice. "Please do not forget – he is your child as well as mine."

I spun round to face her.

"Do you think," I spat, trying but failing to keep the fury from my rising voice, "that I have ever forgotten that? Have you any notion of what it is like to hear him address me as 'Father' – or for me to address him as 'Son' – when he has no idea of the truth of those titles? God help me, it has been as a knife turning in my soul. You at least can be seen to grieve for him. I cannot even do that."

She gasped, then sank to her knees, broken.

"Forgive me, my love." Her voice was so low that I could barely hear her. "I was so absorbed in my own grief that I failed to consider yours—"

Her words were drowned out by a knock at the door.

"Quickly, my love," I hissed, "veil yourself again."

I crossed to the door and lifted the latch.

To my horror, the door opened to reveal the Lord Montecchi. He looked tired and troubled.

"Fra' Lorenzo," he asked, "is my wife with you?"

"Aye, My Lord. She came to me to make her confession."

I opened the door to admit him, as Chiara (taking her cue) crossed herself and rose from her knees.

"My Lord," she addressed him demurely. "How kind of you to come searching for me."

"I was worried about you, Lucia."

"Thank you, My Lord." She stood up and took his arm, before turning towards me again.

"Thank you, Fra' Lorenzo."

"Madam, Sir."

I stiffly accompanied them to the door as they took their leave, then slumped back against it as it closed behind them.

Oh God, I wondered. How long had the Lord Montecchi been standing outside the door before he had knocked?

And how much of our heated discourse had he overheard...?

*** 

Whatever turmoil might now be going on in my own mind, I knew that I must not allow it to detract from the more urgent matter in hand – that of rescuing Giulietta from the vault. I had calculated that she would awaken from her trance in the small hours of the following morning.

In the intervening time I occupied myself by trying to create a small discreet area in my cell where I could hide her until Romeo should arrive the following night. Finally satisfied with my efforts, I made my way to the chapel for Completorium and took my place in the pew.

*May the Lord Almighty grant us a quiet night and a perfect end...*

I knew that I was not to have a quiet night that night. As for the "perfect end," *Deo Volente*, that would not be for a long time.

***

As we left Completorium I signalled to Fra' Gianni that I needed to speak with him.

"What did Romeo say?" I asked.

I could tell, by Fra' Gianni's troubled face, that all had not gone as it should.

"I am sorry, Fra' Lorenzo. I could not find him."

"What?" I gasped.

"I first went to the friary in Mantua and enquired of the brothers there. They told me that they believed there was a young man newly arrived in the town, but they did not recognise the name of Romeo Montecchi."

Of course – why had I not thought of that? Fleeing, as he was, for his life, Romeo would doubtless have not given his real name.

"Did you make any other enquiries?"

"Aye, I asked in the marketplace, and some of the traders said they believed they had seen a young man who fitted the description I gave them. But sadly, none of them were able to tell me exactly where I might be able to find him. I searched around the town for a few hours, but then I realised that I would have to abandon the quest if I were to have any chance of returning to Verona before nightfall."

"So – what became of the letter?" I asked, trying to conceal my growing alarm.

"I have it here," he answered, dejectedly handing it back to me.

I opened my mouth to protest, but then suddenly realised that Fra' Gianni had not been party to the events of the past two days. He remained unaware of the content of the letter, nor of its significance. Had he known how important it was that the message should reach its recipient, he would doubtless have moved Heaven and Earth in his quest to deliver it.

But because Romeo had not received the letter, this meant that he remained in complete ignorance of the Lord Capuleti's decree that Giulietta should marry Count Paris. Nor would he know of the plan we had devised to help her escape from it. I would need to keep the girl concealed at my cell until I could contrive another means of sending word to him.

Who else could I trust? There were only two other people who knew of the marriage – Agnese, and Romeo's servant Balthasar.

What a fool I have been, I thought. Why had I not sought out Balthasar myself, and asked him to deliver the letter?

I resolved to find the youth on the morrow, once Giulietta was safely out of the vault. In the meantime, I took my leave of Fra' Gianni with a nod and a sigh. Whatever might have happened, it was not his fault.

On the way back to my cell I called in at the novices' quarters and borrowed a novice's habit and a spare cloak. Giulietta would obviously need some form of disguise. The sight of two cloaked monastic figures walking together through the city streets at night would not attract a second glance, but a friar and a girl in a wedding dress might possibly arouse a little suspicion.

***

I calculated that if Giulietta had taken the potion around the hour of ten on the preceding evening, she should awaken at around the hour of four of the following morning. Towards midnight, once I was sure that the rest of the friary would be asleep, I gathered up what I would need for the rescue: the cloak and habit, a flask of restorative herbal tonic to help to revive Giulietta as she awoke, the key to the Capuleti family vault (which I had conveniently forgotten to return to the sacristy), a tinder-box and a flambard. I paused only to murmur a brief prayer for a safe outcome, then left my cell by the door which led directly on to the street.

The streets of the city were deserted; the sky was clear but on this night there was no moon. And for once, I was grateful for the additional level of darkness.

It took but ten or fifteen minutes to cover the distance between the friary and the churchyard. The vault, which had looked forbidding enough in the bright light of the morning, by night took on a far more sinister appearance as it loomed above me. Fumbling in the darkness I finally located the keyhole and unlocked the heavy iron gate. The sound as it creaked open filled the night air; I was certain that the whole of Verona would hear it. Once inside, I discovered that the key would only operate the gates from the outside – there was no means of locking them from within. I carefully pushed the gates together so that they would still appear to be closed. Only when I was fully inside the portal of the vault, and thus would be safe from any prying eyes, did I dare to light my flambard.

I waited for a few moments for my eyes to adjust to the light, before I cautiously made my way down the steps into the tomb. Tebaldo and Giulietta lay on their biers, their well-dressed bodies still new and fresh, in stark contrast to the piles of bones and rags littering all of the other slabs and niches. I approached Tebaldo's corpse and let my light fall on his lifeless form. Despite his having come to such a violent end, his face was yet calm and peaceful. For the first time, I thought, this youth looks truly happy. What kind of life must he have led, I wondered, when so much of it had been spent consumed and driven by meaningless hatred?

But whatever harm Tebaldo might have done in his earthly life, he was now beyond harming anyone. And his soul was now in God's hands. Out of prescribed respect for the dead, I murmured:

"*Requiescat in pace*".

And, to my eternal surprise and relief, I found that I meant every word.

*(It is in pardoning that we are pardoned...)*

I moved to where Giulietta was lying, cold and stiff, on the adjacent bier, and cautiously felt her wrist. There was still no detectable pulse, but her pallid face under the muslin sheet was now beginning to show a faint trace of colour. Soon she would awaken. I seated myself on the ground next to the bier, keeping the flambard close to me to give myself warmth as well as light. I retrieved my rosary from whence I had previously secreted it, made myself as comfortable as possible, and settled down to wait.

I have no idea how long I had been sitting there, desperately trying to ignore my cold, dark and dank surroundings, when I suddenly became aware of the noise of footsteps. I held my breath and listened. The footsteps grew louder; I realised that their owner must be coming down the steps into the vault. But concealed as I was behind Giulietta's bier, I remained out of sight of the entrance, and the shaded light of my own flambard was wholly eclipsed by the light of another one, which was now being borne into the depths of the tomb.

Whoever this intruder might be, and whatever business he might have here, I prayed: Please may he go before the lady revives. Otherwise, what he sees will require no end of explanation. And neither she nor I would wish to be the one who would have to give it.

The footsteps came ever closer, eventually coming to a halt at the other side of Giulietta's bier. There was a moment's silence, then I was aware that the muslin sheet which had covered her body was slowly being pulled aside.

The intruder let out a low groan, then a stifled sob, before brokenly murmuring,

"Giulietta! My love! My wife!"

I recognised the voice almost before the words had been uttered.

***

I lifted up my flambard and slowly eased myself to my feet. A ghastly sight met my eyes: young Romeo, his body racking with sobs, was clinging desperately to Giulietta's body, his streaming face buried in the folds of her white wedding dress. So absorbed was he in his prostrate grief for his lost love that he was clearly utterly unaware that I was now standing at his side.

I was so taken aback at his arrival that it took some moments for me to ask myself: What in Heaven's name was he doing here?

I received the answer to that question in the next instant. The broken-hearted boy was reaching into his pouch and pulling out a small glass vial.

Oh merciful Heaven, I thought, as I recalled Giulietta's words: 'I have no doubt that he would wish to follow me to the grave…'

I had no time to wonder what had happened to bring him hither in this desperate state; I knew only that I had but seconds to prevent a true catastrophe.

Romeo, still evidently oblivious of my presence, had now drawn the stopper from the vial. He raised it towards his lips and declared,

"Here's to my love!"

"Romeo, stop!"

The vial, with whatever deadly substance it contained, was inches away from his open mouth as I leapt forward and seized his arm. Romeo screamed. In his shock and amazement he lost his grip on the vial, which fell to the floor and smashed. Its contents trickled across the flagstones, as the musty air of the vault was pervaded by a faint odour of bitter almonds.

\*\*\*

*Hang on a minute – this isn't what's supposed to happen!*
*I reached for another glass of Chianti.*
*By now, I was REALLY intrigued…*

\*\*\*

"Fra' Lorenzo!" Romeo had finally found his voice. "What are you doing here?"

"Son, I will tell you everything. But first – please, may I ask you the same question?"

"Can you not guess?" he answered desperately. "My love, my wife," (he gestured towards Giulietta) "is dead. And I cannot – I will not – live without her. I am come here to die by her side."

"Son," I asked gently, "who told you that your lady was dead?"

"My servant Balthasar. He rode to Mantua to find me, straightaway after he had seen my lady's funeral and burial this morning."

Of course, I thought. Giulietta's cortège had passed through the streets of Verona on its way to the church. The churchyard itself was a public place. Anyone – everyone – could have seen it. Once again, I cursed my stupidity for not seeking out Balthasar to be my messenger.

"And since you have robbed me of the means of joining her," Romeo went on, gesturing towards the broken fragments of the vial and their spilled contents, "I must now use another means."

He drew his dagger.

Again, I leapt forward, seized his arm and held his hand aloft.

"What was in that vial?" I asked. "And where did you obtain it?"

"I bought it from a poor apothecary in Mantua. He told me that it would despatch me straightaway, even if I had the strength of twenty men."

Holy Saint Francis, I thought. This boy is desperate and determined. Will he listen to me? And even if he does listen to me, will he believe me, so incredible is the tale?

"Son, I am going to ask you to trust me – probably more than you have ever trusted anyone in your entire life."

"Why?" he answered fiercely, struggling to free the hand which was still brandishing his dagger.

"Because if you do, you will find that your life may well be worth living after all."

"How can my life be worth living if my love is dead?" he spat venomously.

"Because, son, your love is *not* dead."

He froze, then gradually lowered his arm as he turned to face me. A strange light came into his tearful blue eyes.

"Fra' Lorenzo, in the two years that I have known you as my ghostly father, I have never once had occasion to doubt you. Yet now, I truly believe that you have taken leave of your senses. Look!" He picked up Giulietta's cold, stiff hand, which still wore the ring they had used at their wedding. "Feel!" he shouted, as he took hold of her wrist as if to seek the beat of a pulse. "My love is buried here in her family's tomb! How can you tell me that she is not dead?"

"Romeo, I beg of you, grant me a few minutes. If you can but hear out my story, perhaps then you might understand."

He made as if to protest again, but then capitulated with a defeated shrug.

"Very well," he sighed, laying down his dagger. "Say what you must."

"Son," I began, "has it not occurred to you to wonder why I am here?"

Romeo considered for a moment, but did not answer.

"Do you not think it strange that a friar should seek entry to a burial vault in the middle of the night?"

Again he gave no answer, but continued to stare forlornly at Giulietta's lifeless form.

"Romeo," I pleaded, "are you listening?"

Eventually he raised his eyes, still red-rimmed with weeping.

"Aye."

"Good. Now listen, and take heed."

By now Romeo had forced Giulietta's cold stiff fingers to interlace with his own. But he looked across at me, and muttered,

"Very well, my ghostly father. I am listening."

"It is a wholly incredible story, son, but I swear, in the name of everything that I have ever held as holy, that every word of it is true."

I paused. Romeo waited.

"Years ago, ere I came to Verona, I was at the Franciscan friary in Venice. I worked there, as I do here, as a herbalist, apothecary and infirmarian.

"One night, one of my fellow friars was taken sick and I was called upon to attend him. I quickly realised he needed a particular medicine, but I did not have any to hand, so it became necessary to mix a fresh brew of the medicine there and then. But by some great mischance, the novice who was assisting me that night gathered up the wrong herbs. I failed to notice the error, and during the night the friar died."

Romeo looked up.

"How terrible that must have been for you."

"Aye, son, it was. For I knew not only that I had failed to save his life, but also that I had been responsible for his death."

"Not you, surely? Would the fault not have lain with the novice who gathered the herbs?"

"No, son, I could not blame the novice; he was young and inexperienced. The fault was entirely my own, for I should have made a proper check of the herbs before I made them into the medicine."

"But why are you telling me this now? I am sorry, Fra' Lorenzo, but I do not understand what this story has to do with how my Giulietta came to die—"

"Stay with me, son – it will all become clear, I promise you."

"Very well…" he sighed.

"The friar had died during the night; he lay in state for the whole of the following day, then his requiem was held on the morning of the day after. And it was during that requiem, some thirty hours after I had given him the medicine, that he awoke."

Romeo gasped.

"He – awoke?"

"Aye. At the very moment in the requiem that we looked for the resurrection of the dead."

Romeo, in spite of himself, could not suppress a smile at this.

"How very timely," he murmured.

"Indeed." I smiled too. "It seemed that the medicine which, by accident, I had created, had taken the form of a sleeping draught. But it proved to be a particularly powerful one – one which brought about a temporary likeness of death."

Romeo sat very still as he absorbed the import of these words. When he spoke again, his voice was low and hoarse.

"So – this sleeping draught which you gave to the friar…"

"Aye, son. Your Giulietta has taken a dose of the same potion."

"But why? I do not understand…"

"Believe me, son, it was the desperate action of a desperate young woman."

"Desperate? What had driven my love to such desperation? Why should she wish to assume the likeness of death?"

It was only at this point that I realised that Romeo remained totally in ignorance of the Lord Capuleti's decree that Giulietta should marry Count Paris.

"It was because she needed to escape from a desperate situation – a situation of which, I believe, you have no knowledge."

"What?" He looked genuinely alarmed.

Before I continued, I picked up Romeo's dagger and set it down well out of the range of where he could easily reach it. I would take no risks with his reaction to what I was about to tell him.

"Do you recall, son, that you told me that when you first saw Giulietta at the ball, she was dancing with a kinsman of Mercutio?"

"I can recall every detail of that evening."

119

Once again, the faraway look came into his eyes and he smiled to himself at the recollection.

"The kinsman is a young Count; his name is Paris."

I paused and drew a deep breath.

"Giulietta's father had arranged that he should marry her."

Romeo gasped.

"He was going to steal my wife?"

"Hush, son!" I laid my hand on his arm. "Please remember, only five people in the world knew that Giulietta was already your wife: yourself, Giulietta, Agnese, Balthasar and myself. No-one else, least of all her father or the Count Paris, had any idea that she was no longer free to marry anyone else."

Romeo did not answer immediately. Instead, he bent low over Giulietta, stroked her hair with his free hand, and touched her cold lips with his own.

"She is mine," he murmured.

"Yes, son, she is yours. And she was determined to remain yours."

Romeo glanced up.

"What do you mean?"

"The marriage was being arranged even as you were with her on Monday night. After you left her at dawn on Tuesday, her mother came to her chamber—"

"Aye, I remember," Romeo interposed. "Agnese knocked on Giulietta's door to forewarn us that her mother was approaching. I had to escape quickly, ere she found me there."

I shuddered as I considered this; I had no idea that Romeo had come so close to being discovered in Giulietta's bed.

"Her mother was coming to tell her that she was to be married to Count Paris on Thursday morning."

"Thursday? That is tomorrow morning, is it not?"

"Aye; when dawn breaks it will be Thursday."

"What happened next?"

"Giulietta refused to agree to the marriage, and thus incurred the wrath of her father, who threatened to disown her if she would not obey him."

"It might have been better if he had," Romeo sighed.

"What do you mean, son?" I asked, surprised at his response.

"If he had disowned her, then she would have had no reason to remain in his household. She could thus have come to Mantua to be with me…"

I must own that that possibility had not occurred to me.

"…indeed," Romeo was continuing, "why did she not simply escape and follow me to Mantua in any case?"

"That I cannot say. But this I will ask you: why did you not take her with you when you left?"

Romeo opened his mouth to reply, then closed it again. He looked down at Giulietta, and a tear trickled down his cheek and splashed on her face.

"I do not know," he murmured eventually. "I realise now that I should have done so. But everything came about so quickly… Our marriage… Mercutio… Tebaldo…" He glanced across uneasily at the corpse on the adjacent bier. "Then I had to escape, ere we could make any plans to be together…"

"Be that as it may," I continued hastily, "your Giulietta was determined, even in the face of the most impossible obstacles, to remain a loving and faithful wife to you. So that very same morning, she came to me and begged for my assistance. I have no doubt," I added after a moment's pause, "that had I not been able to help her, she would have even been prepared, in order to avoid this second marriage, to do violence upon herself."

Romeo gasped again, and his fingers closed more tightly around hers.

"Truly, father?"

"Truly, son. And so it was that I realised that if she was strong enough to slay herself for you, then she would also be strong enough, and brave enough, to undertake a difficult and perchance dangerous task: that of borrowing, for a short while, the semblance of death. I remembered the sleeping draught which had deceived us all into believing that the friar had died, and it came to me that we could use this same illusion in order to rescue Giulietta.

"Accordingly, I gave her a vial of the draught and told her that she should go home, beg her father's pardon for having displeased him, and pretend that she now gave her consent to marry the Count, as her father had arranged, on Thursday morning. On Wednesday night she was to drink the potion when she went to bed; she would soon fall into a profound trance, her breathing and her pulse would cease, and she would become cold, pale and stiff – exactly as you see her now. And that is how her parents, and her bridegroom, would find her on the morning of her wedding."

Romeo was looking at me steadily. He still said nothing, but the tears had dried on his cheeks.

"I wrote a letter to you telling you of this plan, and asking that you should return to Verona in secret on Thursday night, in time to be at her side when she awakens."

"But this night is Wednesday, father."

"Aye, son, I know. I had foolishly assumed that when Giulietta went home and agreed to marry the Count, the wedding would indeed take place on Thursday morning. But for reasons which I do not know, the Lord Capuleti then decided that the ceremony should be brought forward to Wednesday. So Giulietta had to take the draught on Tuesday – that very same night."

A faint glimmer of hope appeared in Romeo's eyes.

"For how long does this draught keep her – asleep…?"

The last word came out as a barely audible whisper, as though he hardly dared believe the truth of it.

"For approximately thirty hours."

"And the hour is now…?"

"I am not sure of the exact hour, son, but I calculate that she should wake before dawn."

He turned back towards her and lightly caressed her pale face. Then he looked back at me.

"I never received any letter from you," he murmured, but his voice bore no tone of malice or accusation.

"Nay, son – that was due to a most unfortunate mischance."

"What mischance was that?"

"The friar to whom I entrusted it on Tuesday was detained here in Verona that afternoon, as he was required to conduct Tebaldo's requiem. Thus, he could not leave here with the letter until Wednesday morning. When he reached Mantua he could not find you."

Romeo sighed.

"Aye, by that time I had already received the news from Balthasar that my lady was dead." He shuddered. "I left Mantua forthwith and rode back to Verona; I concealed myself outside the city until I could safely come here to die with her."

"Thank God that I reached this place before you…"

Now it was my turn to shudder, as the image swam before my eyes of what might so easily have happened: Romeo arriving at the vault and drinking the poison… Giulietta awakening to find him dead beside her… I knew not for certain what she would have done, but as I caught a glimpse of Romeo's dagger where it was lying on the ground, I was left in little doubt…

I was jolted away from this hellish vision by a shout from Romeo.

"Fra' Lorenzo! Look!"

The cold stiff fingers, still interlaced with his own, had begun to twitch.

"Praise Heaven! She is beginning to revive!"

Giulietta's pale lips parted slightly as she began to take in a few short breaths, then she uttered a long sigh as her eyes eased their way open.

"Romeo…?"

"I am here, my love." He smiled, bent over her and kissed her.

"Fra' Lorenzo?"

"Aye, daughter, I am here too."

She blinked and looked around.

"I well remember where I should be…"

"Here, daughter, drink this. It will help to revive you."

Romeo slid his arm under her shoulders and raised her head away from the slab. As she sipped the herbal tonic the colour slowly returned to her cheeks. After a few minutes she was able to sit up, then slowly eased her feet to the floor. Romeo, guiding her away from the shards of broken glass littering the ground, carefully supported her as she took her first tentative steps.

"It is almost dawn. We must leave here ere we are discovered," I reminded them. "Giulietta, are you able to walk?"

"I believe so."

"Here, my love, lean on me." Romeo, as if fearful that she yet might be taken away from him again, had still not released his hold of her.

"But first you must put this on."

"What is it?"

"It is a novice's habit; it will disguise you and conceal you from prying eyes. And you," I turned to Romeo as Giulietta slid the scratchy garment over her dress, "keep your hood over your head. You must both keep your faces hidden."

"Where are we going, father?"

"Back to my cell; I will conceal the two of you there for the moment. You can leave for Mantua tonight. Are you ready?"

As one, they nodded.

I began to lead the way up the steps out of the vault. The first grey streaks of dawn were spreading across the sky as I approached the portal. A few paces behind me, Romeo began to guide Giulietta up the stairs.

As I made to open the heavy iron gate, I became aware of movement in the churchyard beyond.

"Stay back!" I hissed to the pair behind me. "There is someone outside!"

***

They froze where they stood, thankfully still hidden from sight by the darkness of the stairwell.

"I will deal with this," I whispered. "Stay where you are, and say nothing. I will come back for you when all is clear."

I pushed the gates ajar and eased myself out through the gap, pulling them close behind me. I discerned that a shadowy figure, his arms full of flowers, was trudging dejectedly towards the tomb. But thankfully, whoever he was, with his head bowed he had apparently failed to notice me in the dim light of the breaking dawn.

I quickly knelt down next to the tomb, pulled out my rosary, and assumed a reverential attitude of prayer.

*"Ave Maria, gracia plena, Dominus tecum, benedicta tu in mulieribus, benedictus fructus ventris tui Jesus…"*

"Fra' Lorenzo?"

I looked up.

"Count Paris?"

I struggled to my feet.

"Why are you here, Fra' Lorenzo?" His tone was unusually sharp.

I held up my rosary.

"I was the Lady Giulietta's ghostly father. I found that I could not sleep this night, and I wished to say some prayers for the repose of her soul."

The Count sighed.

"I am sorry, Fra' Lorenzo. In my grief for the loss of my lady, I fear I have forgotten my manners."

(*'My lady'?* Merciful Heaven, I thought, I hope that Romeo did not hear the Count say those words.)

"It matters not," I answered, in what I hoped was a kindly tone. "But may I ask you, Sir, what brings you to the churchyard at such an early hour?"

"Like you, Fra' Lorenzo, I have been unable to sleep. I have brought flowers and perfumed water for my lady's grave."

(Poor fellow...)

"Please, lay them here. If you wish, I will say a prayer over them."

The Count forced a weak smile.

"Thank you, Fra' Lorenzo."

He knelt down and carefully arranged the flowers on the ground beside the vault, then sprinkled a little of the perfumed water over them. I could not help but notice that the water was being augmented by his own tears.

I knelt down alongside him, and together we recited the Lord's Prayer:

"*Pater noster, qui es in cælis,*
*sanctificetur nomen tuum;*
*adveniat regnum tuum;*
*fiat voluntas tua, sicut in cælo et in terra.*
*Panem nostrum cotidianum da nobis hodie,*
*et dimitte nobis debita nostra,*
*sicut et nos dimittimus debitoribus nostris;*
*et ne nos inducas in tentationem*
*Sed libera nos a malo.*"

125

I concluded with a short benediction:

"*Fidelium animae, per misericordiam Dei, requiescant in pace. Amen.*"

May the souls of the faithful, through the mercy of God, rest in peace…

I said that prayer for all those who were interred in the vault, and everywhere in the churchyard. Though the Count had no idea that the one person for whom it was not being said was the lady Giulietta. And, *Deo Volente*, nor would it be said, neither for her nor for her devoted lord, for many years to come.

***

*Amen to that.*
*So what happens next?*
*I have to find out…*

***

I respectfully allowed the grief-stricken Count a little longer on his knees, but I remained mindful of the fact that Romeo and Giulietta were still waiting, concealed, inside the cold dark vault. Afraid that the Count might go too close to the portal and discover that the gates were not properly locked, I carefully positioned myself between him and the doorway, and after a respectable delay I laid my hand on his arm.

"Sir," I whispered gently, "you can do no more by remaining here. Go home. Your place is with the living, not here amongst the dead."

He looked up and wiped his brimming eyes. He hesitated, then struggled to his feet.

"Perhaps you are right, Fra' Lorenzo. You are very kind and very wise, and I thank you heartily for everything you have done."

(Oh Count, I thought, if you but knew what I have done, and that my deeds are the very cause of your present misery…)

126

Now it was my turn to shed a tear. The Count, mistaking it for a gesture of my own personal grief for Giulietta, extended his hand to me before reluctantly turning and walking away.

I watched him go, his shoulders drooping, and his gait shuffling and stumbling like that of an old man.

What a tragedy, I thought. The Count is a good man, and he is deserving of far better than this. Pray God that one day he will find happiness with a wife whom he can love as he loved Giulietta. One who, unlike Giulietta, can love him in return.

Once the Count was safely out of the churchyard, I leaned back against the gate of the vault and pushed it ajar.

"Romeo? Giulietta?" I hissed into the depths of the portal.

"Aye, Fra' Lorenzo?" Romeo's voice whispered back to me from the darkness beyond.

"All is clear now. Are you ready?"

"Aye."

"Come then. But you must both keep your faces fully hidden. Stay close to me until we return to the friary. If we are approached, say nothing – I will answer any questions."

They stumbled up the steps and blinked against the growing dawn light as I locked the vault gates behind them. As she paused to draw the novice's hood over her face, Giulietta caught sight of the Count's flowers.

"What is this, Fra' Lorenzo?" she asked, her lip trembling.

"Did you hear any of what was being spoken of just now?"

"Nay. We could hear voices – yours and another – but could not tell what was being said."

(Thank goodness…)

"The visitor was the Count Paris. He had brought these flowers for your grave."

She gasped, then cautiously peered at them more closely.

"They are beautiful," she sighed after a few moments. "I had no idea that he cared about me so much."

Romeo also gazed sadly at the display, before placing a comforting arm about her shoulders.

"They are indeed magnificent, my sweet," he murmured. "He must

127

have loved you almost as much as I do."

***

Our journey back to the friary took rather longer than it would normally have done. Although the city streets were mercifully quiet at that early hour, nonetheless we took care to use the back alleys in order to avoid being seen.

Back at my cell, I settled the two of them into the hiding-place which I had prepared for Giulietta, then made my way to the refectory. The larder was well-stocked with bread, cheese, fish and fruit, and I was able to take sufficient for their needs for the day without risk of it being missed from the stores. I next went to find the alms box and took a small amount of money from it. I had no idea how much money Romeo might have, and I feared that the vial of poison which he had procured in Mantua could well have cost him dearly. I resolved to discreetly repay the alms, in the fullness of time, from the coffers of the Conte Da Porto.

Finally, I returned to the novices' quarters and found the cupboard where the lay-clothes were kept. I found a shirt, a doublet, a pair of breeches and a pair of boots which looked as though they would fit Giulietta. The garments smelled slightly musty; they had evidently been stored there for many months. It was very unlikely, I reasoned, that their original owner would have need of them again.

"Here, daughter – change your wedding clothes for these."

"Why, Fra' Lorenzo?"

"You will stand a much greater chance of escaping if you are not recognised. Anyone who sees you thus attired will take you for a boy."

Giulietta fingered the garments gingerly.

"Are you sure they are not needed by anyone else?"

I nodded, then turned to Romeo.

"Where is your horse, son?"

Romeo froze.

"I – left my horse tethered outside the city walls. I had not given the matter another thought."

(No, I thought – when you left your horse, you reasoned that you would not be using it again, believing as you did that your next

128

journey would be your last…)

"Can you remember where?"

"Aye, in the sycamore grove outside the western gate."

"Stay here; I will go and fetch it back here."

I turned to address Giulietta.

"Whilst I am gone, change your clothes."

"What am I to do with the dress?"

"There are some sacks in the cupboard; hide it inside one of those. I will take it back to the vault."

"Why?" Giulietta frowned.

"There is now nothing on your bier. The next time the tomb is opened (whenever that might be) its empty state might well be noticed. But if your clothes remain, it will appear as though the monument still contains the mortal remains of the bride of Count Paris, she who died two nights since."

They looked at each other soberly, then slowly nodded to me. I headed towards the door.

"I will need to lock you in here. Remember, no-one must hear you."

They both nodded and grinned. I did not imagine that they would be overly distressed at being left alone for a while.

The horse was indeed tethered where Romeo had indicated; I presumed this was where he had hidden himself during the remaining hours of daylight yesterday. The poor beast was by now in dire need of hay and water. I led it slowly back to the friary stable and secured it in a vacant stall to rest and recover; it would need to be strong for the journey which would await it that night.

***

Finally night fell, and the fugitives made ready for their escape.

"Where should we go?" Romeo had asked me earlier, during the long hours of waiting.

"What did you do ere now?" I must own that it had not previously occurred to me to wonder.

"I found a deserted barn on the outskirts of Mantua and hid myself in there; there was space enough to conceal the horse as well. I

129

walked into the city to buy bread. It was whilst I was there that Balthasar found me."

I nodded.

"Very well. Go back to the barn for tonight, and stay hidden for as long as you can. If you are desperate, go to the friary in Mantua and ask for shelter there. But do not give your real names. You should be able to claim sanctuary, but even so, it is probably better that the friars do not know precisely who you are."

"Why not?"

"Consider: you, Giulietta, are officially dead. If you were to be discovered alive, here or anywhere else, how should we explain it to your parents or to the Count?"

Giulietta hung her head.

"How indeed," she murmured.

"And as for Romeo," I continued to address Giulietta, "I am sorry to have to tell you this, but I greatly fear what your family might do to him if they were to find him—"

"I fear so too, Fra' Lorenzo."

"Why so?"

Giulietta shuddered and clung to Romeo's hand.

"When my mother came to me to tell me that I was to marry the Count, she found me weeping. Thankfully she knew not that I was weeping for loss of you, my sweet, but instead took my misery for grief at Tebaldo's death."

"Had it not been for that, my love, I should not have had to leave you."

"Even so, my mother promised me that we would have revenge for it. She said that she would find someone who could arrange that you should soon keep Tebaldo company."

(So the Prince had been right in his reckoning…)

"All the more reason, then, that you should conceal your true identities."

"What should we call ourselves?" Romeo asked.

I considered for a moment, then it came to me.

"Son, assume the name of Da Porto. It is a common enough name, and should not arouse any suspicion or attract any undue attention."

"And what of my first name?"

"Call yourself Antonio. It was my father's name."

Romeo gasped, and stared at my monastic habit.

"You had a father…?"

Giulietta giggled.

I grinned.

"Everyone has a father – even those who wear the cowl were first begotten of man and born of woman! And as I have said to you more than once ere now, son, I have not always been a friar."

And nor will I remain a friar for much longer, I added mentally. But there is no need for you to know that. At least, not for the moment…

***

Once again, I was grateful that this night also had no moon. Cloaked and hooded, the three of us led the horse through the dark and deserted streets to the western gate of the city. Once outside the walls, Romeo climbed into the saddle, and Giulietta, now clad in unassuming male attire and with her long dark hair tied back and tucked inside her doublet, clambered up behind him.

She peered at me concernedly.

"You look tired, Fra' Lorenzo – are you quite well?"

I shrugged.

"I did not sleep last night; I will be fine after I have rested."

"Thank you, my ghostly father," Romeo whispered. "Thank you for everything."

"God-speed you both," I answered. "I will send word to you in Mantua."

The horse set off at a slow trot, then cantered away into the darkness.

May Heaven preserve them, I prayed, until I see them again.

I turned back towards the city and reached the gate just as the Watch were turning the corner. I hastily took refuge in a doorway – I had no wish to have to account for my presence – and waited until they were safely past me, before creeping back through the shadows to the friary.

As I approached I became aware of a nagging pain in my chest, and an overwhelming urge to cough. I thought idly that I must have caught a chill during my vigil in the vault, and resolved to mix myself a draught of lemon thyme, elecampane, honey and hyssop, and take some before retiring. Once back inside my cell I began to assemble and crush the herbs, but then another violent fit of coughing took over. I recall nothing more after that.

***

When I awoke I had no idea where I was; I knew only that bright sunlight was streaming in through the windows, and I detected in the air a faint odour of lavandula. I looked cautiously around and gradually recognised my surroundings: I was lying in a bed in the infirmary. Fra' Gianni was sitting at my bedside, reading his breviary.

"Fra' Gianni…?"

"Ah, good morrow, Fra' Lorenzo," he answered cheerily. "You are awake at last! You gave us all quite a shock."

"What happened?" I struggled up on to my elbow, but immediately began to cough again. I abandoned the attempt to sit up and lay back, exhausted.

"We noticed that you had been absent from chapel for some time. That is not like you!"

True; in attending to the needs of my two fugitives, I had missed all of the services on the day of their escape.

"And for almost two whole days!"

I gasped.

"Two days? What day is this, then?"

"Today is Saturday. You did not appear in chapel at all on Thursday, but when by noon on Friday we still had had no sight of you, nor any word to explain your absence, I came to your cell. I found you lying unconscious on the floor by your work bench."

I struggled to recollect. The fatigue, the pain, the cough…

"I – I…"

"Do not try to explain – you have had a bad fever. You must rest and build up your strength. I will bring you some medicine and some broth."

"Thank you, my friend. You are very kind. There is much that I owe you."

Fra' Gianni laid a comforting hand on my arm.

"You owe me nothing. But if you wish to repay me, you can do so by recovering swiftly."

He grinned and left, returning a few minutes later with a laden tray.

As I sipped the broth, it occurred to me that I could not recall the last time I had eaten. And I realised that I was absolutely famished.

The repast over, I lay back and tried to collect my thoughts.

I still had no idea if the Lord Montecchi had overheard any of the heated discourse between myself and Chiara on Wednesday afternoon. Nor did I have any idea of how I could possibly find out. I am not, and have never been, a man who normally gives way to fear, but I nonetheless could not suppress a tremble as I considered the possible consequences. The scandal which would inevitably follow would be devastating for the good name of the Franciscan Order, and utterly catastrophic for Chiara.

But it might still be possible for Chiara to make her escape as planned, and return with me to Venice. This plan had first been hatched a little more than a week ago, but so much had taken place in the meantime that it seemed as though half a lifetime had passed since we had first spoken of it.

And if I were to stand any chance at all of helping Romeo and Giulietta to build a reasonable life of their own, I would no longer be able to keep their marriage – or their whereabouts – a secret from Chiara.

But first, I must try to recover my own strength, and somehow rid myself of this nagging cough.

\*\*\*

I also remembered that my letter to Fra' Roberto, which I had hastily abandoned last Monday afternoon when the distraught Romeo had come crashing into my cell, still lay unfinished on my desk. But I could not recall whether anything I had so far written might betray the theme of the letter to anyone who might have discovered the paper by chance. I shuddered at the thought. The matter of my leaving the Order was a highly delicate one, and I would need to break the news to my fellow friars carefully and sensitively when the time came.

I was shaken out of my musings by the arrival of Fra' Gianni.

"Fra' Lorenzo, you have a visitor."

I blinked as Fra' Gianni ushered in a tall, lithe figure in a dark cloak.

"Good morrow, Fra' Lorenzo."

The visitor threw back his hood as Fra' Gianni withdrew.

"Benvolio! What a pleasant surprise!"

I realised with a shock that I had not seen Benvolio since the debacle in the city last Monday, and that it had been considerably longer since I had spoken to him face to face.

Of my three pupils, he was the only one who had not suffered dire consequences from the appalling events of that fateful afternoon. Save, of course, the consequences of having been a first-hand witness to them. And I had no doubt that the memories of seeing his friend murdered and his cousin banished would remain with him until his dying day.

"How goes it with you, Fra' Lorenzo?" he asked, with a look of genuine concern.

I smiled feebly at him.

"I am still tired, though thankfully I believe the fever is now gone. What brings you here, young fellow?"

Benvolio hung his head.

"I am so sorry, Fra' Lorenzo; I did not know you were ill. My business can wait."

But I sensed that something was troubling him. In my weakened state I might not be able to do very much to help him, but I could at the very least lend him my ear.

"What is the matter, son? Tell me; I can listen for as long as you have need."

"Truly, Fra' Lorenzo? I have no wish to burden you…"

"Truly, son. Please, sit down."

Benvolio drew up a chair alongside my bed and settled himself uncomfortably on its front edge. He seemed unsure of how to begin.

"Fra' Lorenzo, I am worried about my uncle."

My mouth went dry. What could have happened to make Benvolio come to me and say this? I was saved from the need to respond by the timely onset of another bout of coughing.

"The Lord Montecchi?" I finally managed to croak.

"Aye, Fra' Lorenzo. I fear that he is not well. Indeed, he has not been well for some time."

Thankfully, Benvolio appeared not to have perceived my alarm.

"For how long?" I asked.

"For some months since."

"What do you believe to be the trouble?"

"I know not, Fra' Lorenzo, save that he is growing very thin. He has little appetite and very little strength." Benvolio sighed. "I remember that when I was younger he was always bright, and jovial, and energetic. He has been as a father to me—"

"What became of your own father?" I asked gently.

"He was the Lord Montecchi's younger brother. I never knew him. Nor my mother. She died at my birth, and he died of grief not long afterwards."

"Benvolio, I am so sorry. I had no idea…"

"Please, do not trouble yourself, Fra' Lorenzo; there is no reason why you should have known. It is not generally spoken of."

"So – you were brought up in your uncle's household?"

"Aye. Romeo and I are of an age; he is but two months younger. We grew up as though we were twin brothers."

The mention of Romeo reminded me that I had, to my shame, utterly failed to enquire after Benvolio's own health.

"Son, I am sorry; I had not thought to ask you: how are you, after what has happened here?"

Benvolio stared into space.

"I do not know what I feel, Fra' Lorenzo. Stunned, bewildered, confused… In one single blow I have lost both my friend and my kinsman; one dead, the other exiled. I find it hard to comprehend that I will not see either of them again. And both lost so needlessly…" His eyes filled with tears.

"I know, son. It grieves me to think so – and it grieves me too to think that you bore witness to these awful things."

Benvolio shuddered, then turned his brimming eyes towards me.

"Fra' Lorenzo, I do not think that I will ever forget the look in Mercutio's eyes as he lay dying. Yet even at the point of death, he was still able to make a jest."

"What do you mean?"

"He said 'If you ask for me tomorrow, you will find me a grave man.'"

Benvolio's last words were lost in a racking sob.

"Come, son – weep if you wish to. There is no shame in giving vent to your grief."

Benvolio hesitated, then hid his face in the coverlet. I lay back in silence as he wept, then I became aware that he was speaking again.

"A curse on both your houses…"

"What, son?"

"Mercutio's last words. '*A curse on both your houses; they have finished me for this world…*'"

Now it was my turn to shudder.

"A dying man's curse…"

"Aye, Fra' Lorenzo. A dying man's curse – on both houses. The Capuleti have been cursed indeed. First Tebaldo—"

"Son, please do not trouble yourself over Tebaldo. I agree that it is tragic for his family that he is dead – indeed, it is tragic that any young man should die under such awful circumstances. But please remember that he would have suffered the sentence of the law in any case, for having killed Mercutio."

Benvolio was silent as he considered this.

"Be that as it may," he went on, "it was on the very next night that the Lady Giulietta died…"

I nodded, but said nothing.

"… and now I am wondering: what curse awaits the House of Montecchi?"

"Is not Romeo's banishment curse enough?" I asked gently.

Benvolio looked up.

"It is indeed curse enough on its own," he answered. "But I fear that there may yet be something worse in store for us."

"What do you mean, son?"

Benvolio drew a deep breath before answering.

"As I said just now, Fra' Lorenzo, my uncle is not a well man – and my cousin's banishment has affected him deeply. I fear this whole dreadful business may hasten his end."

I was genuinely shocked at his words.

"What makes you say that?"

"It is as though he has lost the will to live."

"Son, whatever may have happened to Romeo, the Lord Montecchi still has you."

This did not appear to comfort Benvolio.

"I cannot replace Romeo. And I fear that I am not good enough."

I struggled up on to my elbows.

"Benvolio, you must never believe that. And you should not even try to replace Romeo in the Lord Montecchi's eyes. But that does not alter the fact that you are nonetheless as good a son as any man could ever wish for. If you were my son, I should be proud of you. The Lord Montecchi may well be grieving for loss of Romeo now, but think how much worse it would be for him if he did not have you either."

Benvolio brightened a little at this.

"Thank you, Fra' Lorenzo. I had not thought of that."

"Go home now, and comfort him – if only by your presence. When I am strong enough, I will call on him. If he needs medicine, I will bring it."

"Thank you again. God speed you a swift recovery."

He bowed and took his leave.

I watched him go. He is a good fellow, I thought. And if ever a youth bore a name which best fitted his character, it was Benvolio: *I wish you well…*

***

I remained in the infirmary for another two full days. On the afternoon of the third day, although the cough was still troubling me, I felt otherwise strong enough to return to my cell. As far as I could ascertain, everything therein remained as I had left it. Thankfully Giulietta had heeded my instruction to conceal her wedding dress, and its accompanying slippers, inside one of the sacks in the cupboard. And as for my unfinished letter to Fra' Roberto, I need not have worried; it contained nothing specific save an oblique reference to a decision I should shortly need to make, and it ended in mid-sentence before any more sensitive facts were revealed. It mattered not if anyone here might have seen it.

I had much to attend to. A pressing priority was to return to the vault and dispose of the wedding dress, but as this could be done only under cover of darkness, I turned my attention to tending and watering the herb garden and resuming the task of harvesting any further honey. This done, I finally completed brewing the potion of lemon thyme, elecampane, honey and hyssop, decanted it into a jar and swallowed a spoonful ere it had cooled. For the first time in almost a week, I found some slight relief from the coughing.

The thought of medicines reminded me of my promise to Benvolio, and I decided that I would pay a visit to the Lord Montecchi the following day. Still uncertain about how much he had overheard, I feared that it would not be an easy interview, and ideally I would have preferred to postpone it until I was feeling stronger. But I was well aware that young Benvolio was relying heavily on me.

I would have to wait until night had fallen before I would be able to return to the vault, but in the meanwhile, I resolved to use the remaining time to finish my letter to Fra' Roberto.

I re-read the opening of my first attempt, then realised that this matter could not easily be dealt with simply by letter. I took up another sheet of paper and began again:

*Salve, Fra' Roberto.*

*I am sorry for the delay in contacting you; unfortunately I have been a little unwell for the past few days.*

*Once again, may I thank you for your kindness to me, both throughout my time as a friar in Venice and more recently at the time of my father's passing.*

*Since returning to Verona I have spent much time in considering the decision which I must make concerning the matter of which we spoke at our last meeting. As I am sure you can imagine, this decision has not been an easy one to make.*

*I should very much like to be able to discuss the matter with you again, face to face. Please could you send me word of when would be a suitable time for me to visit you?*

*In D.no,*
*Fra' Lorenzo*

I sealed the letter and took it across to the novices' quarters, from whence it would be despatched on the morrow.

I had now but to attend the office of Completorium ere I could return to the vault under cover of darkness. I swallowed another dose of the hyssop mixture and prayed that it would control my cough for the remainder of the night.

This night had the faintest sliver of a new crescent moon. It did little in the way of illumination (and for that I was once again very grateful), but its slight presence was nonetheless comforting as I trudged with my bundle through the deserted streets to the churchyard.

As I approached the Capuleti monument I could see, even in the dim moonlight, that the Count's magnificent array of flowers was now looking sad and wilted. I resolved to return in daylight on a legitimate errand to clear away the depressing display, then turned the key in the lock and pushed the vault gates open. As before, only once I was safely inside did I dare to light my flambard.

I was totally unprepared for what befell me next.

As I crept down the steps into the vault, my nostrils were assailed by an overwhelmingly nauseous and putrid stench. I coughed and retched uncontrollably, almost to the point of vomiting. If I had not known differently, I should have said that I could even taste blood in my mouth.

But I could not turn back now. I covered my nose and mouth with my sleeve and steeled myself for whatever horror might await me down in the depths of the tomb. I recalled having said to Giulietta that the people who lay there had no power to harm her. On entering the main burial chamber, I realised now just how much I had been mistaken.

During the six days which had elapsed since my last visit to the tomb to rescue Giulietta, the body of Tebaldo had been reduced to a stinking, oozing mass of rotting flesh, through which his bones were now already beginning to protrude.

Thank God, I thought, that this was not the sight which greeted Giulietta when she awoke from her trance.

Averting my eyes from this ghastly spectacle, I eased my way round to the now vacant bier beyond. I carefully arranged Giulietta's dress and slippers in a suitable pose, then, after a moment's hesitation, ventured into the farthest corner of the crypt and selected one of the oldest skulls from the depths of a dark niche. After murmuring a prayer to the deceased asking for forgiveness for disturbing the remains, I positioned the skull at the head of Giulietta's bier. *Deo*

*Volente*, so speedy was the process of bodily decay that by the time the vault should be opened to admit its next occupant, Tebaldo would be reduced to no more than a stark array of bare bones and faded fabric. And so too, to the untrained eye, would the late and lamented bride of Count Paris. The deception was complete.

Almost suffocated by the stench of putrefaction, I held my breath as best I could as I rushed up the steps. Once outside, I heaved in great gasps of the fresh night air – then finally lost all attempts at self-control and vomited repeatedly into the depths of a nearby bush.

Back in my cell, late though the hour was, I took a few minutes to mix myself a brew of parsley, lavandula and mint-leaves, and copiously swilled out my mouth. But try as I might, I could not wholly purge myself of the lingering taste of bile and decay.

***

The following morning I still felt weak and shaky. Grateful for an excuse to further postpone my visit to the house of the Montecchi, after breakfast I walked back to the churchyard, with the purpose of clearing away the Count's dead flowers from outside the tomb entrance. On the same errand I locked the gates of the vault (which in my haste last night to escape from thence I had forgotten to do) and returned the key to its place in the sacristy, praying that it had not been missed ere now. I could have said (truthfully) that in the general distress of the occasion I had omitted to replace it after Giulietta's burial, and that since then I had been quite unwell and had not been able to bring it back ere now. But in any case, I was grateful that hereafter I should need to have no further dealings with this place of unnatural sleep.

I had been back at my cell only a few minutes when there came a frantic hammering at the door. It crashed open to reveal a dishevelled Benvolio, panting and perspiring, having evidently run all the way hither.

"Fra' Lorenzo – please – you must – come – quickly…"

"Benvolio? Whatever is the matter?"

"My uncle – he is suddenly – become – much – worse… He is – asking – for – you…"

***

I hastily snatched up my breviary. As I followed Benvolio through the bustling streets, it came to me that I had never previously visited the house of the Montecchi; I had only ever seen the Lord Montecchi, Chiara, Romeo or Benvolio when they had come to church or to see me at the friary.

The house was a far more modest building than the ostentatious mansion of the Capuleti. Yet despite the urgency of my errand, I discerned that the place had a pleasant and homely atmosphere which the other sadly lacked.

Benvolio ushered me up the stairs and pushed open the door to one of the chambers. He crossed the room in two strides and drew aside the curtain around the bed.

"Uncle?"

"Benvolio…?" The voice was low and hoarse. My heart sank as I recalled the last occasion I had attended such a scene – back in Venice, less than a month since. Now, as then, the stench of death was poisoning the air. I felt sick.

"Uncle, Fra' Lorenzo is here."

The pale face on the pillow turned painfully toward me, and the hollow eyes met my own.

"Thank you for coming to see me, Fra' Lorenzo. I am sorry to hear that you too have been unwell."

"Thank you, sir." I hesitated, then cautiously asked, "How can I help you?"

The Lord Montecchi turned to Benvolio.

"Please, could you leave us for a few moments?"

Benvolio looked shocked.

"But why, Uncle?"

"I have something which I must say to Fra' Lorenzo in private."

Holy Saint Francis, I thought – what was this…?

***

Once the door had clicked closed behind the reluctant Benvolio, I summoned up my courage and asked a question which I hoped might forestall any unpleasant exchange between us:

141

"My Lord, do you wish for me to hear your confession?"

The Lord Montecchi was silent for a moment, then whispered,

"Aye. But first there is something else I must ask you."

He was clearly not willing to be sidetracked from whatever purpose he had in summoning me hither. My mouth went completely dry, and my tongue felt as though it were seven sizes too large to fit inside it.

"Yes, My Lord?" I croaked.

"I need to ask your advice."

"About what?"

It was as though I were sitting on a knife-edge. What did he know, and what was he about to ask me?

"About my patrimony."

I blinked.

"What of it, Sir?"

"After what has happened here of late, I find I can no longer regard Romeo as my son and heir."

Oh merciful Heaven, I thought – he knows. He must have overheard…

"Sir….?" I finally managed to force out the single syllable.

The Lord Montecchi lay back, closed his eyes and let out a long sigh. As he exhaled I could hear his chest rattle. I had heard that noise elsewhere; a prelude to the final curtain.

My blood ran cold. Was I too about to receive a dying man's curse?

As I waited for him to speak again, I could not help but notice how aged and frail he appeared. That was when it occurred to me that I had never thought to wonder how old he might be, or how many years he had spent as a widower ere Chiara had come to Verona. His brother – Benvolio's father – must have been a good many years younger.

The grey face on the pillow opened its eyes. They were hollow and bloodshot.

"Romeo – is banished…"

"I know, Sir. I was his ghostly father—"

No sooner had the words left my mouth than I silently cursed myself. Why had I not simply said "I was his teacher and confessor"? Instead, I had now stupidly brought to the forefront of our discourse the very subject – the very word, even – which I had been fervently wishing to avoid.

But if the Lord Montecchi had noticed anything untoward in my manner, he gave no sign of having done so. He inclined his head in a slow and evidently painful nod.

"Aye, Fra' Lorenzo. Pray, tell me—"

"What, Sir?"

"As his ghostly father, do you believe that his punishment was just?"

I sighed heavily with relief. I can only hope that the Lord Montecchi took this sigh for an indication of my contemplating the response I should give.

"Sir," I answered after a few moments, "As I am sure you can understand, I cannot break the secret of the confessional. But if by asking me that question, you are asking me if I believe that Romeo is capable of murder, then my answer to that would be: absolutely and indubitably not."

The old man sighed and forced a weak smile.

"Thank you, Fra' Lorenzo. Your words bring me great comfort."

"But, Sir," I continued, "if by your question you mean: do I believe that should Romeo have been pardoned, then that is a much more difficult question to answer."

"Why so?" he whispered. "He had done nothing more than what the law would have done, had it been allowed to take its course."

"I understand what you mean, Sir – but we must consider the position of the Prince. It is my opinion that however much he privately might have wished to pardon Romeo, he could nonetheless not run the risk of being seen to allow a convicted killer—"

"What?" the old man spluttered. "Romeo is not a killer. You have just said so yourself."

His breathing became shallow and fast.

"Sir, please," I hastily tried to calm him. "It is my belief that the Prince found himself in a most difficult position. Whatever his personal preference might have been, he clearly had to be seen to mete out some form of punishment for the death of Tebaldo – if only in order to prevent a full-scale revolt by the Capuleti. I have no doubt that when he exiled Romeo from Verona, he was passing as lenient a sentence as he felt able."

The Lord Montecchi was silent. Finally he whispered:

"Fra' Lorenzo, please answer me truthfully: do you believe that

143

Romeo will ever be permitted to come back to Verona?"

I thought of my discourse with the Prince, and of my solemn promise to keep it secret. I gave the only answer which was possible:

"I know not, Sir."

The Lord Montecchi sighed again.

"That is what I was afraid you would say, Fra' Lorenzo. And I know that my own time in this world is now very short. It is for that reason that I feel compelled to make what is, for me, a very difficult decision."

"What is that, Sir?"

"I wish to make Benvolio my sole heir."

I was stunned.

"Sir, may I ask why you wish to do this?"

"For two reasons. First, as you yourself have just confirmed to me, Romeo may never be able to return to Verona. Or even if he may, that may not be for many years to come. What use to him is an inheritance to which he cannot lay claim? And I cannot leave my estate without an heir."

"Why do you speak thus, Sir?"

"Because I am afeared of what might happen if it is left ownerless. This city has already seen far too much violence, bloodshed and misery. I have no wish that a battle to seize my property should be the cause of any more."

I gasped as I absorbed the import of what he had said.

"Do you really believe, Sir, that that might happen?"

The old man nodded slowly.

"Fra' Lorenzo, I have lived in Verona all my life. And the feud between my household and that of the Capuleti has been ongoing for far longer than that, though for my part I have tried to take no part in it."

"By your leave, Sir, may I ask you: do you know what was the initial cause of this feud? Or why it has continued for so long?"

He sighed again.

"Nay, Fra' Lorenzo. It has been thus for many generations ere now; none living today can even recall how it began. But this I do know: that it will take little short of a miracle to put an end to it."

"Sir, you say that you have taken no part in the feud. If all people were to think and act as you do, such a miracle might yet be possible."

144

He smiled weakly.

"Thank you, Fra' Lorenzo. But until that day arrives, I must take no risks with my household."

"Sir, why are you telling me this now?"

"Because you are a wise man, Fra' Lorenzo – my wife, Benvolio and Romeo have all spoken very highly of you – and your view is one on which I should set great store. I wished to be certain that I am making the correct decision."

"Sir, it is not for me to tell you how you should dispose of your property; that is your decision and yours alone. But this I will say: whatever decision you make, I will support it – and all those whom it affects – wholeheartedly and to the best of my ability."

"Thank you, Fra' Lorenzo. That too gives me much comfort."

He lay back and stared at the ceiling for a few moments, as if collecting his thoughts, before turning his eyes back towards me.

"There is something else which I must also say, on the matter of Romeo…"

I froze. I struggled to speak, but it was as though my throat were paralysed.

"Sir?" I squeaked.

"Fra' Lorenzo, what I am about to tell you is something which I have not revealed to a living soul. But I know that you, as a man of God, may be relied upon to keep this a secret."

"What is that, Sir?"

I still could not force my voice down to its normal pitch.

"You know, I believe, that ere she became my wife, the Lady Lucia had been married previously?"

"Aye, Sir; she told me of that herself. Her first husband had died, I believe?"

"Aye, he miscarried at sea. They had been married but a few weeks."

I hung my head so that I should not have to meet his gaze.

"I was not aware of that, Sir," I murmured reverentially. "But now that you have told me of it, I believe that I now understand why, when I first met the Lady Lucia, she seemed to be so angry and upset."

He nodded.

"She had loved him deeply. As indeed I had deeply loved my own late wife."

I remembered, just in time, that I knew only of the existence of the Lord Montecchi's previous marriage from what Chiara had told me at our first reunion. As far as he was aware, I remained in total ignorance that Chiara was not in fact his first wife. I looked up, duly feigning surprise at his words.

"Sir, forgive me – I did not know of this."

"It was many years ago. She died in childbirth." He sighed deeply, and his hollow eyes filled with tears. "She was truly the love of my life. Never a day goes by when I do not think of her."

I was dumbstruck. Although I already knew that the Lord Montecchi had been previously married, I had no notion of the depth of feeling which he still nurtured, so many years later, for his first wife. Had Chiara known of this? And if so, did it have some bearing on why she appeared to be so keen to return to me? I must own that it had already come as a great surprise to me that she had appeared to have so little conscience about leaving him.

The Lord Montecchi was speaking again.

"And I am glad that I shall soon be reunited with her."

"What of the Lady Lucia, Sir?" I ventured to ask.

"Ah, Lucia. Life has not been easy for her, and now she has taken the news of Romeo's banishment particularly badly. I fear that it may be much worse for her after I am gone. Please, Fra' Lorenzo, will you ensure that Benvolio takes good care of her?"

"Sir," I answered carefully, "I give you my solemn promise that I shall make it my personal business to ensure that the Lady Lucia is well cared for, for the rest of her life."

He smiled gratefully.

"Thank you, Fra' Lorenzo."

He hesitated, then his face grew serious as he spoke again.

"There is something else I must tell you. As I said just now, the Lady Lucia, like myself, had also been previously married. And she was already with child when I first met her. It was her first husband, not I, who is Romeo's father. Although we were married some months before Romeo was born, and I have all along acknowledged him as my son, he is not of my own flesh and blood…"

I looked at him steadily. If he indeed knew the true identity of Romeo's father, his face betrayed no sign as he continued:

"…and now I bitterly regret what I have brought upon him."

146

"You, Sir?" This time there was no need for me to feign surprise. "I am not sure that I understand."

The old man's eyes filled with tears.

"By acknowledging Romeo as a member of the Montecchi family, I brought him, by default, into the feud. And yet, he has not a drop of Montecchi blood in his body. He has been exiled for involvement in a matter with which he has no business. His mother is become utterly distraught at his banishment. And it is all my fault."

I was silent as I considered the implications of what he had said.

"Sir," I replied eventually, "would you be harbouring these thoughts if Romeo were indeed your son?"

"I should regret what has happened; of that there is no doubt. But I regret even more that I should now have brought this great misfortune upon a young man who is completely innocent of any complicity in a bitter and pointless feud."

(Oh merciful Heaven…)

"Sir," I answered after a moment, desperately searching for the right words, "please, do not blame yourself for what has happened. Consider how good a father you have been to Romeo ere now; consider how good a life you have been able to give him. And consider too how much worse he and his mother might have fared if you had not welcomed them into your life. You are a good man, My Lord. And you are utterly undeserving of the misery which you are now bringing upon yourself."

"Truly, Fra' Lorenzo?"

"Truly, sir."

He relaxed, then his features stiffened as he spoke again:

"But please, Fra' Lorenzo, give me your word that you will tell no-one of this."

"Of what, Sir?"

"Of the truth of Romeo's parentage. Least of all Romeo himself, if you should ever see him again."

I nodded slowly.

"Sir, that which people have no cause to know, need not be of any concern to them."

"Thank you." He sighed and laid back on the pillow.

147

"Sir, may I now ask you something?"

He nodded.

"Which of the two – Benvolio and Romeo – is the elder?"

(I already knew the answer to this question – Benvolio himself had told me – but I had particular reason for asking it now.)

"Benvolio, by two months."

"That being the case, Sir, if Benvolio were to ask why you have made him your heir, let that, as well as your concern for your patrimony, stand as the reason."

He smiled in relief.

"Thank you, Fra' Lorenzo. You are indeed very wise. And now, please will you ask Benvolio to come back?"

"Do you wish me to hear your confession first, My Lord?"

"Aye, very well…"

\*\*\*

Benvolio was sitting in the corridor, fidgeting nervously. He leapt up as I emerged from his uncle's chamber.

"Go in, son."

"Will you stay, Fra' Lorenzo?"

"I believe your uncle wishes to speak to you alone. But I will wait outside. If you need me, I am here."

"Thank you."

He pressed my hand and headed for the door. On the threshold he paused and turned back.

"Fra' Lorenzo?"

"Aye, son?"

"Please, will you go and speak to my aunt?"

"The Lady Lucia?"

Benvolio nodded.

"She is become utterly distraught. I fear for her."

Poor young fellow, I thought. What a burden of care he has to shoulder.

"I will try, but only if she is willing to see me. Go now to your uncle."

"Thank you."

The chamber door creaked open and clicked closed behind him.

I wandered down into the main hall and rang the bell. It was answered by a servant whom I did not recognise. This reminded me that I also needed to find Balthasar.

"Please, will you send word to the Lady Lucia that I should like to speak with her?"

The servant bowed and left. He came back a few minutes later, beckoned me to follow him and ushered me into a small reception room.

"Please be seated, Fra' Lorenzo. The Lady Lucia will be down directly."

As I waited, I realised, not for the first time, that a monk's habit was able to open doors which would otherwise remain firmly locked.

I was shocked at Chiara's appearance. Her face was pale and haggard, her lovely blue eyes were still red-rimmed from constant weeping, her hair was lank and tangled, and as the servant withdrew, the hand which she formally extended to me was thin and weak.

But even once we were alone, although I ached to hold her in my arms and comfort her, I knew that here, with the constant risk of interruption, we would need to keep up the appearance of formality.

"My Lady..." I began.

She looked up quickly, evidently shocked at my apparent aloofness. My eyes met hers and flashed a warning, followed by a conspiratorial wink. She read the message and smiled silently in response.

"Fra' Lorenzo," she replied stiffly, "Thank you for taking the time to come here. Benvolio tells me that you have been ill. I trust you are fully recovered now?"

"Not fully, I fear – I still suffer from a slight cough – but I am recovered enough to attend to most of my regular tasks."

She sighed.

"It is comforting to see you."

"Thank you, My Lady. Though I am sorry that I have had to come here under such difficult circumstances."

She sighed again.

"My husband..."

"Aye, My Lady. I fear he is very sick."

"He has been ailing for a long time. But since Romeo was

149

banished…"

Her voice cracked and she began weeping afresh. And I could tell that these tears were not fabricated.

I wanted to tell her that our son was safe. But I could not enlighten her – not for the moment.

"My Lady, I—"

But my words were halted by a frantic knocking at the door. The servant burst in without waiting for a response from within.

"By your leave, Madam, Fra' Lorenzo – please, come quickly. The Lord Montecchi…"

As one, Chiara and I raced up the stairs. A pitiful sight met us as we entered the bedchamber: the Lord Montecchi's waxen face was staring up from the pillow, whilst Benvolio, weeping silently, was clinging to the skeletal hand which lay limply on the coverlet. Chiara shrieked as she rushed to his bedside and flung her arms about his shoulders.

"Luigi…" she whispered.

The incongruous thought came into my mind that I had never, until that moment, known the Lord Montecchi's first name.

"Lucia," he murmured, "I am so sorry… Forgive me… I have…"

But he did not have the breath to finish the sentence.

*"In manus tuas, Domine, confidemus spiritum suum… Requiescat in pace…"*

Benvolio slumped across the bed and sank his head into his hands. Chiara's tears were falling on the old man's hollow cheeks. But whether these tears were being shed for him, or were still being shed for the banished Romeo, I could not tell.

***

I have no idea how long the three of us remained there, in stunned and solemn silence. I dimly recalled the scene of my own father's deathbed, and how Fra' Roberto had gently but efficiently taken charge. Only now did I realise just how grateful I had been for his support – and that this was what I should now do for Chiara and Benvolio.

150

Accordingly, I reached across and carefully closed the Lord Montecchi's staring but sightless eyes, then gently eased Chiara up from the bed so that I could draw the sheet over his face.

"My Lady, Benvolio, come with me."

I motioned to Benvolio to take Chiara's arm as she rose, unsteadily, to her feet. Remembering how weak I myself had felt after the trauma of seeing my own father die, and mindful of how Fra' Roberto had taken care to ensure that I should not neglect my own needs, I guided the two of them out of the room and down the stairs into the dining room, then rang the bell and ordered some broth. Although they both claimed they were not hungry, at my insistence they forced it down, and gradually the colour began to return to their pale faces.

My heart went out to both of them: a bereaved and bewildered young man, barely nineteen years of age and now the master of the house, and a distraught widow who was also grieving for a lost son. Although I had no wish to intrude on their private grief, nonetheless I did not feel happy about leaving either of them in this distressed state.

"Do you wish to be left alone, or would you prefer for me to stay for a little longer?" I asked at length.

Benvolio looked up.

"That would be most kind, Fra' Lorenzo, if you are able?"

I nodded.

"I can remain here for as long as you need."

"Could you stay here until tomorrow? There are some matters on which I would much appreciate your advice, but I do not feel able to think about anything tonight."

"By your leave, My Lady…?" I turned to address Chiara.

Her face was expressionless, but she inclined her head in a barely perceptible nod.

"In that case, I should be honoured."

Benvolio gave me a grateful smile as he stood up and rang the bell. It was answered by a young man whom I recognised as one I had seen elsewhere before now, but I could not recall who he was until I heard Benvolio address him by name.

"Balthasar, Fra' Lorenzo will be staying here tonight. Please will you arrange for a room to be prepared for him?"

"Aye, Sir."

Balthasar bowed and withdrew. I made a mental note to seek out the youth again ere I left; here was someone whose help I should soon be needing on another pressing matter.

We remained in sad but nonetheless companionable silence until Balthasar returned to say that my room was now ready, at which point we were all relieved to be able to retire. The young servant respectfully led me up the stairs and showed me into a small but tastefully furnished chamber.

"Balthasar, I need your assistance. But this is not an appropriate time or place to discuss it. Please, will you come and see me at the friary?"

"Gladly, Fra' Lorenzo. I will come as soon as is possible. And I hope you will sleep well tonight."

In the privacy of my room I took off my habit and slid between the crisp linen sheets, lightly scented with lavandula. Tired though I was, I remained mindful of my monastic obligations, so I opened my breviary and began to read the office of Completorium.

"May the Lord Almighty grant me a quiet night and a…"

I was asleep ere I had even reached the end of the first sentence.

***

The following morning I encountered Benvolio in the garden. He timidly raised the matter of the Lord Montecchi's funeral arrangements.

"My uncle was a good and God-fearing man, Fra' Lorenzo. And he held you in very high regard. Please, will you conduct his requiem?"

I was taken aback at Benvolio's words. During his lifetime the Lord Montecchi had always treated me with politeness and respect, but I had always taken this to be his normal manner in his dealings with men of the church. That he had evidently held me in high esteem came, therefore, as a complete surprise.

"Benvolio, I am truly humbled at what you have just said. I should feel it a great honour to conduct your uncle's requiem – but would it not also be appropriate to consult the Lady Lucia on this?"

Benvolio sighed.

"My aunt appears to be content to leave all these arrangements to me, Fra' Lorenzo. I cannot see how she would raise any objection. And you are also her confessor, are you not?"

"Aye, but all the same, by your leave, I should like to ask her permission before I agree. In her present state of mind, I would not wish to do anything which might possibly upset her further."

Benvolio looked up.

"I am worried about her, Fra' Lorenzo. When I asked you yesterday to speak to her, I was hoping that you might be able to help her."

I was stunned.

"I? Why do you believe that I might have been able to help?"

"Because of – of – something that my uncle once said."

"What was that?"

"You may not know this, Fra' Lorenzo, but before you came to Verona, my aunt had been totally opposed to the church. I never discovered the reason for it, but I know that for many years it had caused great distress to my uncle. She would accompany him to church just once a year, at Easter, simply because she knew it would please him, but for the remainder of the year she wanted no part of it. But after you arrived, she seemed to change completely, and would be happy to go to Shrift and to Mass each and every week. My uncle said that it was as though you had worked a miracle with her. It seemed that you were able to speak to her in a way that no-one else could achieve. So I – I – I had dared to hope that you might be able to work another miracle with her now."

"I cannot work miracles, Benvolio!" I hastened to assure him. "But what did you hope I might be able to achieve with her?"

Benvolio sighed.

"I had hoped that you could persuade her not to give way to her untold grief over Romeo's banishment. But that was yesterday. Now that my uncle is also taken from her, I greatly fear that she may never recover."

"Son, your aunt must be allowed to have time to grieve, both for your cousin and for your uncle. But if you wish, and if she will agree to speak to me, I will gladly tell her that you are worried about her."

"Thank you, Fra' Lorenzo." He managed a weak smile. "And now, please may I ask you something else?"

"Of course."

"My uncle told me yesterday, just before he died, that he wished to make me his heir. Did you know of this?"

I nodded.

"He told me so himself."

"Do you know why he suddenly wished to do this? I am not his son."

I cast my mind back to the discourse which I had had with the old man the previous day. Although I had promised him that I would tell no-one that he was not Romeo's father, as far as I could recall I had made no such promise about any other matter we had discussed. And Benvolio did deserve some form of explanation for what had now been thrust upon him. I could, at the very least, tell the young man of the reasoning which I and his uncle had agreed would be appropriate.

"Yes, Benvolio, I do know. And although you may not be his own son, you are his brother's son – and so you are nonetheless his own flesh and blood."

Benvolio remained unconvinced.

"But what of Romeo? Should he not be my uncle's rightful heir?"

"In an ideal world, yes, he should. But sadly, the world in which we live is far from ideal."

"Aye, indeed it is," Benvolio acknowledged despondently.

"And you must believe me when I tell you that this was a decision which your uncle did not take lightly."

"That I find slightly reassuring. But I still do not understand…"

I laid what I hoped was a comforting hand on his arm.

"After Romeo was banished from Verona, your uncle was uneasy about bequeathing his estate to someone who might not be able to return to claim it."

Benvolio sat very still.

"But Romeo is nonetheless my uncle's son…"

Again, I found that I was having to choose my words very carefully. I knew, and Chiara knew, and the Lord Montecchi knew, that Romeo was not his son – but Benvolio remained none the wiser.

"Be that as it may, Benvolio," I replied after a moment's hesitation, "under the present desperate circumstances, your uncle wished to make sure that his property should remain secure."

"But why me? A patrimony should pass to the first-born, should it not?"

(But circumstances alter cases – as they did in my own…)

154

"You told me yourself, and your uncle has also told me, that you are two months older than Romeo."

"Aye, so I am. What of it?"

"In that case, perhaps you should now regard yourself as the first-born of your generation. And it was for that reason that your uncle decreed that in Romeo's absence, you should now become his heir."

The relief on the youth's face was almost tangible.

"Thank you, Fra' Lorenzo. My uncle was indeed right in his opinion of you."

"It is kind of you to say so, Benvolio. Though I have been well-taught."

(I thought of Fra' Roberto, whose wisdom and compassion had been so vital to my own life.)

"But what if...?" Benvolio hesitated. His face had once again creased into a frown.

"If what, son?"

"What if Romeo does ever return to Verona? I have no wish to be the one who has usurped what is rightfully his."

(Benvolio. *I wish you well.* True to his name now, as ever before. The peacemaker and well-wisher.)

"Please, Benvolio, do not add to your present troubles by worrying about that."

"But what if he does return? What will happen then?"

What indeed, I wondered. I considered for a moment before answering.

"If that situation should ever arise – and there is every possibility that it will not – we will address the question at that time. I am sure that there is a solution which will benefit everyone, even if we cannot see it now. But for the moment, please do not concern yourself with it. Devote your energies to carrying on here, for the sake of your late uncle."

It was only after the words were spoken that I realised they applied just as much to my own situation as they did to Benvolio's. What would happen in the matter of the Da Porto estate, if Filippo should

155

ever reappear? I only hoped that I could apply those words to myself with as much conviction.

Benvolio sighed.

"Thank you. For my uncle's sake, I will try to do my best. Though I fear I am not worthy."

"Benvolio, you must never say that. Do you believe that your uncle would have placed such great faith in you, if he had truly thought that you were not worthy?"

Benvolio relaxed a little and his face brightened.

"I hope not."

I rose to my feet and laid a comforting hand on his shoulder.

"And now, before we speak again about your uncle's requiem, I must go and see if your aunt is willing to talk to me. I would not wish to progress this further until I am sure she has no objection."

Benvolio smiled.

"Thank you, Fra' Lorenzo. I will wait for you here."

I left Benvolio in the garden and approached the house with some trepidation. I had no idea if Chiara would agree to see me. And even if she did, for the first time in my life, I had no idea how she might react…

*** 

As on the previous afternoon, I was ushered into the same small reception room, whilst one of the servants was despatched with the message to the Lady Lucia that Fra' Lorenzo wished to speak to her. Each waiting minute seemed more like an hour. Finally the servant returned and informed me that the Lady Lucia was resting, but that she had agreed to come down and see me for a short while.

Chiara herself appeared a few minutes later. But she was accompanied by a slightly older lady whom I had not seen before, and who showed no inclination to leave us alone together.

"My Lady…" I began.

"Fra' Lorenzo," she answered, with an air of stiff formality. "I understand that you wished to speak to me?"

"Aye, My Lady. Thank you for agreeing to see me. I assure you that I will not detain you for long."

"Very well – what is it that you wished to say to me?"

"Merely this: that Benvolio has asked me if I will conduct the requiem for your late husband. I have told him that I should be honoured to do so, but only if this also meets with your approval."

She gazed at me steadily.

"I am surprised that you should feel the need to ask me."

"Why so, My Lady?"

"My late husband held you in the highest regard, Fra' Lorenzo. I know that he would wish his requiem to be conducted by none other than you. And for my part, I cannot imagine it otherwise."

"Thank you, My Lady. I am most grateful for your good opinion. I will return to Benvolio directly and inform him of your decision. Good day to you."

"Good day to you also, Fra' Lorenzo."

She gave a small inclination of the head before turning and making for the door, indicating that our short interview was now at an end. But as she reached the threshold she paused and turned back, almost knocking over the shuffling matron who was following a little too close behind her. The effect was almost comical.

"Fra' Lorenzo, I am sorry if I have appeared inhospitable."

The older woman, who was still trying to regain her balance, failed to notice the momentary flash in Chiara's eyes as her glance met my own. I responded with an appropriately sanctimonious smile.

"There is no need for you to apologise, My Lady. I fully understand that you have much to occupy your mind at this sad time. Please, think no more of it."

"Thank you, Fra' Lorenzo. You are most kind."

And with that, she was gone.

***

Benvolio was still waiting where I had left him in the garden. He leapt to his feet as I approached.

"Did you see her? What did she say?"

"Aye, Benvolio, I did see her, and she is happy for me to conduct the requiem. But I am afraid I did not succeed in talking to her on the other matter."

"What do you mean, Fra' Lorenzo? Why not?"

"She was accompanied throughout by another lady. I did not feel it

157

would be appropriate to discuss matters of such a delicate nature with a stranger present."

Benvolio considered for a moment.

"That would be Gertrude. She was my nurse, and has stayed with us since my birth." He sat down again, despondent. "What can we do, then?"

"There is perhaps one thing," I replied after a moment, speaking as though the idea had only just entered my head.

"What is that?"

"I will have the opportunity to speak to your aunt alone when she next comes to me for Shrift."

Benvolio brightened.

"I will ensure that she does not miss her next visit."

"Thank you – but please, Benvolio, do not pressurise her. She has much on her mind at the moment, but I am sure she will come to Shrift in her own good time. And now, perhaps we might discuss the arrangements for the requiem?"

***

I finally returned to the friary in time for luncheon, having arranged with Benvolio that the Lord Montecchi should be laid to rest the following afternoon.

I sought out Fra' Gianni and offered a brief explanation of my hasty absence the previous afternoon and night.

"We were on the point of raiding your cell again, Fra' Lorenzo!" he answered with a grin.

"I am sorry. But when it became apparent that I should have to stay the night at the house of the Montecchi, it was by then too late to send a message to the friary."

Fra' Gianni smiled.

"We were not unduly worried, as we already had some idea of where you had gone. One of the novices had seen you leaving in great haste yesterday with young Benvolio." His face then grew serious. "I am sorry that you went there on such a sad errand."

I sighed.

"There are occasions when doing the Lord's work is not for the faint-hearted."

Fra' Gianni nodded sympathetically.

And aside from the requiem, there still remained the delicate matter of how Romeo should be informed. I was well aware that this would not be an easy task. As far as Romeo was concerned, the man who had just died was his earthly father. And he would not even be able to return to Verona to say his final farewell.

Back in my cell, I sat down at my desk and hesitatingly began to write:

*Romeo,*
*It is with the greatest regret that I have to tell you that—*

I threw down my quill.

This was news which could not be delivered by letter.

\*\*\*

"Fra' Gianni?"

"Aye?"

"I find I must go out again, and I must take one of the horses. Please do not worry if I do not return until late."

"Where are you going?" He appeared slightly alarmed.

"I have a message to deliver."

"Are you sure you are well enough? Can you not send one of the novices to deliver it?"

I shook my head.

"This is a message which I must deliver in person."

He made as if to argue further, but then sighed and shook his head.

"God-speed you, then – thither and back again…"

\*\*\*

It was a hot, clammy afternoon; hardly ideal conditions for an urgent gallop along a straight, dusty, unshaded road which at times appeared to shimmer in the heat. It seemed an eternity before the towers of Mantua rose on the horizon through the yellow cloud of cornfields and sunflowers. I slowed the horse to a canter, and as I approached the city I began to look out for the barn which Romeo had described.

It did not take long to find it; I dismounted and searched, as my horse took a desperate drink from a nearby ditch. The barn bore signs of recent habitation, but now there appeared to be no sign of the fugitives. Realising that I could easily spend hours fruitlessly searching for them, I decided instead to head for the friary, in case, as I had suggested, they had sought shelter there.

I was greeted by a young novice who, once I had introduced myself, bade me wait in the cloister whilst he summoned the Guest-Master. As I waited, I tried to rehearse in my mind what I might say. This would be the second time within the space of little more than a week that someone had sought out Romeo in Mantua, with the purpose of delivering tragic news concerning someone whom he loved. But this time, unlike the last, the death was not a masquerade.

"You are Fra' Lorenzo?"

I looked up to behold a friar of around my own age.

"Aye."

He held out his hand and smiled.

"I am Fra' Stephano, and I am the Guest-Master here. How may I assist you?"

"I am looking for a young man by the name of Antonio Da Porto. I believe he is recently arrived here in Mantua, and I wonder if he might have come to the friary to seek lodgings?"

It seemed an age before he answered:

"Aye, Fra' Lorenzo. The young man came hither yesterday, with another young man who appears to be a mute."

"A mute?"

My momentary surprise at this was not feigned; it was a few moments ere I realised that Giulietta would doubtless have had the presence of mind to assume such a guise, lest her feminine voice should betray her.

"His page, it seems."

"May I speak to him?"

"I will see if he is here," Fra' Stephano answered diplomatically. "Please, Fra' Lorenzo, will you wait?"

He returned to the cloister a few minutes later and beckoned me to follow him.

The guest quarters were plainly though comfortably furnished. The room in which Romeo and Giulietta were housed contained two narrow beds, a table and two chairs. Romeo leapt up to greet me as I entered. Giulietta, still assuming the persona of a mute page-boy, gave me a respectful bow as Fra' Stephano withdrew.

"Fra' Lorenzo! It is good to see you! What brings you to Mantua?"

The smile died on Romeo's lips as he read my sorrowful countenance.

"Fra' Lorenzo? What is wrong?"

"Son, please sit down. I am sorry to be a bringer of bad tidings—"

"What is it? Please, tell me." His eyes widened with fear.

"I am afraid the Lord Montecchi is dead."

He gave no answer. It was as though he believed that by not acknowledging my words, he might somehow render them unsaid.

Giulietta leapt to his side and took his hand, interlacing his fingers with her own.

It fell to me to break the silence.

"Romeo, I am sorry."

"When – did – this – happen?" he asked flatly.

"Yesterday evening."

"And you have ridden hither today to tell us?" Giulietta's concerned whisper was barely audible.

I nodded.

"You needed to be told, son."

"When is his requiem to be held?"

"Tomorrow afternoon."

Romeo answered without looking up.

"I should like to be there."

I had been afraid of this. But thankfully Giulietta spared me the need to reply.

"My love," she whispered, "you cannot. You must not."

"He was my father," Romeo persisted. "How can I not be there when he is laid to rest?"

"Son, do you wish to follow him to the grave yourself?"

"What?" Romeo spun round to face me.

"If you return to Verona whilst you are still under sentence of exile…"

I could not bring myself to finish the sentence; the prospect was too dreadful to contemplate.

Giulietta, catching my unspoken drift, let out a strangled gasp. Her free hand leapt up and grasped Romeo's arm.

"I have done so once before." Romeo protested.

"Fortune favoured you on that occasion, son," I replied sternly. I glanced at Giulietta, whose concerned eyes met my own. "Far more so than you can ever imagine."

"But—"

"Romeo, I am sorry, but your presence at the requiem would not help your father…"

(Oh son, if you but knew the truth of those words…)

"… and do you truly believe that he would have wished you to place yourself in mortal danger on his account? Indeed," I added, as much to myself as to him, "what father on earth would wish that on one of his children?"

Romeo said nothing. Giulietta's fingers tightened around his. The two of them stood, totally still, totally silent; he staring into space, she staring at him.

Finally Romeo spoke again.

"I have failed him."

"No!" Giulietta and I spoke the word together.

"It is true! I have brought shame upon him, and upon his household, with what I have done—"

"Romeo, listen to me. I was with the Lord Montecchi in his final hours. And he told me that he knew in his heart that you were not a murderer. He even said so to the Prince himself."

"What?" Romeo gasped.

"Aye. After you had—" (I hastily corrected myself) "After what happened, it was he who personally pleaded with the Prince that you should not be put to death."

"Truly?"

"Truly. And is that not all the more reason why you should not dice unnecessarily with death now, simply in order to be able to walk behind his corpse? That is not what he would have wished of you."

Romeo said nothing, though his shoulders heaved and he raised his free hand to wipe away a tear. Giulietta guided him towards the table and gently released his other hand as he slumped onto one of the chairs, buried his face in his hands and sobbed.

Giulietta left him alone with his grief for a short while, then she bent over him and murmured something in his ear. I did not hear what she said, but it seemed to have had some effect, for Romeo raised his head and looked tearfully up at me.

"You are right, Fra' Lorenzo. I should not go. But please, my ghostly father, will you say a prayer with me now for my earthly one?"

Fra' Roberto's words sprang to my mind:

*"A ghostly father should complement an earthly one, not replace him…"*

"Of course."
We knelt down.

*"Ave Maria, gracia plena…*
*Ora pro nobis peccatoribus,*
*Nunc et in hora mortis nostrae…"*

*"Pater noster, qui es in cælis, sanctificetur nomen tuum…"*

*"Fidelium animae, per misericordiam Dei, requiescant in pace…"*

\*\*\*

"How fares my mother?" Romeo asked at length.

"Benvolio is taking care of her. But she is nonetheless very worried about you."

Romeo hesitated, then asked:

"May I write to her?"

"I am sure that a letter from you, however brief, would set her mind at rest. Wait here; I will find you some paper and a quill."

I left them briefly and sought out the Guest-Master's office.

"Fra' Stephano, may I ask you: has Antonio Da Porto told you anything about his circumstances?"

"Only that he and his page needed shelter here for a short while. They both seemed to be tired and hungry when they arrived, but I did not enquire further."

163

"Thank you. Whilst I am not at liberty to tell you exactly why he is come here, I feel you should know that when he arrived here, he was in great distress. And now I have just had to bring him the news of his father's death. Please, will you be mindful of this in your dealings with him?"

"Of course, Fra' Lorenzo. Thank you for telling me of this. I will make sure that the other brothers are also informed. Rest assured that we will take good care of him and his page for as long as they remain as our guests."

"Thank you, Fra' Stephano. I have known the young man for many years, and you may rest assured that he will not abuse your hospitality. And now, may I please borrow a quill and some paper and ink?"

***

"What shall I write?"

I considered for a few moments before answering.

"Tell her only what is absolutely necessary for her own peace of mind. Tell her that you are well and safe, but do not divulge where you are; if the letter were to fall into the wrong hands, it might well put you in renewed danger. For the same reason, do not tell her of your marriage."

"Why not?" He seemed shocked at the suggestion.

"Do you wish to also place Giulietta in danger? Remember that in Verona she is officially dead. Do you wish that her parents – or the Count Paris – should try to find her? Which doubtless they would, if they heard word that she was still living?"

Romeo opened his mouth to reply, then closed it again. Giulietta reached out and took his hand.

"I, for one, have no wish for that to happen, my love," she murmured. "If they found me, they would try to take me away from you."

Romeo shuddered and gripped her hand tightly, then turned to me.

"But we cannot stay here for ever..." he began.

"Be that as it may," I interrupted, "you can stay here for the present; the brothers here will take good care of you for as long as you have need. As to what happens in the future..."

164

I left the sentence unfinished. I had begun to form a plan in my own mind, but for now, that would need to remain a secret.

Romeo sat down at the table and began to write:

*My dearest Mother,*

*I am devastated to have been told the news about Father. He, and you, are constantly in my thoughts.*

*Please do not be worried about me; I am safe and well where I am hiding.*

*I will try to send word to you again soon.*

*Your loving son,*
*R.M.*

He folded the letter and I secured it inside my saddlebag.

"I will deliver it to her personally," I promised him. "And now, I must go back to Verona. But I will be back here anon. Until then, may the Lord preserve you and keep you."

"And you also, my ghostly father," Romeo answered. "God-speed."

I was halfway through the door when Romeo called me back.

"Fra' Lorenzo, a few days ago I wrote a letter to my father. I have it still. He will never read it now, but I have no wish for it to be found here. Please, will you take it and dispose of it as you think fit?"

"Of course."

He handed me another paper, which I added to the contents of my saddlebag.

\*\*\*

I took my leave of them, returned the quill and ink to Fra' Stephano, then set off back to Verona. By now the oppressive heat had dissipated, and my return journey was altogether more relaxed – not least because I was no longer encumbered by the worry of my errand.

By the time I reached the friary, the troublesome cough had returned, though I attributed the attendant pain in my chest to a bad cramp resulting from having spent too long in the saddle. I swallowed another dose of the hyssop mixture before taking my place in the chapel for Completorium. Fra' Gianni smiled with relief when he saw me, but we did not have the opportunity to speak again that night.

Back at my cell I secreted the two letters in the same hidden corner where I had previously concealed the vials of the sleeping potion. The letter to Chiara I would deliver when she next came to Shrift. As for the other, it would have to wait. Whatever it might contain, I was too tired to deal with it now.

*** 

The following morning I took the opportunity to spend an hour or two gathering and preparing the ingredients which I would need to make a fresh supply of my cough mixture. As I was mixing the herbs in the dispensary, there came a knock on the door. It opened to reveal young Balthasar.

"I believe you said you wished to see me, Fra' Lorenzo?"

Of course I had. And it had been my intention to ask him to deliver a letter to Romeo in Mantua. But that letter had never been written – and I had in the meantime spoken to Romeo face to face.

I thought quickly. The original reason for my wishing to see him now no longer existed, but here nonetheless was an opportunity to seek out some other information.

"Balthasar, I need to ask you something – something which I could not ask you in your master's house, for fear that we might be overheard."

Balthasar looked a little alarmed, but nonetheless asked:

"What is that, Fra' Lorenzo?"

"I believe you knew of your young master's secret marriage to the Lady Giulietta?"

Balthasar nodded sadly.

"Aye, Fra' Lorenzo. It pains me to think of it. My master, who had doted for so long on the Lady Rosaline who had spurned him, had been so happy to have at last found his true love. And then, for her to have been taken from him so soon after they had married…"

I nodded sympathetically.

"It is tragic indeed. I conducted her requiem."

"I know, Fra' Lorenzo. I saw her cortège pass through the streets. I rode straight away to Mantua to tell my master of what had happened."

I recalled, just in time, that I had heard of this only from Romeo,

166

during our long vigil in the Capuleti family vault. Accordingly, I feigned surprise at Balthasar's words.

"You rode to Mantua? How did you know to look for him there?"

"On the day when he was bani… the day of his wedding, he came late at night in secret to his father's house. He took care to ensure that none should see him, save I. He told me that he was on his way to spend the night with his lady, but said that he would be leaving for Mantua at first light. He took a little money with him there and then, but requested that I should meet him outside the western gate at dawn, with his horse and a bundle containing a few of his clothes."

(This also answered a question which I had been asking myself: how had Romeo had money to buy food?)

"So when you saw the Lady Giulietta's cortège…"

"Aye, I saddled my horse forthwith and rode to find him." He hesitated. "I – did not wish to be the one who would have to tell him, but there was no-one else…"

Balthasar's last words were lost in a strangled sob.

"And when you found him – what then?" I asked gently.

"He asked me if I had brought him any word from you, Fra' Lorenzo, and he seemed to be shocked and surprised that I had not…"

(Yet again, I cursed my stupidity for not seeking out this honest young man to be my original messenger…)

"… then he asked how fared his lady, and if his father was well."

"In that order?"

"Aye. It was then that I had to tell him about the Lady Giulietta. Such was his reaction to that news, that I never had the opportunity to tell him that his father was also not in good health."

"What was his reaction?"

(I already knew the answer to this in part, but I nonetheless needed to know how much Balthasar knew about Romeo's intentions.)

"At first I thought that he did not believe me. Then, when he

167

realised that I was indeed telling the truth, he shook his fist at the heavens and cried 'Stars, I defy you!' Then he gave me money and asked me to go and buy him paper and ink; he said that he had to make another errand, and that I should meet with him again in half an hour."

"And then?"

"I did as he had bidden me. When I met with him again he bade me farewell, and told me to return to Verona directly, lest anyone should have noticed my absence."

"Do you know why he wanted the paper and ink?"

"Aye, he said that he wished to write a letter to his father. I asked him if he wanted me to deliver it, but he said that the letter would take a long time in the writing and that he did not wish to delay my departure."

"And he gave no other indication of what else he might have been intending?"

"Nay, Fra' Lorenzo. Though I must tell you that I was afeared to leave him thus."

"Why so?"

"His face was pale and his eyes were wild; he had the air of a desperate man. And yet despite his own distress, he remained concerned for my well-being. I wanted to remain with him, but he repeated his insistence that I should not linger in Mantua."

"And since you left him that day in Mantua, have you heard any further word from him?"

Balthasar regretfully shook his head.

"Please, then, will you tell me if you do?"

"Aye, Fra' Lorenzo, gladly. Though I greatly fear that that may not happen."

I paused to reflect. As far as Balthasar was aware, Giulietta was dead and buried, and Romeo had disappeared. Much as I should dearly have loved to enlighten him on both matters, to have done so at this stage would, I reasoned, incur far too great a risk. Two people may keep a secret, if one of them does not know it.

"Balthasar," I asked after a moment, "do you know if the Lord Montecchi ever received the letter which your master was intending to write?"

(Again, this was a question to which I already knew the answer, but the question was nonetheless necessary if the deception were to be maintained; Balthasar might well have become suspicious if I had not enquired after it.)

"That I know not, Fra' Lorenzo, though it has never been mentioned in the house, so I believe that he did not. Why do you ask?"

"It matters not," I answered. "In any case, whatever that letter might have contained (even if it was ever written at all), it can do the Lord Montecchi no good now."

This reminded me that the hour was fast approaching for the Lord Montecchi's funeral.

"Balthasar, by your leave, I must prepare for your late master's requiem. But if you would care to wait for a few minutes, I will walk back to the house with you."

\*\*\*

This was the third requiem I had conducted in less than two weeks. First Mercutio, then Giulietta, and now the Lord Luigi Montecchi.

Looking back, it is difficult to determine which of the three of them was the most difficult or traumatic. I realise now that I am not comparing like with like: a young murder victim, a girl who was undertaking an elaborate deception upon which life and happiness depended, and an old man who had died of a painful and wasting disease, but whose end had been hastened by overwhelming grief and guilt.

Suffice it to say that the Lord Montecchi's requiem was a solemn affair. The mourners were led by Chiara and Benvolio, with the remainder of the household in attendance. Despite their evident distress, they somehow succeeded in maintaining a quiet dignity throughout. I mentally added Romeo's presence to the occasion; I knew that he was here in spirit if not in body.

The Montecchi family vault was at the opposite end of the churchyard to that of the Capuleti. As both monuments were already several hundred years old, I was forced to the conclusion that the two families' apparent willingness to share the same consecrated ground must indicate that the tombs had already been in existence long before the feud had begun. How sad, then, that only in death did they now seem to be able to tolerate each others' company.

As with their house, the Montecchi tomb was a much more tasteful and modest affair than that of their adversaries. It had clearly not been broached for some time, for the lock on the gates showed signs of rust, and once inside it was evident that the other occupants had all long since been reduced to dust and bones. Benvolio accompanied me into the vault, but at his insistence Chiara, left in the charge of the ever-faithful Gertrude, remained outside.

The deceased Lord was laid to rest in a vacant niche.

"*Fidelium animae, per misericordiam Dei, requiescant in pace…*"

As the mourners were dispersing, I noticed two figures – a young man and an older woman – in the distance at the opposite end of the churchyard. They were bending down by the tomb of the Capuleti; I became aware that they appeared to be placing fresh flowers. It was only as they straightened up that I discerned who they were: the Count Paris and the Lady Capuleti. As they caught sight of the funeral party they hesitated, then after a moment the Count slowly made his way across the churchyard towards us. As he approached he doffed his hat.

"Fra' Lorenzo," he greeted me quietly. "I am so sorry to see that you have had to conduct another requiem so soon after the last one."

"Thank you, sir," I responded, equally quietly. "It is indeed a sad time."

"May I ask who it is who has recently passed on?"

"The Lord Montecchi. It seems that he had been very ill for some time."

The Count seemed momentarily to be at a loss for words – after all, the Montecchi were the sworn enemies of the family into which he had been intending to marry. But then he squared his shoulders and, turning towards Chiara and Benvolio, bowed respectfully.

"Madam, Sir, please accept my sincere condolences on your sad loss."

Benvolio thanked him graciously, then the Count turned and walked back to where his companion was waiting at the other end of the churchyard. What he said to her I could not hear, but I could see that she stiffened with shock, and her hand flew to her mouth as she glanced across at us…

\*\*\*

When I returned to the friary I found a letter waiting for me. It bore the seal of the friary in Venice.

*Salve, Lorenzo.*
*Thank you for your letter. I am sorry to hear that you have been unwell; I trust that you are now fully recovered.*
*I should be delighted to see you again to discuss the matter further. Please can you come to Venice on Monday next? As before, I will ensure that a room is prepared for you here.*
*God speed you on your journey.*

*In D.no,*
*Fra' Roberto*

That gave me two full days to attend to matters here in Verona in the meantime. Most pressing, of course, was the need to deliver Romeo's letter to Chiara. But that would have to be done in person, and so could only be done when she came to the friary. And that, in turn, could only be as and when she felt ready.

In the event, I need not have worried. The following day was a Saturday, and Chiara appeared at my cell in the afternoon – ostensibly for Shrift, in advance of attending Mass on Sunday.

I was unsure how she would greet me; after all, this would be the first time I had seen her alone since the Lord Montecchi's death. And I had been in no doubt that she had held him in great affection and that her grief had been genuine. Whatever she might have thought – or might still be thinking – about our plans for a future together, I knew that I must be careful not to put her under any undue pressure.

Accordingly, I opened our discourse with the simple concerned enquiry which any ghostly father might make to one of his flock:

"How are you?"

"I do not know," she answered after a moment, with a faraway look in her blue eyes. "At times I still find it hard to believe that he is gone."

"Benvolio has told me that he is very worried about you."

She smiled ruefully.

"Benvolio is a good and virtuous youth. I am glad that Luigi has made him his heir, now that... now that..."

Her composure crumpled as she tried unsuccessfully to finish the sentence.

*(Where there is despair, let me sow hope...)*

"Would it help if you knew that Romeo was safe?"

She gasped.

"You have had word of him?"

By way of answer I handed her Romeo's short letter. She read it and her eyes widened.

"How did you come by this?"

I cautiously took her hand. I had been afraid that she might withdraw it, but instead her fingers, as if of their own accord, interlaced with my own.

"I have seen him."

"When? Where? Where is he?"

"I saw him the day after the Lord Montecchi died. I realised that he needed to be told of what had happened, and I could think of no other way of informing him than by seeking him out and telling him face to face. As to where he is, that I am afraid I cannot tell you – at least not for the moment."

"Why not? I am his mother—"

"And I am his father."

She fell silent.

I continued,

"One of his parents knows of his whereabouts. Please, be content with that for the present."

"Can you take me to see him?"

"No. That would be much too dangerous – for you as well as for him."

"Is he – far from here?"

"Not so far away that I could not find him, but far enough away for him to be safe."

172

She was silent for a moment, then asked brokenly,
"Do you think that I will ever see him again?"
I squeezed her hand gently.
"*Deo Volente*, my love…"
Her hand returned the pressure as she looked up at me.
"*Deo Volente*," she murmured. "God willing."
We sat in companionable silence for a few moments, then Chiara suddenly withdrew her hand and fumbled in her reticule.
"I almost forgot – this morning I received this. I am not sure what to make of it. Please, read it."
She handed over a small piece of paper. The writing was in an unfamiliar hand.

*Lady Montecchi,*
*I was most distressed to learn of the recent death of your husband.*
*Having myself recently suffered the loss of a dear daughter, I have some notion of what you must be enduring.*
*Please accept my deepest sympathy.*

*Sincerely,*
*Giovanna Capuleti.*

I was dumbstruck.
"You received this this morning, you said?"
She nodded.

(Of course. The Lady Capuleti had been with Count Paris in the churchyard…)

"Do you know who delivered it?"
She shook her head.
"It never occurred to me to wonder."
"Have you answered it?"
"Not yet. I wanted to ask your advice first."
I considered this new development and wondered what significance it might have. Some say that Death is the ultimate leveller. Could it be that after so many deaths on both sides, this small gesture of compassion might, at long last, be signalling a possible end to this pointless long-running conflict?

"I would suggest," I said after a moment, "that you send a simple reply to her, merely thanking her for her kind expression of sympathy. Say no more than that for the moment. If she responds, tell me; we can decide then what to do next."

"Have you paper and ink? I will write a reply now."

She settled herself at my desk.

*Lady Capuleti,*
*Thank you for your letter. Your kind expression of sympathy is greatly appreciated at this sad time.*

She looked up.

"She wrote of the loss of her daughter – would it be appropriate for me to mention that?"

I considered, then nodded.

"If you wish, my love."

Chiara continued to write:

*May I also offer you my own condolences on the loss of your daughter.*
*Sincerely,*
*Lucia Montecchi*

"What should I do with it?"

"Leave it with me if you wish; I can arrange for one of our novices to deliver it."

"Thank you."

She handed me the paper, then suddenly looked up at me. Her eyes shone as of old.

"Forgive me, my love, I have not asked you – how are you? Are you recovered now from your illness? I have been so worried."

"I am much better, thank you. I still have a slight cough, and I am a little tired, but otherwise…"

She smiled.

"Thank goodness. I could not bear to lose you too."

I took her hand again.

"It is good to hear you say that. But I must tell you: I shall have to go away for a few days."

"Where? And why?"

"Back to Venice. I need to see Fra' Roberto."

"When do you leave? And will you be gone for long?"

"On Monday. And only for as long as is necessary. I will be back as soon as possible."

She hesitated before asking,

"Does it concern – your future…?"

"Aye, in part. Though I can say no more for the present. I will tell you more when I am able."

"May I ask you, though – does that future hold a place for me?"

I squeezed her hand again.

"If you wish it, my love, then there will always be a place for you."

She smiled contentedly, then let out a long sigh.

"I must go. Benvolio will be wondering why I am gone for so long."

"Wait – I still have not heard your confession. That is the reason why you came hither today, is it not?"

She knelt down and bowed her head demurely.

"I have only one thing to confess to you," she murmured coyly. "And I believe you already know what that is…"

\*\*\*

As I left the chapel after Mass the following morning, I found Benvolio waiting for me outside. He looked brighter and happier than I had seen him for a long time.

"Fra' Lorenzo, may I speak to you in private please?"

"Of course."

I motioned him to follow me back to my cell.

No sooner had the door clicked closed behind us than he grasped my hand and pressed it firmly.

"Fra' Lorenzo, I must thank you."

"For what, Benvolio?"

"You have worked another miracle with my aunt. She came to see you for Shrift yesterday, I believe?"

I nodded.

"When she returned, it seemed as though she was a changed woman."

"Indeed, son? In what respect?"

175

"She seemed so much more lively. She even smiled, for the first time since my uncle died. Indeed, for the first time since my cousin was banished. Whatever did you say to her?"

"Very little," I answered carefully, "save that rather than grieving for the past, she should perhaps begin to look to the future – whatever future the Lord might have in store for her. Neither your uncle nor your cousin would wish that she should pine away for them. But any change in her demeanour has come from her, not me. And that is how it should be. I am merely a guide. People may come to me for direction, but the choice is theirs as to whether or not they elect to take it. Ultimately they must find their own way."

"Do you believe, then, that this is what the Lord had in store for me?"

"Aye, son. There is a purpose to every event, even though we mere mortals may not see or understand it at the time."

"What of Romeo, then?"

Despite his own good fortune, Benvolio was still evidently concerned about his cousin – exiled, and now disinherited.

"I am sure that the Lord has his own plans for Romeo, wherever he is. And if those plans also involve you, then I have no doubt that this will become clear in the fullness of time. In the meanwhile, remember him in your prayers. But for now, concentrate on your own affairs – you have much to concern you."

Benvolio smiled and pressed my hand again.

"Thank you, Fra' Lorenzo. Thank you for everything."

As he made for the door I called him back.

"Son, tomorrow I shall have to go away for a few days. I will be back as soon as possible, but if you need a priest in the meantime, Fra' Gianni will be happy to assist you."

Benvolio bowed.

"God-speed, Fra' Lorenzo."

I spent the remainder of the day attending to routine matters in advance of my forthcoming absence: weeding and pruning the herb garden, tending to the apiaries, and ensuring that the dispensary was well-stocked. I made my way to the chapel a little in advance of the hour of Completorium, in order to be able to spend a few minutes alone at prayer.

I recalled the occasion when, back at the friary in Venice a mere

176

two years ago, I had been standing on the threshold of a new life here in Verona. Now, it seemed that the wheel had come full circle; I was being offered the gift of another new life back in Venice. Was this indeed the life which the Lord had in mind for me?

And, as Benvolio had said, what of Romeo?

Could it be that my own new station in life might also hold the key to my son's future?

"O Lord, you who have the steerage of my course, direct my sail…"

I was roused from my meditation by the familiar sound of the opening of Completorium:

"*Noctem quiétam, et finem perféctum concédat nobis Dóminus omnípotens…*"

May the Lord Almighty grant us a quiet night and a perfect end… Amen to that.

***

The following morning I arose at first light. Fra' Gianni, considerate as ever, had arranged for the refectory to serve me with an early breakfast, so that I should be able to set off for Venice as soon as I was ready. He had also left instructions that I should be provided with a basket of food for the journey. I carefully packed a few lavandula plants and three jars of our home-produced honey, as a modest gift for Fra' Roberto.

As I was climbing into the saddle, Fra' Gianni appeared at my side.

"God-speed, my friend. And please commend me to Fra' Roberto."

"Gladly. And thank you for everything. I will return as soon as possible."

He smiled sympathetically.

"Do not rush yourself. Take as much time as you have need."

Although I had given him no indication of the nature of my errand, he seemed to know, instinctively, that it was not a trivial matter.

The journey was far more enjoyable than on the previous occasion, only a few weeks since, when I had ridden along this same road. Then,

I had been pressed to complete the ride in the shortest possible time, and at the end of it I was awaited by a dying man whom I had not seen for almost twenty years. Now, I could take my time and relish the fine weather and the fair countryside, and at the end of my journey I was awaited by a kind and understanding friend.

I finally arrived at the friary late in the afternoon. The novices had again been forewarned of my arrival, for I was welcomed as an honoured guest; my horse was taken to the stable to be fed and watered, and I was ushered into the refectory and a most welcome and refreshing pitcher of ale was put before me. It was there that Fra' Roberto came to find me.

"Lorenzo! It is good to see you again. I trust that you are now fully recovered?"

"All save the cough, which seems to be most persistent."

Did I imagine it, or did a faint look of alarm cross his face as I spoke? Whether it had been there or not, it was gone in an instant.

"I expect you have been working too hard!" he declared cheerfully. "Whilst you are here with us, you must take the opportunity to rest. So many of our brotherhood work themselves into the ground by attending constantly to the needs of others, whilst all the while neglecting their own. But even men of God do not have limitless physical resources!"

Once again, I marvelled at his unfailing sense of care, compassion and worldly wisdom. He was, and had always been, the antithesis of all that I had been led to believe about men who take holy orders. If, during my time as a friar, I had succeeded in being one-tenth as good a ghostly father to my flock as he had been to me, then I would have been more than satisfied that I had done my job well.

"Thank you," I whispered.

"How fare the friars in Verona?"

"All fare well, thank you. Those who know you have asked to be commended to you."

"Thank you. Please return my greetings to them when you see them again."

I nodded.

"Supper will be served in half an hour." Fra' Roberto went on. "Would you like to have our talk after that, or would you prefer to wait until tomorrow?"

"As you wish, Fra' Roberto – whichever is the more convenient for you."

He smiled warmly.

"This evening, then?"

***

Back in my room I carefully unpacked the lavandula plants and the jars of honey from my bag, thankful that they had not suffered during the ride from Verona. As we strolled out into the herb garden and settled ourselves comfortably on one of the benches, I handed the plants to Fra' Roberto.

"A gift from the friary garden in Verona."

He took one of the plants and breathed in its sharp sweet scent.

"What plant is this, Lorenzo?"

"It is called lavandula. I had not encountered it in its living form until I arrived in Verona, but it is perhaps the singular most useful herb I have ever known."

I was reassured to see that the garden, which had been my own province until only two years earlier, was still being well cared for.

"Who takes care of the herb garden now?" I asked.

"It is the responsibility of Fra' Pietro."

The name struck a chord.

"He who had previously been Novice Pietro?"

"Aye, the same who was once your apprentice. He has proved to be a good and worthy successor to you."

Novice Pietro – he whose simple error all those years ago had been the accidental source of the potion which would bring about the likeness of death. And who, to this day, had no inkling of what he had unwittingly created.

I smiled.

"That is good to know. I should like to see him again whilst I am here."

"I have no doubt that you will do so tomorrow. If you come out into the garden during the morning you will find him here. And that would be a good opportunity for you to give him the lavandula bushes."

I nodded.

"One of its many virtues is that it is greatly favoured by honey bees!" I indicated the jars of honey on the bench beside us. "This is also for you; we have our own apiaries."

Fra' Roberto grinned.

"That is very kind of you, Lorenzo. Maybe you should suggest to Fra' Pietro that we should also keep bees here."

"Would he be receptive to such a suggestion, do you think?"

"If it came from you, whom he has always held in very high regard, then I am sure that he would."

"I feel very humbled."

"Do not be; you have done much good, and that is something of which you can rightly feel very proud."

"But pride is a sin, is it not?"

"Only when it is used for self-glorification. But if you have achieved something which benefits other people, if you are not proud of it then you are undermining its value. Modesty is one thing, but self-effacement is something else entirely."

I blinked.

"Truly?"

He answered my question with another.

"Do you recall the Parable of the Talents?"

I nodded.

"What of it?"

"The two servants who made good and wise use of the talents with which they had been entrusted gained more, and were well-rewarded by their master. But the servant who hid his talent, and made no use of it whatsoever, lost everything."

"You mean...?"

"Aye; we too are entrusted with talents, in the form of particular abilities, or perhaps gifts of the spirit – and it is our duty to make the best and wisest use of them. God did not give us these gifts with the intention that they should be hidden away and wasted. And your particular talents have been of great value to many people. If you had concealed them and not made use of them, many of those people might not be living today. You should be very content with that."

I was silent as I thought of the all hundreds of people I had treated during my time as an infirmarian. At the time I had merely regarded this as part of my regular daily duties. It had never occurred to me to think that they might not otherwise have recovered.

I hung my head.

"Thank you," I murmured.

"And," Fra' Roberto continued gently, "God also has plans for us all. For some, that may mean the life of a religious order. But holy orders is a calling, and those who enter it must do so happily and of their own free will." He sighed. "During my time as a friar, and latterly as a Superior (oh, how I detest that title – it suggests that I am in some way better than my fellow friars!), I have seen many fine young men, all talented and with promising futures, and all sadly ruined by having been forced into the cloister against their wishes."

I looked up.

"Men like myself, you mean?"

He smiled.

"Nay, not you, Lorenzo – for you have made a good life for yourself as a friar, even though it was not the life that you might have wished. And that too is something of which you should be proud, for it shows great strength. But when thinking of others who came to us as you did, I have come to believe, very strongly, that the cloister should not be regarded merely as a convenient means of disposing of surplus progeny. And that applies to daughters just as much as to sons. To do so is a disservice to the individuals themselves, and it is also a great insult to God. These are people whose true destiny should lie in the world outside."

I could now see which way this discourse was leading. I silently thanked him for raising the subject so delicately.

"Do you believe," I asked timorously, "that that is where my future lies?"

"Before I answer that, Lorenzo, may I ask you: is that what you believe yourself? After all, I cannot make the decision for you."

I opened my mouth to speak, but no words came.

Fra' Roberto, after a moment, gently added:

"As I said to you at our last meeting, whatever decision you make will have my blessing."

"But what if I make the wrong decision? Or make my decision for the wrong reason?"

"What do you think might constitute the 'wrong' reason, Lorenzo?"

181

I hesitated.

"Selfishness, I suppose," I answered finally, "and perhaps the notion that I might be putting my own wishes before the will of God."

"Has the possibility not occurred to you that it might be the will of God that you should return to Venice as your father's heir?"

I caught my breath.

"No," I replied after a moment. "No, it has not."

"May I ask why not?"

"I suppose it is because… because…"

The words stuck in my throat.

"Because what, Lorenzo?"

I drew a deep breath and blurted out:

"Because it seems to be too good to be true."

Fra' Roberto looked at me steadily.

"Just because something is good," he said slowly, "that does not necessarily mean that it is not the will of God."

I blinked.

"What?"

"Indeed. Quite the opposite, in fact. If God is good, why should He not want what is good for His followers?"

"You mean…?"

"Aye. Think of what has happened ere now: your father had but two sons, the elder of whom will produce no issue and who has now disappeared. If it was not God's will that you should become your father's heir, then would not your elder brother have married and had children?"

I stared at him, open-mouthed. This notion had never crossed my mind.

Fra' Roberto continued:

"Your father realised, long before he died, that you would make a far better successor than your brother, and that he had made a grave error in sending you into the friary. That is why he recalled you hither."

"Did he tell you of this himself?" I found my voice at last.

Fra' Roberto nodded.

"He also told me that he bitterly regretted his actions in forcing you into the Order, and he asked me to ensure that you should have no feelings of guilt at leaving it."

182

"So…" I hesitated again, "you truly believe that it is God's will that I should follow my father's wishes?"

"I do, Lorenzo. I believe that it is the will not just of your earthly father, but also of your Heavenly Father. But consider this: your time as a friar has made you the man you are today. You have lived through many years of poverty, chastity and obedience, and you have learned wisdom and compassion which will stand you in good stead in your new position. I truly believe that you will prove to be as good a Count as you have hitherto been a friar – and a far better Count than one who had previously known no other walk of life."

"Fra' Roberto, you do me a great honour by speaking thus. I hope that I am worthy of your good opinion…"

"Keep on as you have done thus far, and you will be more than worthy."

"Thank you," I murmured.

Fra' Roberto stood up.

"Come, Lorenzo, it is growing late; we should go in to Completorium. Come and see me again after breakfast tomorrow."

***

The following morning I was eased into consciousness at first light by the crowing of a cockerel. Wandering out into the garden and following the sound, I crossed the herb garden to a hedge on the far side. Behind this was a small enclosure, strewn with piles of straw, which was home to half a dozen farmyard fowl: five broody hens and a single rooster. Stooping over them, with his back to me, was a figure in a Franciscan habit. Lying on the ground at his feet was a basket of grain, of which he was scattering copious handfuls to the birds.

"Good morrow, Brother!"

He straightened up and turned to face me, and his face creased into a broad smile.

"Fra' Lorenzo, is it not?"

"Aye. And you must be Fra' Pietro?"

"The same. Your apprentice of many years ago. It is good to see you again."

"You too, my friend. I am glad to see the herb garden is still thriving!"

183

"I was merely continuing the good work which you started!"

"And adding to it as well, I see!" I gestured towards the chickens.

Fra' Pietro grinned.

"We have had these birds for only a few months. Do you have hens at your friary?"

"Nay, though we do keep bees."

Fra' Pietro nodded enthusiastically.

"That is something which I should like to do here. Perhaps next year, once the birds are properly settled. One task at a time is enough, I think!"

(One task at a time… Wise words indeed, I thought.)

"I have brought some lavandula for you from our friary garden. The plants are stored in my room; I will bring them outside after breakfast and we can find a place in the garden for them. By next year the bushes should be well established; if you introduce your bees next summer, they will thrive on the flowers."

"Thank you."

He crouched down again and plunged his hand into the depths of the straw. It emerged clutching two smooth brown eggs.

"How many of those do you find each day?"

"At the moment, not many; perhaps four or five at most. But one of the hens is sitting on a nest, so we are hopeful that in the fullness of time our flock will increase. Come, I must take these to the refectory, then we should go in to Mass."

He carefully placed the eggs in the basket and stood up.

"Until later, Fra' Lorenzo?"

"Until later, my friend. I have business with Fra' Roberto in the meantime, but I will come and find you afterwards."

\*\*\*

"What happens now? How long does it take?"

Fra' Roberto grinned.

"It is very straightforward, and takes about five minutes!"

"Five minutes? That is not what I meant! I meant how many weeks until everything is completed?"

"All stages save one are already completed, Lorenzo."

"What?"

"After your last visit I made some enquiries, and I discovered that the whole procedure is surprisingly simple. All the preliminary stages have already been taken care of. All that remains is a simple ceremony, in the presence of two witnesses, during which I can formally release you from your vows to the Order."

I gasped.

"How did you know in advance what I would decide?"

"I did not; at least, not for certain – but nothing of what I have done thus far would commit you to leaving the Order if you had decided to remain as a friar. It is only the final stage which would release you."

"So when do I...?"

"Whenever you are ready. Though I imagine you will need a little time to finalise your affairs in Verona."

I nodded.

"At the very least I must inform my fellow friars that I am leaving the Order."

"That is your choice, Lorenzo; you need only tell them if you wish that they should know."

This statement came as a complete surprise.

"Why should I not wish that they should know?" I asked in amazement. "And what could I say to them otherwise?"

"Merely that you have arranged with me that you will be returning to Venice. It is, after all, no more than the truth."

"But not the whole truth..."

"It is truthful enough, for any who might find the whole truth difficult to accept."

I caught my breath.

"Do you believe that there are some who might?"

Fra' Roberto nodded gravely.

"I am sorry to have to say that amongst those who came to us under the same circumstances as your own, there may well be some who find themselves falling prey to another of the seven deadly sins – one which has the power to corrode and destroy."

"Jealousy?"

Fra' Roberto nodded again.

"Jealousy of someone who has now been offered something which has been cruelly denied to them."

I hung my head humbly.

"I had not thought of that. And I would have no wish to become the cause of it."

Fra' Roberto smiled sympathetically.

"You have always looked for the good in your fellow friars, Lorenzo. There is no reason why you should have thought of it. But even men of God are not immune from human emotions – bad ones as well as good. Sometimes there are things which are best kept hidden: what people do not know can have no power to hurt or harm them."

Wise words indeed… Whatever my own experiences might have taught me, I now realised that in comparison to this wise and kind ghostly father, I still had much to learn.

"What of the two witnesses?" I asked after a moment.

"You need have no fears about that. They will be carefully chosen, and will be sworn to the same level of secrecy as that of the confessional. As indeed will I."

I was silent as I considered what he had just said.

"After this ceremony of which you speak, will I no longer wear the monastic habit?"

"Nay, Lorenzo, you will not. Your habit is a part of your life as a friar, and will play no part in your life outside the cloister. You will hand it back as part of the ceremony."

"So I will need to finalise my affairs at the friary in Verona beforehand?"

"Aye. And you will also need to procure some other garments for yourself!" Fra' Roberto grinned mischievously. "It would not be seemly for you to leave here wearing only the attire of Adam!"

I returned his grin.

"Indeed not! I will give some thought to that matter later."

"How much longer do you think you might need in Verona?"

I tried to call to mind all the matters which would need my attention. I found that my mind had become a complete blank.

"Please may I have a little time to think about that?" I replied eventually. "I should be able to give you an answer later today."

Fra' Roberto nodded.

"Of course. Come and see me again after supper. And in the meantime, it might be wise if you make another visit to your family home. I am sure you will also have much to attend to there."

"Thank you. I will go thither this afternoon."

***

I returned to my cell to collect the lavandula plants, then wandered back into the herb garden. Fra' Pietro was busy with a spade, preparing a place in the flower-bed in readiness for their planting.

"I see you have allowed plenty of room for the bushes to spread!" I remarked, as I handed them over to him.

"Aye," he grinned. He carefully positioned the plants in the holes which he had already dug in the ground, two spans' width apart, and watered them thoroughly.

"What is to go there?" I asked, indicating a large area to one side which he had purposely left unplanted.

"I am surprised that you should need to ask!" He grinned again. "The beehives, of course!"

I made a mental note to ensure that he would receive these as soon as was appropriate. If it was not possible to transport some from Verona, then they would be a personal gift from the Conte Da Porto.

Back in my cell I forced myself to think of all that I should need to do in Verona before leaving the Order. I soon realised that matters relating to the friary were all things which could be easily and quickly delegated. Even the garden and the dispensary could now safely be left in the hands of my competent apprentices.

More complicated, though, were the matters of Chiara, and of Romeo and Giulietta. The latter were still hiding at the friary in Mantua, but all three of us were fully aware that this could not continue indefinitely. Would it be possible, I wondered, to transport them hither to Venice, where they were known to no-one else, to begin a new life here?

And as for Chiara – I now knew that the prospect of spending the rest of my life without her was impossible to contemplate. But even though she was now a widow, I still needed to devise a means of spiriting her away from Verona which would not arouse suspicion or scandal…

187

After luncheon I left the friary and made my way to my old family home. I found that I still thought of it as my father's house. I had not yet fully grasped the notion that it was now my own, even when the servants bowed to me and addressed me as "Sir" or "My Lord."

I called them all together (chief retainer, valet, housekeeper, cook and a few kitchen staff) and announced to them that following my father's death I was now their employer, and that I hoped that they would wish to remain to serve me as they had previously done so with my father, though stressing that if any of them wished to leave they would be free to do so. The chief retainer made a low bow and thanked me profusely on the others' behalf.

"We will all be pleased and honoured to remain in your employment, My Lord."

"Thank you. Please, now return to your tasks; I will need to speak to some of you separately on individual matters."

First of all, mindful of Fra' Roberto's advice about clothing, I sought out the valet – a young and quietly-spoken fellow named Giuseppe, who it transpired had been with my father for the past five years.

"How may I assist you, My Lord?"

I indicated my Franciscan habit.

"I will shortly be needing some different clothes!"

If Giuseppe had noticed any incongruity in my monastic attire, he showed no reaction. He merely inclined his head reverentially.

"If you would care to follow me, My Lord?"

He led me upstairs to the room which had previously been my father's chamber – the same room in which the old man had recently taken his leave of this world. Giuseppe crossed the room and opened a door in the far corner, which led into a generously-sized dressing-room, and opened one of the closets.

"My Lord, these clothes belonged to your late father. As you will see, he favoured simple good quality over showiness and extravagance. I believe that you and he are of similar height and build. If any of these garments would suit your purpose, then they are at your disposal."

As I peered into the closet, having been accustomed for so long to only a single monastic habit, I was overwhelmed at the sheer quantity of garments inside. I extended my hand into the interior and cautiously drew out a linen shirt, a silk doublet and a pair of woollen breeches. As Giuseppe had indicated, although the cut and the cloth were of fine quality, the overall appearance was one of subdued and understated elegance.

Giuseppe nodded and smiled approvingly.

"My Lord, would you care to try these?"

Dumbstruck, I could manage only a silent nod as I clumsily struggled to remove my monastic attire. Giuseppe, seemingly unfazed, gently helped me to ease it over my head, and appeared utterly unconcerned as I stood, as Fra' Roberto had so delicately described it, in the attire of Adam. But I had no time to be embarrassed, for within seconds he had helped me on with the shirt and the breeches, and was holding out the doublet. As I silently blessed his quiet professionalism, I realised with a shock that I had worn a friar's habit for more than half of my life; for so long, in fact, that I had all but forgotten how it felt to wear anything different.

Giuseppe gave another approving nod and moved across the room towards a fine curtain which hung on the wall in the corner. He drew it aside to reveal a full-length mirror.

As monastics we had long since learned to dress without the use of mirrors. Even essential activities such as shaving, which could not easily be accomplished without them, were done by a weekly session where all the brothers gathered together and shaved one another. Truth to say, I had almost forgotten that mirrors existed.

Fra' Lorenzo of the Order of Saint Francis stepped cautiously forward. Staring back at him from the depths of the looking-glass was the Count Sebastiano Lorenzo Matteo Giovanni Battista Da Porto.

I gasped.

"My Lord?" Giuseppe had appeared at my side bearing a velvet cloak and a pair of fine leather boots.

"Thank you." I found my voice at last.

"My Lord, your late father was a great and a good man, and it was a pleasure and an honour to serve him. I am most grateful that you have given me the opportunity to serve you as his heir."

"Thank you, Giuseppe. I hope that I will prove to be a worthy successor to him, once I return hither for good."

"By your leave, My Lord, when will that be?"

"In a few weeks' time, I hope; possibly sooner. In the meantime, I will need some clothes for when I am released from the friary. Please, may I borrow these?"

Giuseppe looked shocked at the question.

"My Lord, that is not for me to say! All of these garments are yours already, to wear and use as you wish!"

I managed an embarrassed laugh.

"Forgive me, Giuseppe, I had not thought of that, so accustomed have I become to having no possessions! Now, please, will you help me to change back into my habit, and pack these clothes ready for me to take away?"

\*\*\*

My next interview was with the chief retainer. Unlike Giuseppe, this man (who was named Emilio) was one who had been with the family for many years; for so long, in fact, that I found I could not recall a time when he had not been there.

"My Lord Sebastiano!" He greeted me formally but with a sincere smile. "It is very good to see you again, and thankfully under much happier circumstances than those of your previous visit."

He was referring, of course, to the night of my father's death. I vaguely recalled him answering the door to me and Fra' Roberto; though I am ashamed to admit that on that occasion, with much else on my mind, I had taken but scant notice of him.

"Thank you, Emilio. It feels good to be home again."

(Holy Saint Francis – did I say that...?)

"My Lord, I cannot tell you how glad I am that you will soon be returning to us. When do you anticipate that you will be back here for good?"

This was the very same question which Giuseppe had just asked. Clearly they were anxious to have a master again.

"In a few weeks' time, once I have completed my unfinished business with the friars. But in the meantime, I have one request to make of you."

"Name it, My Lord."

"Will you be able to accommodate two guests here, in advance of my returning?"

If Emilio was surprised at the question, he gave no sign of it.

"Of course, My Lord. May I ask who they might be?"

I thought carefully before answering.

"A young man and his wife; they are friends of mine from Verona. At the present time they are lodging in Mantua, but I should like to be able to offer them hospitality here."

"It will be our pleasure, My Lord. I will ensure that a room is made ready for them forthwith."

"Thank you. I will give them a letter of introduction. I envisage that they should arrive here within a week or two."

"Very good, My Lord."

Thinking of my two young fugitives, I recalled that I had vowed to repay the money which I had borrowed from the alms box.

"One more thing, Emilio. I should like to make a gift to the friary in Verona before I depart. Please could you arrange for me to have a small amount of money?"

Emilio nodded.

"I will arrange it immediately, My Lord."

"Thank you."

Emilio bowed and turned to leave, then paused and turned back. He opened his mouth as if to speak, but hesitated.

"What is it, Emilio?"

"Forgive me, My Lord; I fear I may be speaking out of turn. I should not wish to shock you."

At that moment I realised that years of hearing other people's confessions had rendered me fairly difficult to shock. Fra' Roberto had (as always) been right – my years as a friar had indeed made me the man I had now become.

"Please, say what you wish to say, Emilio."

Emilio hesitated, then drew a deep breath.

"My Lord, on the day when you left us to enter the friary, your father withdrew into his chamber and did not emerge for over a week."

"Truly?"

"Aye, My Lord. And when he did reappear, he was never the same

191

again. It is my belief that he never recovered from losing you."

I gulped.

"What?"

Emilio, evidently emboldened by my encouragement, went on:

"You were always his favourite, even when you were but a babe in arms."

I gasped again.

"Even though I was the cause of the death of my mother? His wife?"

Emilio nodded.

"Even in the depths of his grief after her death, he was nonetheless able to accept that even though your mother had died whilst giving birth to you, you yourself could not be held to blame. And in one respect, you were his last link to her. For that reason at least, you were particularly precious to him."

Again I was dumbstruck.

"My Lord? Are you all right?"

I finally regained the power of speech.

"I am sorry, Emilio; I had no idea. I had always believed that he had favoured my brother over me."

Emilio's face grew stony.

"Nay, My Lord. Your father was very disappointed in your brother. Even before he… he…"

"He disappeared?" I suggested tactfully.

Emilio smiled gratefully.

"Please forgive me for speaking so frankly, but I can think of no other way of telling you. Your father believed that your brother was lazy and profligate, whereas you had always been conscientious and sensible. Believe me, My Lord, it broke your father's heart that you had not been the elder son."

I was silent again. Eventually, for want of a means of breaking the silence, I asked:

"Emilio, what was your opinion of my brother?"

"My Lord, it is not my place to offer an opinion on such matters. But, by your leave, I will say this: Your father was a very wise man – and during all the years I knew him, I have only once known him to have made a mistake."

"What was that?" I asked, though I imagined I already knew the answer.

"Sending you into the friary."

"How did you know about that?"

"My Lord, on the night of your father's death, as he was waiting for you to come to him, he called me to his deathbed and told me everything. He was afraid that he might not survive for long enough to see you. He entrusted me with the story, with instructions that I should tell it to you, if he had died before you arrived."

"What did he say about Filippo?" I asked cautiously.

"Nothing that I did not already know."

"So you knew about…"

Emilio nodded.

"Aye, My Lord; I had been suspicious of it for some time. Truth to say, I believe that so had your father – but for many years he had fervently hoped that he was wrong."

\*\*\*

I returned to the friary with my mind in turmoil. During the space of the past two hours, I had learned far more about my father than I had known during the eighteen years which I had spent living in his household.

After supper I sought out Fra' Roberto again.

"How was your visit this afternoon?"

"Very good, thank you. And I have even succeeded in solving the problem of clothing!" I indicated the bundle which Giuseppe had so carefully packaged. "Please, can you store this for me here until I need it?"

"Of course. And have you given any further thought to when you might be ready?"

I nodded.

"Very soon. One month at most, very possibly less."

"That is good; it is better that you should keep the transition time as short as possible. The sooner you embrace your new life, the easier it will be to leave the old one."

"I will set off back to Verona tomorrow morning. And – thank you for all your good advice."

"I am glad that you have found it to be helpful. God-speed, and come back as soon as you are ready."

"Thank you." I hesitated. "Please, may I ask you one more thing?"

"Of course."

"Afterwards, when I am no longer a friar, will you please continue to be my ghostly father?"

Fra' Roberto smiled.

"I am surprised that you should need to ask!"

\*\*\*

During the ride back to Verona, I thought again of Fra' Roberto's advice about how much I should say to my fellow friars. Whilst I could feasibly give the bare minimum of information to most of them, there was at least one from whom I felt I could not conceal the whole truth. But then I realised, with a sickening lurch of the stomach, that I knew nothing of Fra' Gianni's own circumstances, nor of the reason why he had originally become a friar. If he, like myself, had been what Fra' Roberto had described as "surplus progeny," how would he react to the news?

The following morning after Mass, I sought him out. He greeted me warmly.

"Good morrow, my friend! It is good to see you back so soon. I trust that your mission was successful?"

"Aye, thank you."

"Are you able to tell me about it?"

"Before I answer that, may I first ask you something?"

"Of course."

"Why did you become a friar?"

He appeared surprised at the question, but answered readily enough:

"I was brought up in the Pietà. The Sisters who cared for me told me that I had been left in the *ruota dei trovatelli*, a mere few hours after my birth."

I gasped.

"I am so sorry."

He smiled.

"Do not be. If I had not been left with the Sisters, I should doubtless have died in the gutter. So I decided that by becoming a

194

friar, I could somehow repay their kindness – by serving others as they had served me. Why do you ask?"

"I had to be sure that what I am about to tell you would not cause you distress."

"Why? Why should it?"

"It might have done, if your circumstances had been the same as my own."

"What do you mean?"

By way of answer, I knelt down and crossed myself.

"Bless me, Father, for I have sinned—"

Fra' Gianni gasped.

"What is it, Fra' Lorenzo? It is not your usual day for Shrift."

I looked up at him steadily.

"What I am about to tell you must remain secret."

He held my gaze for a moment, then nodded.

"Ah, I see – the secret of the confessional?"

"Aye. Fra' Roberto advised me that it would be better if as few people as possible know about this."

He looked at me in alarm.

"Why? Have you done something wrong?"

"Nay," I hastened to reassure him. "But the circumstances are – er – somewhat unusual."

Fra' Gianni's eyes widened, though he said nothing.

I struggled to my feet.

"Perhaps it might be better if we both sit down."

\*\*\*

"Before I go on, perhaps I should tell you of the reason why I became a friar."

"Why? It is of no relevance to me."

"Be that as it may, it may help you to understand what I am about to tell you."

Fra' Gianni settled himself more comfortably in his chair.

"Very well, go on."

"Unlike you, my friend, I was not a willing recruit to holy orders."

Fra' Gianni looked up in amazement.

"I find that very hard to believe, Fra' Lorenzo."

"Indeed? That is comforting to know; I have tried my best during my time as a friar."

"So – why did you enter the Order?"

"I was a second son. It seems that there was a rule in the family that only the first-born son could inherit. All other children, of either sex, were destined for the cloister."

Fra' Gianni gasped in horror.

"Did you know of this at the time?"

"Nay, I found out about it only a few weeks since. My father told me of it on his deathbed."

"I must own, my friend, that I find this somewhat shocking."

"Why so?"

"It cannot be right that anyone should come into this kind of life if they do not do so willingly."

I nodded.

"That is also what Fra' Roberto believes. But it seems that there are many who do enter the Order against their will. And it is for that reason that he advises that the details of my news might be best kept concealed."

"What news is that?"

"In brief, my friend, I will soon be leaving the Order."

He gazed at me, open-mouthed.

"I do not understand…"

I drew a deep breath.

"It seems that my elder brother disappeared, some ten years since. My father has now appointed me as his sole heir."

Fra' Gianni was silent. Finally he said slowly,

"Now I understand why you asked about my own circumstances before telling me of this."

I nodded.

"Fra' Roberto indicated that it might be upsetting to those who, like myself, had come here as conscripts rather than as volunteers. For that reason, he suggested that to most of the brothers, I should say merely that I am returning to Venice."

Fra' Gianni smiled wistfully.

"I am going to miss you, my friend. But I am nonetheless very pleased at your good fortune."

"Thank you." I shook him warmly by the hand.

"When will you go?"

"Quite soon; certainly within one month, perhaps even sooner. I have a few items of unfinished business to attend to first."

"If by that you mean your spiritual duties, then please do not worry about those. They can be delegated very quickly."

"Thank you, my friend. But there still remain one or two other matters which are quite separate; things which I must deal with on my own. Please do not worry if I am absent from time to time for the next few days."

Fra' Gianni nodded sagely. He seemed to know, instinctively, when it was not appropriate to ask too many questions.

***

After paying back my debt to the alms box, I returned to my cell, took up paper and quill and began to write:

*Emilio,*
*These are the two young friends of whom I spoke at our last meeting. Please make them welcome as my guests until I return to Venice.*

I paused. How on earth should I sign it? This letter was being sent by the Count, not the friar. I had no idea that the simple act of signing my name might prove to be so challenging.

I drew a deep breath and wrote:

*Sebastiano Lorenzo Da Porto.*

After luncheon, I saddled up the horse and set off for Mantua.

***

"Fra' Stephano?"

"Fra' Lorenzo! It is good to see you again!"

"How are your two young guests?"

He grinned.

"Very well, though I think they might be becoming a little bored by now! I expect that they will be grateful for the diversion of a visit

197

from you!"

"Thank you. May I come and speak to you again before I leave?"

"By all means. I think you will find them in the cloister."

Romeo and Giulietta were indeed sitting reading on a bench in a shady corner of the cloister garden. As one, they leapt up to greet me as I approached.

"Fra' Lorenzo! What news from Verona?"

"I have much to tell you both, but we must not be overheard. Is there somewhere where we can converse in private?"

Romeo nodded.

"It is fairly private here, but we can return to our room if you prefer?"

We retired to the privacy of their simply-furnished chamber.

"First of all, are you both well?"

Giulietta nodded.

"Very well, thank you, Fra' Lorenzo."

"Well enough to travel?"

Romeo looked up.

"I believe so. Why do you ask?"

"Would you like to be able to begin a whole new life together, in a place where your past cannot haunt you?"

The look of sheer joy on their faces was a delight to behold.

"Truly, Fra' Lorenzo?" Romeo found his voice at last.

"Truly, son."

"Do you have somewhere particular in mind?" asked Giulietta.

"Aye. Venice."

They both gasped.

"Why Venice?"

"That, son, is a long story. Please, make yourselves comfortable; it may take a while in the telling…"

\*\*\*

By the time when, ten minutes later, I had finished my tale, they were both staring at me open-mouthed.

"Fra' Lorenzo, you are indeed a man of many surprises," Giulietta said at last.

I grinned.

"I have never had any wish to be regarded as dull."

Romeo laughed.

"In all the time I have known you, you have never been dull. Frustrating and infuriating on occasions, but never dull!"

"Thank you. But at the risk of sounding dull for a moment, there are some practical matters we must speak of. First of all, you will need this letter. The chief retainer at the palazzo (his name is Emilio) will be expecting it when you arrive. And here too is a little money – Giulietta, please go and buy yourself some more suitable attire."

Giulietta's face broke into a broad but cheeky smile.

"Thank you, Fra' Lorenzo, but I find I have grown rather fond of wearing breeches. They are much more practical and comfortable than a gown, and certainly far more suitable for a long journey on horseback!"

Having undertaken similar journeys wearing a monastic robe, I could sympathise fully with her sentiment.

"In that case, wait until you arrive in Venice."

Giulietta nodded approvingly.

"When should we go?" Romeo asked.

"As soon as you wish; Emilio will be ready for you. But I suggest that you should go as soon as you are able. Indeed, if you feel ready to travel, you can set off from here tomorrow at first light. I will tell Fra' Stephano that you will be leaving, and ask him to arrange for you to have some food for the journey. It is a long way, but if you ride all day you should reach Venice before sundown."

They glanced at each other for a moment, then turned to me and nodded.

"How will we find the palazzo?" Giulietta was as practical and sensible as ever.

"The address is on the outside of the letter. But I will also draw you a small map. It is not difficult to find."

Romeo's face grew serious.

"What of my mother?"

"Do not worry about that. I will arrange for her to visit you in Venice…"

(And, I added mentally, very possibly for much longer than you think.)

199

"… and then," I winked at Giulietta, "she can then have the opportunity to meet her new daughter-in-law!"

Romeo took hold of Giulietta's hand and squeezed it.

"I know that she will love you, my sweet. Almost as much as I do."

I stood up to leave.

"I must go now. God-speed, and I will see you again in Venice."

Romeo leapt to his feet, stepped forward and hugged me.

"God-speed to you also, my ghostly father. And thank you. Thank you for everything."

I was halfway to the door when Giulietta called me back.

"Fra' Lorenzo, what names should we give when we arrive?"

I must own that I had not given this matter much thought. I had told Romeo to call himself Antonio Da Porto whilst he was living in Mantua, but this name would hardly be an appropriate introduction to the household who, until very recently, had served the real Antonio Da Porto for so many years. But nor would it be wise for them to have recourse to their real names, whilst there still remained a chance that they might be discovered.

"For the moment, simply give your first names; Emilio will expect no more of you than that. Romeo, you should continue to call yourself Antonio. Giulietta, I once had an aunt named Caterina. Are you happy to assume her name for the moment?"

Giulietta nodded.

"Aye, Fra' Lorenzo. After all, we are still the same people inside, whatever name we might bear."

Not for the first time, I marvelled at how this young woman could display a wisdom so far beyond her tender years. My son had indeed made a good choice.

***

"Fra' Stephano?"

"Aye?"

"Your young guests will be leaving tomorrow at first light. They have a long journey ahead of them; please can you arrange for them to have some provisions for the trip?"

"Of course, Fra' Lorenzo."

"Thank you. And thank you also for your great and generous

hospitality to them. Please, accept this small contribution to the cost."

"I can assure you, Fra' Lorenzo, there is no need. As you well know, we friars have a duty of care to anyone who requires it."

"Even so, please accept it," I insisted.

Fra' Stephano briefly made as if to argue further, but then reluctantly held out his hand and took the purse which I offered. He peered inside it and gasped.

"This is a most generous gift, Fra' Lorenzo. Thank you."

"Nay, it is I who must thank you. Sadly I cannot tell you more, but suffice it to say that I cannot envisage what might have happened to those two young people if you had not given them food and shelter."

Fra' Stephano hesitated.

"May I ask, Fra' Lorenzo – from whence has this money come?"

I looked at him steadily.

"It is a gift from the estate of Antonio's father, in token of his family's gratitude."

\*\*\*

I arrived back in Verona in time for supper. Afterwards, Fra' Gianni called me to one side.

"Fra' Lorenzo, young Benvolio came to the friary this afternoon. He said that he wished to see you."

"Did he say what it was that he wanted?"

"Nay, but he seemed quite agitated. He said that he will return tomorrow morning and hopes to see you then."

What could possibly have happened to make the placid and sensible Benvolio 'agitated'? As I entered the chapel for Completorium, I offered a silent prayer that this did not signal yet another catastrophe...

\*\*\*

The following morning I turned my attention to the beehives. In particular, I wished to ascertain whether it would be possible to transport one of them to Venice, as a gift for the friary when I returned thither for good. But it was not long before I was interrupted.

"Fra' Lorenzo?"

"Good morrow, Benvolio! I am sorry that I was not here yesterday when you called."

"No matter, Fra' Lorenzo. What I came to tell you would not suffer from being delayed by one day."

I tried surreptitiously to interpret his demeanour. Yes, he did seem agitated – but as far as I could ascertain, he did not seem to be unduly distressed.

"What is it that you wish to tell me?"

He gazed at me steadily and his face creased into a broad smile.

"Fra' Lorenzo, I am going to be married."

\*\*\*

"And," Benvolio continued, as I stared at him open-mouthed, "I should be honoured if you would perform the ceremony."

"When?" I eventually managed to reply. "I did not even know that you—"

"As soon as possible. And no, until a few days ago I myself knew nothing of it. Everything has happened so quickly."

"Son, are you sure you know what you are doing?"

"Fra' Lorenzo, I have never been more sure of anything in my entire life."

I drew a deep breath and asked:

"Who is the lady?"

Whatever answer I might have been anticipating, I could not have been more astounded by his response.

"The Lady Rosaline."

\*\*\*

"The same Lady Rosaline who—?"

"Aye, Fra' Lorenzo." Benvolio nodded.

"But is she not of the House of Capuleti? Sworn enemies of your family?"

"Of the House of Capuleti, aye. But sworn enemies of my family – nay, no longer."

"What?"

I could not believe what I was hearing. If I had not known Benvolio to have always been a sensible and level-headed youth, I should have sworn that he was giving way to fanciful and irrational imagination.

"How has this come about?"

Benvolio looked at me earnestly.

"It was last Monday afternoon. My aunt and I had just finished eating our luncheon, when it was announced that we had a visitor. When the visitor was shown in, it was none other than the Lady Capuleti, who was accompanied by her niece – the Lady Rosaline."

"What?"

"Indeed, Fra' Lorenzo – that was also my reaction. But the Lady Capuleti was gracious and courteous to my aunt, who – I must own – did not seem to be overly surprised to see her."

"I think I can tell you why that might be, son."

Benvolio's eyes widened.

"Why so, Fra' Lorenzo?"

"When your aunt came to me for Shrift last Saturday, she showed me a letter which she had recently received. The Lady Capuleti had written to her to offer her condolences on the death of your uncle. I advised your aunt to send the Lady Capuleti a short reply, thanking her for her kind thoughts. It would seem that the Lady Capuleti came to visit your aunt in response to that reply."

Benvolio nodded.

"That would seem feasible. But after a moment or two, my aunt and the Lady Capuleti asked if they might be left to converse in private. Accordingly, I offered to take the Lady Rosaline outside to show her the garden."

"Did you not find her presence difficult, remembering how she had previously caused so much pain to your cousin?"

Benvolio's face grew serious.

"Aye, Fra' Lorenzo, I did – at first. I was at a loss about what to say to her; however it was she who first spoke of the matter."

"Indeed? What did she say?"

"She said that she was sorry to hear that I had lost so much in such a short time. First my friend, then my cousin, and now my uncle. For want of a suitable reply, I thanked her, then offered her my condolences on the sudden deaths of her own cousins."

"Tebaldo and the Lady Giulietta?"

I remembered, just in time, that Benvolio – in the same way as everyone else in Verona – still believed that Giulietta was dead. In order to be a good liar, I realised, it is essential to have a good memory.

Benvolio nodded.

"She thanked me for that, then went on to say how much she regretted that our two households should have lived at odds for such a long time." He paused, and his face coloured. "As she was speaking, I began to understand why Romeo had doted on her for so long. She is beautiful, gently-spoken…"

His voice tailed off.

"Go on, son," I said gently.

"It is difficult to describe. Even though this was the first time I had met her face to face, it was as though I had known her all my life. It may sound strange, but it seemed as though I had suddenly realised that until now, half of my soul had been lost and it had just been found. I have never felt like that before, Fra' Lorenzo. Do you understand?"

I nodded.

"Aye, son, I do."

"Rosaline then said that she was most saddened that the quarrel between our two households had resulted in her cousin's death and my cousin's banishment. What a terrible and pointless waste it had been. And I cannot help but agree with her."

"As indeed do we all on that point," I replied.

"And then," Benvolio went on, staring into space as if he had not heard me, "I suddenly felt very bold. I realise now that I might have been speaking out of turn, but I asked her if she had known that my cousin had been very fond of her."

"What did she respond to that?"

Benvolio turned to face me.

"That is what is so remarkable, Fra' Lorenzo. So much so that I wonder what might have happened if I had not asked."

"Go on."

"She said 'Aye, I did know. Your cousin was a good and virtuous youth, and it pained me to think that I could not return his affection.'"

"Holy Saint Francis!"

Benvolio nodded.

"Indeed, Fra' Lorenzo. I then asked her 'Why not? Was it because of the quarrel?'"

"And was it?"

"Nay." He paused before continuing. "At least, not entirely. The quarrel might have been one reason, but apparently it was not the real reason."

"What, then? What other reason could there have been?"

"That is precisely what I asked her. And her answer was, 'Because I loved another'."

I gasped.

"It had been my understanding – from what you, and Mercutio, and Romeo himself, had all said – that the Lady Rosaline had sworn to remain chaste!"

"That had also been my understanding, Fra' Lorenzo. But when I repeated this to her, she smiled and said, 'Nay, I had sworn only to remain chaste because I believed my true love to be unattainable.' I asked her 'Who, then, is your true love?' She simply looked at me and asked me 'Can you not guess?'"

"So – the Lady Rosaline had rejected Romeo because—"

"Aye, Fra' Lorenzo – because, it seems, she had been in love with me all along."

***

He smiled ruefully.

"The night of the ball at the Capuleti mansion, where Romeo and I had gone in disguise, Rosaline and I had even danced together – though neither of us had been aware of it at the time."

"So when did you decide that you wished to marry?"

"That very same afternoon."

"And – what of the quarrel?" I ventured, almost afraid to ask the question.

Benvolio smiled again.

"The quarrel, as I told you just now, is no more."

"Please, tell me more."

"When Rosaline and I returned to the house, my aunt and the

Lady Capuleti were sitting talking quite happily. It seemed that they had both agreed that the feud, whatever might have been the original reason for it, had long since run its course, and that from now onwards our two households should put an end to the quarrelling and live peacefully together as friends and colleagues."

"Amen to that!" I uttered, as much to myself as to Benvolio.

"I accompanied the Lady Capuleti and Rosaline back to the Capuleti mansion, and formally asked the Lord Capuleti for Rosaline's hand in marriage. He was happy to give his consent, saying that he was delighted that centuries of rancour might now be ended by true love."

"And what of your aunt? What does she feel about this?"

"She is very happy for us."

"In that case, son, I should be honoured to perform your marriage. When do you wish for it to take place?"

"Can you do it tomorrow?" He smiled sheepishly. "Or do you think we are being too hasty?"

I thought of Romeo and Giulietta (who had married less than four and twenty hours after they had first met), and of the ill-fated nuptials of Giulietta and the Count Paris, which had been arranged for a mere three days after their first encounter. Benvolio and Rosaline had met on a Monday and were asking to be married on the following Saturday. Their courtship seemed positively leisurely by comparison.

"If you both truly love each other, son, and you wish to be together, then no, I do not think so. I will go and see the Lord and Lady Capuleti later this morning. And please commend me to your aunt, and tell her that I will call on her this afternoon."

"Thank you, Fra' Lorenzo!"

He shook my hand, bowed and left.

When, less than two weeks earlier, I had agreed to marrying Romeo and Giulietta in secret, it had been my vision that their union might eventually serve to unite the two warring households; the one good thing which I might achieve ere I departed from Verona. Now, it seemed, that this would indeed be achieved after all. It would come about by a different and far more public marriage than theirs, but it would nonetheless be one which I would have the honour of conducting.

And for that, I murmured a private prayer of thanks.

***

My interview with the Lord and Lady Capuleti was brief and businesslike. They were, it appeared, more than happy for the marriage to take place as soon as Benvolio and Rosaline should wish.

"It will not be a lavish affair, I fear," the Lord Capuleti said apologetically.

"I do not think that it will need to be, Sir," I hastened to reassure him. "The young Lord Montecchi and the Lady Rosaline love each other and wish to be together. Is that not enough?"

He sighed.

"You are right, Fra' Lorenzo." He turned to his wife. "Perhaps we have had our priorities wrong for too long."

The Lady Capuleti nodded.

"There have been far too many tragedies here of late. Let us be grateful that something good has happened at last."

I nodded.

"Amen to that."

It seemed that their recent double-bereavement had at last made them appreciate that life is too short for pointless feuding, and that happiness, when it is found, is precious and must be nurtured. How tragic, then, I thought, that it should have required four deaths in close succession (three real, one simulated) to have finally brought them to their senses.

"By your leave, My Lord, My Lady – do you think it would be appropriate to inform the Prince?"

They looked briefly at each other, then nodded.

"Would you like me to tell him?" I asked. "I have to speak to him on another matter in any case."

The Lord Capuleti smiled gratefully.

"Thank you, Fra' Lorenzo. That would be much appreciated."

***

"Please will you tell the Lady Lucia that I am here? I believe she is expecting me."

"Aye, Fra' Lorenzo." Balthasar bowed and left.

A few minutes later Chiara appeared. And once again,

infuriatingly, she was accompanied by the ubiquitous Gertrude.

"Fra' Lorenzo! Benvolio told me you would call this afternoon. It is good to see you."

But the flash in her eyes (again, thankfully, unnoticed by Gertrude) belied her excessively formal tone.

"You too, My Lady. I trust you are well?" I too entered fully into the charade.

She nodded.

"Much has happened since I saw you last."

"So I understand! It seems that the Lady Capuleti has responded to your letter in person?"

"Aye, last Monday. I was surprised that she should have replied so soon, but all the same I was pleased and grateful that she did."

"May I ask what you spoke of during her visit?"

"Of course. It is no secret! We acknowledged that we have both recently lost people who were very dear to us, and we agreed that the time has now come to put the past behind us and to put an end to the feud. Giovanna – the Lady Capuleti – said that she had already spoken to her husband ere she came to see me, and it seems that he too is of the same mind. I believe that the Lord Montecchi, had he still been alive, would have been very happy to see this day." She sighed. "Life is short; far too short to harbour an ancient grudge."

"Wise words indeed, My Lady. It is only sad that it has taken so long to resolve."

"Aye, Fra' Lorenzo." She nodded sadly.

"But, My Lady," (I laid particular stress on those words) "I understand there is to be a wedding soon?"

I looked directly into her eyes. She held my gaze, nodded and smiled.

"Aye, Fra' Lorenzo. Good news, is it not?"

"Very good news indeed. I have no doubt that I shall see you there?"

"Aye." Her eyes flashed again as she caught my drift.

"In the meantime." I continued, "I must go and make the necessary preparations. And I also need to pay a visit to the Prince. Will you be coming to Shrift as usual on Saturday afternoon?"

"Of course."

"Until Saturday, then, My Lady."

208

I bowed and took my leave.

***

The sentry on duty at the gate of the Prince's palace was the same as had been on duty on the afternoon of the fateful brawl. He greeted me formally, but his tone was not unfriendly.

"Good day, Fra' Lorenzo! May I ask if you are expected?"

"Good day to you also. Nay, I do not have a prior appointment, but I should be most grateful if the Prince could see me for a few minutes if he is available."

"Please, come inside. I will send a message upstairs."

"Thank you."

A few minutes later I saw the manservant Paolo striding towards me across the courtyard.

"If you would please care to come with me, Fra' Lorenzo?"

He led me into the same reception room where my previous audience with the Prince had taken place.

"Please be seated, Fra' Lorenzo. The Prince will be down to see you in a few minutes."

"Thank you, Paolo."

How much has happened since I was last in this room, I thought.

"Fra' Lorenzo?"

"Sir!" I rose to my feet as the Prince entered. "Thank you for finding the time to speak to me."

The Prince looked concerned.

"Please, Fra' Lorenzo, be seated."

He gestured towards the chair I had just vacated, then settled himself in another.

"I know you would not come to see me on a trivial matter. How may I assist you?"

"Sir, I have the honour of bringing you some excellent news. The feud between the Montecchi and the Capuleti is at an end."

"What?" the Prince gasped.

"Aye, Sir. It seems that the two households have at last agreed to lay aside their differences and make their peace."

"This is indeed excellent news, Fra' Lorenzo. But it is a pity that it could not have happened sooner."

209

"Indeed so, sir. It is sad that it should have taken so much tragedy to bring it about."

The Prince nodded sadly.

"We have all suffered losses…"

His voice trailed off.

"But there is more, Sir. The new Lord Montecchi – young Benvolio – is to marry the Lady Rosaline, the niece of the Lord Capuleti."

The Prince's eyes widened and he whistled under his breath.

"Heaven be praised! When is the wedding to take place?"

"Tomorrow morning, Sir. I will be conducting the ceremony myself."

The Prince hesitated, then cautiously said,

"I should like to come to the service, if I may. I should like to share in their happiness, and the peace which it will bring to the city."

"Sir, the service will be held in a public church and everyone will be welcome to attend. But your presence would be a pleasure and an honour."

He smiled gratefully.

"Thank you, Fra' Lorenzo." He paused, then slowly asked, "Have you had any news of young Romeo?"

"Not for some time, Sir," I answered carefully.

"Do you know where he is now?"

"Nay, Sir, I do not," I replied truthfully. "By your leave, Sir, why do you ask?"

The Prince sighed.

"If it is ever appropriate that I should be able to grant him a pardon, I should like to know how I might inform him of it. Would you be able to pass on a message to him from me?"

"Sir," I hesitated, "Much as I should dearly love to be able to do so, I must in all honesty admit that I do not know. And there is something else which I must tell you."

His face grew serious again.

"What is that?"

"I shall soon be leaving Verona."

The Prince raised his eyebrows.

"Why so, Fra' Lorenzo? And where will you go?"

"I must return to Venice, Sir," I answered carefully. "I have other business there."

He sighed.

"I shall be very sorry to see you go. But I wish you well."

"Thank you, Sir. But if you wish to contact me, please send a message to the Franciscan friary in Venice. The friars there will ensure that I receive it."

"Thank you, Fra' Lorenzo." He rose to his feet. "Until tomorrow, then?"

I bowed.

"Until tomorrow, Sir."

***

The wedding of Benvolio and Rosaline took place the following morning. It was, as the Lord Capuleti had indicated, a quiet affair, attended only by the Prince, the immediate families and the members of the two households – their rancour at last vanquished by the love of the two young people who knelt together at the altar as I joined their hands. The wedding feast, to which the Prince was invited as guest of honour, was a simple but happy repast. The Lord Capuleti, in drinking the health of the bride and bridegroom, warmly welcomed Benvolio into the Capuleti family, but also made mention of two people who sadly could not be there to share the couple's joy: Benvolio's uncle the Lord Montecchi, and his own daughter Giulietta.

"She was a good and beautiful girl," he declared sadly, "and it broke our hearts that she should have died so suddenly and so tragically, on the day of what would have been her own wedding." He turned to address his niece. "Rosaline, as you are now my closest relative, I wish to name you as heiress to the Capuleti estates. It is my great hope that the union of our two households may ensure that Verona will at last become a peaceful and happy city."

The Prince stood up and raised his glass.

"Amen to that!" he declared.

Amen to that indeed, I added mentally. How sad, though, that it did not transpire thus for their cousins…

***

Chiara arrived for Shrift a full half an hour earlier than her usual time.

"Forgive me, my love, I could wait no longer."

"No matter – we have much to discuss."

"I know." She looked at me eagerly.

"Please, sit down."

She settled herself at the table. I sat down opposite her and reached across for her hand.

"Were you surprised at the news of Benvolio and Rosaline?"

She smiled.

"Only at first. Then, the more I thought about it, the more I realised there was a certain inevitability about it. As you know, it happened very quickly."

"There is nothing wrong with that," I reminded her. "Do you recall, My Lady Lucia, a story of a young woman named Chiara and a young man named Sebastiano?"

She returned my grin.

"I do indeed, Fra' Lorenzo. And I recall that they fell in love even more quickly than Benvolio and Rosaline!"

"And they remained in love for many years," I added with a wink, "even when faced with insurmountable obstacles."

She nodded.

"If someone were to tell me such a tale," she sighed, "I doubt that I should believe it."

"Nor I. But I believe that the ending of the tale might prove to be even more incredible."

"Truly? How, then, do you believe it might end?"

"I believe that all the obstacles which had remained in their way for such a long time suddenly disappeared, and that Chiara and Sebastiano were free to marry at last. Provided, of course, that they wished to."

"And did they wish to, do you think?"

"I cannot speak for both of them, but I know that it was certainly Sebastiano's wish."

Her fingers interlaced with my own.

"And I know," she murmured, "that it was also Chiara's wish."

***

"When we first spoke of this, my love, you said that you would be willing to fake your own death in order to escape with me. Do you still wish to do that?"

She looked up.

"That was when Luigi was still living. I could see no other way, as I had no wish to cause him pain or disgrace by leaving him. But that does not apply now."

"What will you do, then?"

"I will simply announce that I am returning to Venice, from whence I came, to begin a new life there. After all, my husband has died and his nephew has married. There is no reason for me to remain here in Verona."

"Have you spoken to Benvolio of this?"

"Not as yet, but I cannot foresee him raising any objection. I know that he made a promise to Luigi that he would take care of me, but now he has a new wife, and I should have no wish to intrude on their life together!"

I realised that I should soon have to break the news to her that our son also had a new wife, and that we should be sharing our home with them. But this was neither the time nor the place for such an announcement. We still had to finalise the details of our own future.

"When do you envisage that you will be able to leave here?" I asked her.

"In about a month, I expect; perhaps less. And you?"

"I have done most of what I need to do here; I expect to be free within a day or two."

"So soon?" She gasped.

"Aye. But I have no cause to stay here once my work is finished, and Fra' Roberto in Venice said that I should not linger once I was done."

"What will happen when you go back to Venice?"

"I will need to go back once more to the friary to be released from my vows, then I shall be able to return to the palazzo. What will you do?"

She smiled.

"I will go to the Convent of the Poor Clares and lodge with them at first, as I did when I first came to Verona. I will send word to you when I reach there. God-speed, my love."

"God-speed. Send word to me at the friary, and address your letter to Fra' Lorenzo. The Superior will ensure that the message is passed on to me. In the meantime, whilst I am waiting for you to arrive, I shall give some thought to the arrangements for our own wedding." I squeezed her hand, which still wore the simple patterned ring, fashioned in silver. "And this time, thankfully, it will not need to be a secret!"

***

My impending departure was announced by Fra' Gianni, in a suitably discreet manner, at luncheon on the following day – a Sunday. The two of us had agreed, during a private discourse after supper the previous evening, that I should depart after breakfast on the Monday morning. I do not know what kind of reaction I had been expecting, but I was most surprised at the level of sadness which it appeared to cause. So much so, in fact, that I do not wish to dwell on the memory. Suffice it to say that during the course of the afternoon I was visited in my cell by a steady procession of friars and novices who came to bid me farewell. All said that they would miss me, but nonetheless wished me well for my new venture. It transpired that none, save Fra' Gianni, appeared to know the real reason for my leaving Verona. And for that, I realised, I was most grateful. As had happened so many times before, Fra' Roberto's far-sighted advice had been correct.

It but remained for me to clear and tidy my cell in readiness for its next occupant (whoever that might be). There was, in fact, very little which I would need in my new life, though I realised that in order to give some credibility to the story that I was to continue as a friar once I had returned to Venice, I should need to take with me, at the very least, my breviary, my rosary, and one or two utensils from the dispensary. It was whilst packing these latter items that I recalled that I still had, concealed in their hiding place, the vials of the sleeping potion.

Although there was now (thankfully) no further need for the potion, it was nonetheless certainly not advisable to leave the vials in a place where they might subsequently be found, and possibly accidentally administered (with Heaven alone knows what

214

consequence). Accordingly, I went to the place where I had hidden them. As I put in my hand to remove them from their cache, my hand touched something else. I reached in further and drew out a piece of paper.

The paper was carefully folded and sealed, and addressed on the outside to "My dear father."

I gasped as I recognised Romeo's hand. It was the letter which he had given to me on my first visit to him and Giulietta in Mantua, when I had brought them the tidings of the Lord Montecchi's death. Romeo had, I recalled, given me instructions to dispose of it as I thought fit.

I sat down at the table, cautiously broke the seal, and began to read:

*My dearest Father,*
*If you are reading this, it is because I have died by my own hand.*
*Father, I am deeply and truly sorry if this causes you pain and distress.*
*But if you allow me to explain to you how this has come about, then I dare to hope that you may understand.*

*On Sunday evening last, Mercutio and Benvolio persuaded me to accompany them, in disguise, to a banquet and ball at the house of the Capuleti. It was during that feast that I met a young and beautiful lady whom I loved at first sight. It was only later that I learned that she was none other than the Lady Giulietta, the daughter of the Lord and Lady Capuleti - the sworn enemies of our family.*

*Later that evening I met her again, in secret, and I learned that she too had fallen in love with me as swiftly and deeply as I had with her. On that same night we arranged to marry. This we did, the following afternoon, at Fra' Lorenzo's cell.*

*It was as I was returning from our wedding that I became drawn into the dreadful fight which resulted in the deaths of Mercutio and Tebaldo - for which, as you know, the Prince sentenced me to immediate exile from Verona. I was able to pass that night with my dear wife, but was forced to leave her at first light on Tuesday and flee from Verona to Mantua.*

*Today is Wednesday. My servant Balthasar has today come to me in Mantua with the news that my Giulietta, my beloved wife, is dead.*

*I cannot, and I will not, live without her. Accordingly, I have just purchased, from an impoverished apothecary here in Mantua, a dram of poison which, he has promised me, would despatch me forthwith even if I had the strength of twenty men.*

*I am now about to return to Verona, where I will make my way to my dear lady's tomb and end my own life by her side.*

*Please forgive me, my dear Father. And please commend me to my lady Mother and ask her forgiveness for the pain and shame which I have caused to both of you.*

*Your ever-loving son,*
*R.M.*

I already knew, from the discourse which Romeo had had with me during our long vigil in the Capuleti vault, of the depth of his feelings for his beloved Giulietta. But only after reading this passionate suicide note did I realise just how close their story had come to having a very different ending.

I folded the letter and packed it carefully into my saddlebag. And for the first time since the death of my own father, I burst into tears.

\*\*\*

There still remained one letter which I myself needed to write before my departure.

*Benvolio,*

*It was with great joy that I conducted your marriage yesterday. I rejoiced not only in the happiness of you and the Lady Rosaline, but also in the end of the feud which has blighted your household and hers for so many years.*

*I am sorry, however, that I have not had the opportunity to explain to you in person that very shortly I shall be leaving Verona. My Superior has arranged that I will be returning to Venice, from whence I came originally. All this has happened very swiftly, and I expect that by the time you receive this letter I will have already left.*

*Fra' Gianni has indicated to me that after my departure he will be happy to assume the role of your ghostly father. I commend him to you; he is a good and kind man and has been a true and trusted friend.*

*If you wish to write to me, please send me word by Fra' Gianni. He will ensure that your letter is forwarded to me at the friary in Venice.*

216

*I wish you and your dear wife a long and happy life together.*

*In D.no,*
*Fra' Lorenzo*

I sealed the letter and laid it on the table, then for the last time made my way to the friary chapel for Completorium.

*May the Lord Almighty grant us a quiet night and a perfect end...*

\*\*\*

My departure, after an early breakfast the following morning, was mercifully quiet and discreet. Fra' Gianni met me in the stable and handed me a bundle of food for the journey.

"God-speed, my friend. Commend me to Fra' Roberto. And I wish you every success in your new life."

"Thank you. Please, may I ask you one last favour?"

"Of course."

"I have left a letter on the table in my cell. Please will you ensure that it is delivered to young Benvolio?"

"Indeed I will, my friend. But in return, will you please do something for me?"

I blinked. Never, in all the years I had known him, had Fra' Gianni ever asked for anything for himself.

"Of course. What is it?"

"Please take good care of yourself. And in particular, be mindful of your cough."

\*\*\*

Back in Venice, Fra' Roberto greeted me with surprise.

"Lorenzo! It is good to see you again, though I had not expected you to return so soon."

"Nor I, Fra' Roberto – but Fra' Gianni was able to reallocate my friar's duties much more quickly than I had anticipated. And once I had disposed of the few other outstanding matters, there seemed to be little reason to remain."

"How many of your fellow friars know of the real reason for your leaving Verona?" Fra' Roberto asked cautiously.

"Fra' Gianni only. And he is bound by the secret of the confessional."

"How did he receive the news?"

"He was surprised, but wished me well. And his own circumstances, thank the Lord, were not the same as my own."

"He was a foundling, was he not?"

"So I understand, though I only discovered this a few days since. How did you know?"

"He told me so himself. It seems that he wished to repay the debt which he owed to the Sisters of the Pietà who had saved his life." Fra' Roberto sighed. "He is truly selfless. It is a great pity that there are not more men like him."

"Aye."

I repeated Fra' Gianni's parting words to me as I had left Verona.

Fra' Roberto gasped, and his face grew serious.

"He had also noticed it? I too have been worried about it, Lorenzo; I became aware of it during your last two visits."

I realised, with a shock, that I had become so accustomed to the cough that I had long since ceased to notice it. Had it indeed been going on for so long?

Fra' Roberto hesitated, then added,

"Please do not forget, Lorenzo, that one of your uncles died of consumption."

I froze.

"Do you believe that that might be the cause of it?"

"That I cannot say – at least, not at this stage. But it seems that one of the first indications is a cough which no medicine seems able to cure." He looked at me steadily. "At the very least, Lorenzo, please take care of your health. Fra' Pietro will doubtless be happy to help you, in the same way that you have helped so many others."

*(It is in giving that we receive…)*

"Thank you, Fra' Roberto."

He remained pensive for a moment, then his face brightened.

"There is still the small matter of your release, Lorenzo. I have decided on the witnesses; it but remains to advise them of the time.

Would tomorrow morning be suitable for you?"

I nodded.

"Very well. Come at the hour of ten."

He opened a cupboard and removed the bundle which I had given to him at our last meeting.

"Here is your ordinary attire. Do not forget to bring it with you!"

\*\*\*

I had no idea of what to expect as I presented myself in Fra' Roberto's office at the hour of ten the following morning. Fra' Roberto was seated at his desk; the two witnesses (neither of whom I recognised) occupied two chairs which had been positioned to one side. All three rose to their feet as I entered; we shook hands formally and I was directed towards a fourth chair which had been positioned opposite Fra' Roberto's desk.

The ceremony, in the event, was extremely simple and mercifully brief. After I was asked to confirm that it was my wish to leave the Order, Fra' Roberto pronounced that I was forthwith released from my vows – after which all four of us signed an official document to that effect. Fra' Roberto and the two other friars then discreetly turned their backs as I removed my monastic habit for the final time, and assumed the attire – and with it the identity – of the Count Sebastiano Lorenzo Matteo Giovanni Battista Da Porto.

I carefully folded up the habit and handed it back to Fra' Roberto, formally signifying the end of my time as Fra' Lorenzo of the Order of Saint Francis. The two witnesses, their work now officially completed, bowed and took their leave. Fra' Roberto and I were left alone.

Eventually, Fra' Roberto broke the silence.

"How are you feeling, My Lord?"

As he was speaking I had opened my mouth to reply, but hearing myself thus addressed rendered me speechless.

"I – I – "

"Do not worry!" Fra' Roberto smiled sympathetically. "No-one – least of all me! – will be expecting you to step from being a cleric to being a Count in an instant!"

I found my voice at last.

"It is strange, Fra' Roberto – the staff at the palazzo all addressed me as 'My Lord' when I was wearing the attire of Fra' Lorenzo, and I thought nothing of it. But to hear you say it… Somehow it does not seem right. I feel as though I am no longer the same person."

"Lorenzo, you are still the same person inside, even if you now bear a different name. And it is reassuring to find that I am not the only one to feel uncomfortable about his official title!"

I laughed with relief.

"I had not thought of that! Though I am sure that, like you, in the fullness of time I shall learn to live with it!"

Fra' Roberto smiled again, then picked up another piece of paper from his desk.

"Please, Lorenzo, take this with you as a memento of your time with us. It is as good a rule for all those outside the cloister as for those within it."

It was a copy of the prayer attributed to the founder of the Order:

*Lord, make me an instrument of Your peace. Where there is hatred, let me sow love; where there is injury, pardon; where there is doubt, faith; where there is despair, hope; where there is darkness, light; where there is sadness, joy.*

*O, Divine Master, grant that I may not so much seek to be consoled as to console; to be understood as to understand; to be loved as to love. For it is in giving that we receive; it is in pardoning that we are pardoned; it is in dying that we are born again to eternal life.*

A lump came to my throat.

"Thank you, Fra' Roberto," I murmured.

Fra' Roberto gestured towards the portrait of Saint Francis of Assisi which still hung on the wall beside his desk.

"He was a truly great man," he said simply. "If all people lived by his rule, this world would be a much happier place."

I re-read the Saint's words – *Where there is hatred, let me sow love* – and thought of the decades (possibly centuries) of futile feuding in Verona. And I found that I could not help but agree.

***

Within the hour, the Count Sebastiano Lorenzo Matteo Giovanni

Battista Da Porto had taken his leave of Fra' Roberto and was presenting himself at the door of the palazzo. The door was answered by Emilio.

"My Lord!" His face broke into a broad smile as he greeted me warmly. "It is very good to see you back here so soon. Are you now finished with your business at the friary?"

"I am."

"In that case, My Lord: welcome home!"

"Thank you, Emilio. It feels good to be back."

"Come, My Lord; I will arrange for an additional place to be laid for you at luncheon. Your young guests will no doubt be pleased to see you."

I looked up.

"When did they arrive?"

"On Friday last, but quite late in the day. They were both exhausted; I understand that they had ridden all the way from Mantua."

"Are they now recovered?"

Emilio nodded.

"It would appear so, my lord – though I have no doubt that they will tell you themselves when you see them!"

"Where are they now?"

"I believe they have gone for a walk in the city. They have done that each morning since they arrived."

It had not previously occurred to me that to a pair who had spent the past two weeks in hiding (and in Giulietta's case, also in mute disguise), being now able to walk freely in the streets, and without fear of arrest or discovery, would be something to be treasured.

***

When I presented myself at luncheon, Romeo and Giulietta were already seated at the table. As one, they leapt up in surprise at my approach.

"Fra' Loren – I beg your pardon – My Lord!"

Romeo (who had clearly also been taken under Giuseppe's wing with regard to his clothing) grasped my hand and pressed it firmly. He took a step backwards and surveyed my new attire.

221

"You look – quite different."

"And so, my young friends, do you!"

Giulietta, who was now wearing a simple but elegant dress, dropped a discreet curtsey.

"My Lord," she murmured.

"Please, no formality! Let us eat. We will have plenty of time to talk afterwards."

***

"How was your journey hither?"

"Long and tiring," Romeo sighed. "I had not realised just how far it is between Mantua and Venice. Even setting off at first light, as you had advised us, it was still evening ere we arrived here."

"But all the members of your household have treated us as honoured guests," Giulietta added. "Even your housekeeper has taken it upon herself to find me some new clothing." She gestured towards her dress. "How can we ever repay you?"

"By remaining together and happy," I answered with a grin.

Romeo took hold of Giulietta's hand and squeezed it.

"Of course," he murmured, though more to her than to me.

"But where shall we go from here?" Giulietta frowned. "You have been most kind, My Lord, but we cannot impose on your hospitality for ever—"

*(Not to be served, but to serve… It is in giving that we receive…)*

"Please," I held up my hand for silence, "you are welcome to remain here for as long as you wish. This palazzo is far too large for one person alone. And after all the many troubles and adversities which you have endured, I feel that you have earned the right to a little comfort and relaxation!" I paused. "One thing which I learned during my time as a friar was that we should always give help where it is needed. And it would give me great pleasure to be able to help you."

"Truly, My Lord?"

"Truly. And one more thing – please do not address me as 'My Lord'!"

They looked embarrassed.

"What shall we call you, then?" Romeo asked eventually.

I had been giving some thought to this matter as I had been waiting for them to return from their walk. And I was still no nearer to finding an answer to the question.

"My real name is Sebastiano," I ventured. "Do you feel happy calling me by that?"

Romeo hesitated.

"If you wish, but I find it difficult to think of you as anything other than Fra' Lorenzo." He paused. "Why were you not called Fra' Sebastiano?"

"That was because when I was received into the Order, there already was a Fra' Sebastiano. It was preferable that each brother should be known individually, so it was recommended that I should assume another name. I chose Lorenzo because it is my second given name."

Giulietta looked up.

"Whatever name we might use, we are still the same inside."

Romeo glanced at her.

"You said that on the night we first met, my love."

She met his gaze.

"And it is true... Do not forget, my sweet, that we too have been living under assumed names for some time."

"Of course," I mused. "You are now Antonio and Caterina, are you not?"

Giulietta nodded.

"But in private we are still Romeo and Giulietta!"

I looked at them gravely.

"I believe that it would be best if those names were not generally known."

"Why so?"

"You now have a new life here in Venice. Do you wish to run the risk that your past might come back and blight your future?"

Their eyes widened in horror at the prospect.

"I suggest, then, that for public purposes we should all use our official first names. Though if we wish to retain other names as our second names, and use those names in private..."

Antonio Romeo and Caterina Giulietta glanced at each other, then both turned to me and nodded in agreement.

223

"Very well, My Lord Sebastiano Lorenzo…"

I turned to Giulietta.

"By your leave, may I ask for a few minutes alone with Romeo?"

If Giulietta was surprised at the request, she gave no sign.

"Of course. I will take a walk in the garden. Come and find me there afterwards, my sweet."

She kissed Romeo lightly on the cheek, then curtseyed and left us.

\*\*\*

Romeo's face had again become serious.

"What is it, Fr – er, Lorenzo – that you need to say to me which you cannot say in the presence of my wife? We have no secrets between us."

"That is good, Romeo – a husband and wife should not conceal things from each other. But I needed to speak to you alone because I do not know how much Giulietta knows of the reason for your initial return from Mantua."

"What do you mean?"

By way of answer, I handed him the letter which he had written to the Lord Montecchi. He read it in silence and his eyes widened.

"You wrote this letter ere you left Mantua?"

Romeo nodded.

"How had you intended that the Lord Montecchi should have received it?" I asked gently.

Romeo was silent.

"I do not know," he answered eventually. "In my desperate state I wished only to die…"

"When Giulietta awoke in the vault," I continued, "you were waiting by her side – which is what I had promised her ere she took the sleeping draught. But did you ever tell her that that is not why you had come to the tomb? Does she know that you had heard only that she had died, and that it was your intention to die with her?"

Romeo stared miserably at the ground. Eventually, he shook his head slowly.

"I did not see the need to distress her at the time. And since then…"

"Then perhaps you should tell her now."

"Why?"

"You yourself said just now that the two of you had no secrets between you. And yet you have not told her that you were prepared to die rather than to face life without her?"

Romeo said nothing.

"I have often wondered," I continued gently, "what might have happened, if she had awoken and found you dead at her side."

He shuddered.

"And there is more which I must tell you."

"What?"

"Your mother is planning to come to Venice."

"When?" he asked eagerly.

"I am not certain, but quite soon. But she does not know that you are here – nor does she know of your marriage. Hence, she knows nothing of the events which you described here." (I indicated the letter in his hand). "She knows only that you were exiled from Verona after the death of Tebaldo."

"Did you deliver my letter to her?"

"I did, and it brought her much comfort. But ere she sees you again, I believe that she will have to be told the whole story."

Romeo sat very still.

"I am prepared to tell her myself, if you are happy that I should do so…" I continued.

Romeo nodded.

"… but it would be made much easier if I could first show her this letter – which tells the tale in your words rather than my own."

"Very well…"

"And there is more. But first we must go and find Giulietta, for she also needs to hear this."

As we walked out into the garden, Romeo asked,

"Do you think I should show Giulietta the letter?"

"If you wish. Would you like me to leave you alone for a short while?"

He shook his head.

"It will be easier, by your leave, if you are present."

***

225

Giulietta was sitting in a shady corner of the garden, reading. She leapt up as we approached, but on seeing Romeo's troubled countenance, her radiant smile faded.

"What is it, my love? What is wrong?"

"There is nothing wrong," I hastened to assure her. "But there is something which you need to be told – something of which I believe, at present, you are blissfully ignorant."

"What?"

We settled down on the bench, and Romeo took her hand in his. He opened his mouth to speak, but no words came. It fell to me to break the silence.

"Giulietta," I began gently, "do you recall the plan we made for your escape from Verona?"

"Aye," she answered in surprise. "What of it?"

"It came dangerously close to miscarrying."

"Why? What happened?"

"The letter which I wrote to Romeo, advising him of the plan and asking him to return to Verona to rescue you, never reached him. Instead, he heard only that you were dead."

Her eyes widened and her hand flew to her mouth in horror.

"So how did—"

Romeo found his voice at last.

"Please, my love, read this."

Giulietta was silent as she did so. As she finished, the paper fell from her hand. She turned to Romeo and gazed at him through tearful eyes.

"I had no idea… Would you truly have done that?"

Romeo nodded.

"Aye, my love."

Giulietta shuddered.

"If I had awoken and found you dead, I should have ended my own life then and there."

They clung to each other. I bent down to retrieve the letter from where Giulietta had let it fall.

"That is what might have happened," I whispered. "Praise Heaven that it did not."

Giulietta looked up.

"So why did it happen differently?"

"Because Fra' Lorenzo arrived at the vault before I did," Romeo answered. "He prevented me from taking the poison."

*(Where there is despair, let me sow hope…)*

Giulietta leapt up and hugged me.

"It seems that we both have a very great deal for which we must thank you."

***

"And now, there is something else which I must tell you."

"What is that?"

"The feud between your two households is at an end."

"What?" they answered in unison.

"Aye. I had hoped that this might have been brought about by your own marriage, though sadly that did not happen. But it now seems that your two mothers have met together and have made their peace. And—"

"And what?"

I drew a deep breath – I had no idea how they would react to what I was about to tell them.

"Your two cousins, the Lord Benvolio and the Lady Rosaline, have recently married."

I kept my eyes firmly fixed upon Romeo as I spoke. He showed no reaction.

There was silence for a moment. Then Giulietta asked calmly,

"Do they love each other?"

"Aye."

She smiled.

"That is good. I hope that they will be happy together."

Romeo took hold of her hand again.

"If they are half as happy as we are, then they are very fortunate."

"It seems that it happened almost as swiftly as with the two of you," I added.

Romeo smiled, then his face froze.

"Did you say 'the Lord Benvolio'?"

I nodded.

"Since when has Benvolio been a lord?"

Again, I drew a deep breath; again, I had no idea how he might react.

"Since the death of the Lord Montecchi. On his deathbed, he named Benvolio as his heir."

Romeo let out a long sigh.

"I had wondered what he might do about that, after I was exiled."

Now it was my turn to gasp.

"You do not object?"

"Why should I object? Benvolio was older than I. But in any case, I have no claim to the House of Montecchi. It is no longer my home; indeed, I can no longer even use it as my name. And I can never return to Verona—"

"Even if the Prince were to issue you with a pardon?"

"Even then. I will not return without my wife, and to do so would reveal that she is not dead after all. How could we ever explain the deception? That would implicate you also."

"How indeed…" I mused.

Romeo suddenly stiffened.

"You said that my mother is coming hither?"

"She is?" Giulietta asked in surprise. I had forgotten that she had not been present when this had previously been discussed.

I nodded.

"And you said also that our two mothers have now made friends…"

"Yes, but… Holy Saint Francis…!"

I had suddenly realised Romeo's train of thought.

"So how can we prevent my parents from finding out the truth, when the Lady Montecchi returns to Verona?"

Giulietta was genuinely alarmed.

I opened my mouth to answer, then realised, just in time, that I could not yet tell them that Chiara would not be returning to Verona. I was certainly not in a position to tell them the reason for it.

"I will explain everything to her when she arrives, but before she sees you. Do not forget, she has no idea where you are."

"Why is she coming to Venice?"

I hesitated.

"I do not know for certain," I answered carefully. "Nor do I know

228

exactly when she is expected, nor for how long she is intending to stay. But it seems that she came from here originally."

"Indeed?"

I had sometimes wondered if Chiara had ever told Romeo of this. His surprised reaction suggested that she had not.

"Aye. On hearing that I too would soon be returning hither, she asked if she might visit me whilst she is here. I understand that she will send word to me at the friary when she arrives."

"Does she not know, then, that you are no longer a friar?" Romeo asked.

"There are very few people in Verona who know that I am no longer a friar," I answered, carefully and noncomittally. "And that is how I prefer it should remain. But if your mother sends word to the friary, the message will be sent on to me here."

As we returned to the house, I reflected – not for the first time – how necessary it is to have a very good memory if one is to maintain a convincing deception.

And oh, how I longed for the day when I no longer needed to conceal the truth…

***

It was a little over two weeks later that the message was delivered to the palazzo that the Lady Montecchi was staying at the nearby Convent of the Poor Clares.

Accordingly, I presented myself at the door of the Convent and asked if I might see her. But I was totally unprepared for the reception which I received. Whereas previously I had had the advantage of a monastic habit (which, as I have previously remarked, had the ability to open up all manner of locked doors), on this occasion I was attired in my new incarnation as a nobleman. And this, it transpired, imposed all manner of hitherto-unknown restrictions.

First of all, the outer gate of the Convent remained firmly locked whilst I was interrogated through a spyhole. I was asked (none too politely, I might add) if the Lady Montecchi was expecting me to call. On being assured that she was, the elderly and stony-faced sister grudgingly drew back several bolts and admitted me to the courtyard, but then firmly instructed me to remain exactly where I was, whilst she summoned one of the novices to go and find the Lady Montecchi and to escort her downstairs.

As I waited for Chiara to appear, I began mentally rehearsing how I might reasonably converse with her (and, in particular, convey to her the important message about Romeo and Giulietta), if we were forced to endure the constant presence of an unsympathetic chaperone. Out of the corner of my eye I surreptitiously studied the grey and wrinkled face surrounded by the wimple and veil. Under what circumstances, I wondered, had this woman entered this Convent? Had she been a foundling like Fra' Gianni? Or a young woman who had been unlucky in love? Or another example of what Fra' Roberto had described as "surplus progeny"? Whatever the reason, here was someone for whom the cloister was clearly a prison rather than a home. I searched my memories of my time as a friar for a recollection any monastic, of either sex, who had appeared as openly miserable as this poor lady. I found, thankfully, that I could call none to mind.

I was recalled to the present by the sight of Chiara approaching across the courtyard.

"My Lord!"

Her evident surprise at my changed appearance was swiftly disguised by her bowing her head and dropping a low curtsey.

"My Lady!" I returned her formal greeting and bowed. "It is good to see you again. I trust you are now recovered from your journey?"

"I am indeed, thank you, My Lord. And I have brought you a letter from my nephew."

As she rose to her feet she handed me a piece of paper; I recognised the handwriting as that of Benvolio.

This letter, whatever it contained, appeared finally to convince the elderly sister that my intentions in visiting the Lady Montecchi might, after all, not be of a wholly dishonourable nature. But although she appeared to relax slightly, she still showed no inclination to leave us alone together.

Once again racking my brains about how I could tell Chiara about Romeo and Giulietta, I suddenly realised that the problem had in fact provided its own solution – and indeed a compelling reason for my having called on her at all.

"My Lady," I declared, "I have news of your son."

Chiara's face brightened as her eyes met my own.

"You do, My Lord?"

"Aye. He is staying here in Venice as my guest."

She gasped.

"May I see him?"

"Of course. Please, may I escort you to the palazzo?"

"That would be an honour, My Lord."

I offered Chiara my arm. The elderly sister, her face expressionless, silently drew back the bolts on the heavy outer gate and released us into the street outside.

Once we were free of the confines of the Convent, and out of the earshot of its gloomy inmate, we were at last able to converse without restriction.

"Is he truly here?"

"Aye. But there is something you must first know, ere you see him."

She gasped in alarm.

"What? Is he hurt?"

"Nay, he is very well and very happy," I hastened to reassure her. "But much has happened since you saw him last."

I drew a deep breath and produced his letter from my pocket.

"Please, read this. It will tell you much, but not everything..."

\*\*\*

Chiara handed back the letter to me with a trembling hand.

"How did you come by this?"

"He gave it to me himself, after your husband had died. It was never delivered; he asked me to dispose of it as I thought fit."

"And is it true?"

I nodded.

"Why did you not tell me of this ere now?"

Her eyes were wet, though there was no tone of accusation in her voice.

"For two reasons. Firstly, it is not the whole story – there is more which you need to know ere you see him. And then, the second reason will become apparent."

"Please, then, tell me the rest."

"First of all, Giulietta was not dead."

Chiara gasped.

231

"So why—"

"Her father had promised her in marriage to the Count Paris. She faked her death so that she would be able to avoid the second marriage, and then escape with Romeo to Mantua."

"How?"

"I had given her a sleeping potion which would cause her to appear to be dead, for a period of around thirty hours. On the day when she should have married the Count Paris, she was discovered apparently dead. The plan was that she would be laid to rest in her family's vault, and when she awoke, Romeo would be there to take her away. But my letter to Romeo, advising him of our plan, never reached him; instead, he heard only from Balthasar that Giulietta had died."

Chiara gasped again.

"How, then, did he survive?"

"I went to the vault alone, to await the time when Giulietta would awaken from her trance. It was whilst I was there that Romeo arrived."

"And had he brought – poison…?"

"Aye. I know not what it was, for it was a liquid which I have never encountered, before or since. But it had a strange odour – bitter almonds. Truth to say, the mere sight and scent of it was sufficient to make my flesh crawl. I have no doubt that had he taken it, it would indeed have done its work very quickly…"

She shuddered.

"What happened next?" she asked after a few moments.

"I explained the escape plan to him, and together the two of us waited until Giulietta awoke. Then I hid them both at my cell for the rest of that day, and at nightfall they left and fled together to Mantua. They stayed there, under assumed names, for a short while, then I arranged for them to come to Venice."

Chiara was silent as she absorbed the full import of what I had said.

"So – was that why you could not tell me where he was?" she asked eventually.

I nodded.

"Giulietta was officially dead. We could not risk the danger of her being discovered."

"And – is Giulietta also here in Venice?" Chiara asked slowly.

"Aye."

"And are they happy?"

I smiled.

"Come and see them, and decide for yourself!"

She relaxed and returned the smile.

"Very well, My Lord – please escort me to your house, so that I may meet my new daughter-in-law!"

\*\*\*

The emotional reunion took place in the gardens of the palazzo. Romeo and Chiara embraced tearfully. Giulietta stood respectfully to one side, until Romeo took her hand and presented her formally to his mother.

Giulietta gave a deep curtsey.

"My Lady Lucia. I am honoured to meet you at last."

Chiara helped her to her feet and embraced her warmly.

"Please, we are members of the same family now. So – no formality. My name is Chiara."

Romeo gasped.

"Mother? I had always thought that your name was Lucia!"

Chiara smiled.

"Lucia was the name which the Lord Montecchi called me. It seems that his first wife, who had died many years earlier, had also been called Chiara. It did not seem appropriate. We decided on Lucia because the two names are very similar in meaning."

This story was news to me. If Chiara was inventing it in order to cover her momentary slip of the tongue, she was doing so with great conviction. I almost believed it myself.

Romeo, on learning that his mother had lodgings at the Convent, drew me to one side and asked if a room could be prepared for her at the palazzo.

"Of course, if she wishes to stay here."

It was necessary, for the sake of appearances, to extend a formal invitation – although I already knew in advance what Chiara's response would be. Accordingly, the housekeeper was instructed to prepare a suitable chamber for Her Ladyship, whilst Chiara and I returned to the Convent to collect her possessions.

As before, I was forced to observe the rule stating that all males (other than priests and monks) were prohibited from entering most of the Convent's precincts. As I waited in the courtyard for Chiara to bring her luggage down from her room, I asked the elderly sister if I might speak with the Guest-Mistress.

"That is me, My Lord," she answered stiffly.

"Forgive me, madam, I had not realised." I answered. "Please, as a token of my gratitude for your hospitality to my dear friend, accept this small contribution to the Convent's funds."

Her basilisk face expressed surprise, then softened a little.

"Thank you, My Lord. You are most generous."

"Please, think nothing of it."

I too have been in your position, I thought. I know only too well how it is to have to rely entirely on the charity of others.

*(It is in giving that we receive…)*

As we made our way back to the palazzo, Chiara remarked,

"I think that Giulietta and I will be great friends. It seems to me that we have much in common!"

"What do you mean?"

Chiara's eyes flashed.

"Can you not guess? Here is a girl who has been prepared to sacrifice everything – even to the extent of faking her own death – for the sake of the man she loves. Does that not remind you of someone else?"

I grinned.

"I seem to recall someone, almost twenty years ago, in this very city…"

\*\*\*

Back at the palazzo, I remembered that I had not yet opened the letter from Benvolio.

*Fra' Lorenzo,*

*Thank you for the letter which you left for me before you left Verona. It now transpires that my aunt is also returning to Venice, so I am entrusting this letter to her in the hope that she will find a means of delivering it to you.*

*I too am sorry that we were not able to make our farewells in person. I shall miss you very much, but I have already made the better acquaintance of your friend and colleague Fra' Gianni. He is, as you yourself have indicated, a great and good man and will be a worthy successor to you.*

*My new wife and I are extremely happy together, and Verona is once again a peaceful city. For both of these I am very thankful.*

*My only sadness is that I still have no knowledge of what has happened to my dear cousin. If news should ever reach you of what might have befallen him, please write and tell me. Even to be told the worst would, I believe, be easier to accept than this dreadful uncertainty.*

*I wish you every happiness and success in your new life in Venice.*

*Benvolio Montecchi*

I read and re-read the letter several times. As I perused the final paragraph, a seed of an idea planted itself in my mind, and slowly began to grow...

I rose, folded up Benvolio's letter, and went to find Chiara.

\*\*\*

Later, as the four of us were seated at the dinner table, I drew a deep breath and turned towards Romeo.

"Are you happy here in Venice?"

"Of course!" He seemed surprised at the question. "Why do you ask?"

"Would you be happy to live here for the rest of your life?"

Romeo gasped.

"What do you mean?"

I handed over Benvolio's letter.

"Read this, both of you."

"I do not understand," Romeo said as he handed it back to me. "What does this have to do with what you have just asked me?"

By way of answer, I produced Romeo's own letter to the Lord Montecchi.

"This is what so nearly happened," I said gently. "Thankfully, it did not. But if it were to be generally presumed that this is in fact what did happen..."

235

Giulietta's eyes widened.

"You mean…?"

"Aye," I nodded. "After all, Giulietta, you can never return to Verona in any case, as there you are already officially dead. If, then, the story were to be put out that Romeo had also died at your side, then that would mean that the two of you could truly begin a whole new life here, with new names, and with no fear of future discovery."

Giulietta reached across and took hold of Romeo's hand. Romeo remained very still, staring fixedly at the table. Finally, he raised his head and turned to Chiara.

"Mother, what do you think?"

"The Count and I have already spoken together of this," she answered. "In my view, I believe that this would be an ideal solution."

Romeo turned back to his wife.

"What do you say, my love?"

Giulietta squeezed his hand.

"My sweet, I am still overwhelmed at the thought that you would be prepared to die rather than to face life without me. And if that should eventually be how Verona will remember you, then I shall be very happy."

Romeo sat in silence for a moment, then looked up at me.

"Very well," he declared finally. "So be it."

I nodded.

"I will write to Benvolio this evening."

"Would it not also be appropriate to inform the Prince?" Chiara asked.

"I had not thought of that," I answered truthfully. "But yes, I believe it would."

***

Later that evening, I installed myself in my father's old study, mentally assumed my former identity as a friar, and set about composing what was to become the official final chapter of Romeo's story.

It proved to be far more challenging than I had imagined, for I realised there was much that I still needed to conceal. Eventually, after almost an hour, I had finally written what I hoped would serve:

236

*My Lord Prince,*

*I trust that this letter finds you in good health.*

*Since my return to Venice, I have recently been sent, by an unknown hand, a letter which I believe you should see; accordingly, I enclose herewith a copy of the text of it. I am unable to explain by what means this letter came into my hands, but I have no doubts whatsoever as to its authenticity.*

*The letter was evidently written by young Romeo Montecchi to his father, on the day of the tragic death of the Lady Giulietta Capuleti. I do not know – nor do I now have any means of ascertaining – if the Lord Montecchi ever received this letter before his own untimely death only a few days later.*

*As you will see from Romeo's letter, he writes that he and the Lady Giulietta had, on the previous day, been secretly married. This much I can confirm, for I conducted the clandestine ceremony myself. I did so in the hope that the union of these two young lovers might finally bring about the reconciliation of their warring families. I most earnestly beg your pardon that I was not able to reveal this fact to you previously; however, I was at the time sworn to absolute secrecy. And as you well know, this hope of reconciliation was all too soon dashed by the tragic events which took place later that same day.*

*Please also forgive me for having to impart such sad tidings, at a time when Verona is now a peaceful and happy city.*

*In D.no,*
*Fra' Lorenzo*

The letter to Benvolio was, if anything, even more difficult. How much, or how little, should I tell him?

*Benvolio,*

*Thank you for your letter, which your aunt has now delivered to me.*

*I am pleased to learn that you and your dear wife are well and happy. But sadly I must now ask you to prepare yourself for some bad news.*

*I have recently received tidings that your cousin Romeo is dead. It seems that he had died by his own hand following the tragic death of the Lady Giulietta, to whom he had recently been secretly married.*

*Please accept my deepest sympathy in your loss, which I too feel very strongly. My thoughts and prayers are with you at this sad time.*

Until that point, I had had no idea just how frighteningly easy it is to tell a convincing lie, when one knows that one is in a position of absolute trust.

I laid aside my quill, sealed the letters and wandered miserably downstairs in search of company. Romeo and Giulietta had already retired for the night, but Chiara was sitting reading in a corner of the drawing room, evidently waiting for me. She looked tired, but leapt up at my approach.

"Is it done?"

"Aye, my love."

She smiled and held out her arms.

\*\*\*

The following morning, whilst Romeo and Giulietta went for their usual morning walk in the city, I made my way to the friary and asked to speak in private with Fra' Roberto.

"Greetings, My Lord!"

"Greetings to you, my ghostly father! But no formality! Please call me Lorenzo."

"As you wish! I trust you are well?"

"I am, thank you."

"I am glad to hear it. How may I assist you?"

"I have two requests, Fra' Roberto. First, please could I ask that these two letters be despatched to Verona?"

"Of course. And what is the second request?"

I hesitated.

"Please forgive me if what I am about to say sounds strange – or even incredible."

Fra' Roberto smiled.

"I have heard many strange and incredible things during my lifetime, Lorenzo. I very much doubt that what you are about to say is the strangest of them! Please, tell me more."

He settled back in his chair and gestured me towards the other.

I sat down and relaxed a little.

"Do you recall, Fra' Roberto, my telling you that I had once been in love?"

"I do indeed. It was during the talk we had on the day after your father's death. What of it?"

"I – I – I have now met the lady again."

Fra' Roberto's face was expressionless.

"And do you find that you still have feelings for her?" he asked laconically.

"I do. And so, it seems, does she for me."

"I see." He paused, then continued in a more formal tone, "Do you wish for me to hear your confession, My Lord?"

I suddenly realised his train of thought.

"Nay, my ghostly father," I answered hastily. "The lady, although she had previously been married, is now a widow. And I am come to ask you if you will consent to marry us."

Fra' Roberto smiled and sighed with relief.

"It would be an honour, Lorenzo. When do you wish for this marriage to take place?"

I looked at him steadily.

"We wish only for a very simple and quiet ceremony. Are you available this afternoon?"

\*\*\*

When the four of us reassembled for luncheon, I asked Romeo and Giulietta if they had any plans for the remainder of the day.

Romeo shook his head.

"Why do you ask?"

"Can you spare an hour of your time this afternoon?"

"Aye; for what?"

"To attend a wedding."

They blinked.

"Whose?"

I reached across the table and took Chiara's hand.

"Ours."

Giulietta's knife clattered to the floor. Romeo's jaw dropped and he stared at his mother in disbelief.

"But – but –"

"But what?" Chiara asked gently.

Romeo said nothing, but continued to stare at us, open-mouthed.

"Do not look so taken aback," I added. "Love is not confined to the young. And you two are not the only ones who can fall in love very quickly."

Chiara caught my eye and shot me a brief conspiratorial smile.

"And Romeo, as you will thus become legally my stepson, I intend to adopt you formally as my heir. Provided, of course, that you consent to assume the name of Da Porto."

Romeo found his voice at last.

"You never cease to amaze us, Lorenzo. How many other surprises do you have in store?"

Only one, I thought sadly, as I carefully avoided his mother's eye.

***

*"Ego conjugo vos in matrimonium, in nomine Patris, Filii et Spiritus Sancti…"*

***

As one, we were roused us into consciousness by the song of the lark.

"Good morrow, My Lady!"

"Good morrow, My Lord!" Chiara returned my kiss.

"Tell me, my love," I murmured sleepily into her ear, "Why did you never have any other children with the Lord Montecchi?"

She blinked against the morning sunlight, raised herself up from the pillow and looked down into my eyes.

"Can you not guess?"

"Nay."

"It is because we…" Chiara hesitated, then continued shyly, "we did not have that kind of marriage."

"What?" I gasped, now fully awake.

Chiara nodded.

"Our union was based upon companionship. And do not forget, my love, that Luigi's first wife had died in childbirth. I truly believe that, even after I had survived having given birth to Romeo, Luigi was

240

afraid to take the risk that it might happen again."

"So you never…"

She shook her head wistfully, but her eyes shone.

"Never. We never even shared a room, let alone a bed. I have remained wholly true to you, my love, ever since the day I left Venice."

\*\*\*

In the fifteen years which have elapsed since those events, the four of us have lived happily together in the palazzo in Venice. During that time Romeo and Giulietta have been blessed with three fine sons. In deference to an old-established custom of the Montecchi family, which decreed that the eldest son should be named for his paternal grandfather, their first-born was baptised Luigi.

Chiara did, however, prevail upon them to give him the second name of Sebastiano.

Their second and third sons were named, respectively, Mercutio and Benvolio.

This happy state of affairs continued until the time when, less than a year since, Chiara was suddenly taken from us. Her loss was felt terribly by all whom she left behind, though we were all thankful that her end had been swift and peaceful, and that she had been spared from prolonged suffering, or from the feebleness which comes with advancing years.

I never discovered what had become of Filippo. Emilio said that he had heard a report that he had died, of some unknown affliction, in Sorrento. But that story has never been confirmed, and now I do not imagine that I will ever know for certain. But whatever became of my brother, I hope with all my heart that he was happy in the life he had chosen.

But during the past few months, I have become aware that the consumption which once claimed the life of my uncle has now also ensnared me in its ugly and vice-like grip. With Fra' Pietro's faithful assistance I have fought it for many years, using medicines which treat the symptoms (if not the cause) of my affliction. I know that by continuing thus, I could probably delay my demise for a little longer. But, truth to tell, I have no wish to do so. I have had a good and a happy life, and I am not afraid of dying.

241

But be that as it may, I find that I cannot take my leave of this world with a truth left untold. For that reason, and knowing that my days on this earth are now every one of them numbered, I have now decided to set down this tale.

Romeo, you already know those elements of this story in which you were directly involved. But now I dare to hope that by telling you more of the details of which you have previously been in ignorance, you will thereafter be better placed to understand fully why I acted as I did.

Only two people ever knew the whole truth about your parentage: your mother and me. The Lord Montecchi, although he was fully aware that you were not his own son, never knew of your real father's true identity. And I promised both of them that I would never shatter your illusion that the man whom you had always called "Father" was ever anything other than precisely that. The deaths of the Lord Montecchi and of your dear mother have, in one respect, released me from that promise, but I will nonetheless honour their wishes during what little remains of my own lifetime.

But you will doubtless by now have realised what it is that I have yearned, for so long, to be able to tell you: that I am not merely your ghostly father, nor (as I have been for the past fifteen years) your stepfather, but also your earthly father. Your entitlement to succeed me as the next Conte Da Porto comes not only from your position as my stepson and my legally-named heir, but also from your own direct bloodline.

And that honourable bloodline will, after you, be continued by my three grandsons. Though I must own that the irony of Luigi's given name has not been lost, on either me or your mother!

As for young Mercutio and Benvolio, I have left provision that they should each receive a modest income from the Da Porto estate, to enable them to train for whatever professions they choose. Though if either of them should find that they wish to enter holy orders, I make only one condition to that: that they must do so of their own free will.

Romeo, I am fiercely proud of you, and I am truly sorry that I have never been able to acknowledge you publicly as my own flesh and blood. And I fervently hope that you will find it in your heart to forgive me for having deceived you for so long.

I will now entrust this manuscript to Emilio, and give him

instructions that he should hand it to you after I am gone.

I am not afeared of death, for I know that your dear mother – who was the love of my life in the same way that your dear Giulietta has been the love of yours – will be waiting for me in the hereafter. And as the great Saint Francis himself declared: It is in dying that we are born to eternal life.

*Noctem quiétam, et finem perféctum concédat mihi Dóminus omnípotens.*

May the Lord Almighty grant me a quiet night and a perfect end.

My son, live and be prosperous.

Your loving father,
Sebastiano Lorenzo Da Porto

*"Happy birthday Grandpa!"*

*His face lit up.*

*"Have you done it?"*

*I handed him a bulging A4 ring-binder. He laid aside his card from the Queen, and took it from me as though it were the Holy Grail.*

*"Well – what's in it?"*

*I grinned.*

*"You'll find out when you read it! But can I ask you something? You remember that you mentioned an Italian connection?"*

*"Yes…"*

*"Does the name of Da Porto mean anything to you?"*

*He frowned for a moment as he thought, then slowly nodded.*

*"Yes. I found some mention of the name in my grandfather's family on his mother's side. I think they came originally from Venice, or somewhere around there. Why?"*

*"Can you remember how far back it goes?"*

*"Not precisely, at least not without looking it up – but quite a long way. Off the top of my head I would guess probably sometime in the 1500s. Why do you want to know?"*

*"It seems to figure in this book. I wouldn't want to spoil your surprise – but I think you'll find that it's worth waiting for."*

\*\*\*

*So had the "official" story of Romeo and Juliet, as so famously portrayed by Shakespeare, in fact been nothing more than an extremely elaborate cover-up?*

*I vaguely remembered, from the dim and distant past when I'd been studying the play at school, having been told that the idea for the plot had not, originally, been Shakespeare's own. He had apparently based it on an earlier (and much less well-known) account of the same story, which some believe might even have had its basis in fact. I was, by now, sufficiently intrigued to try to track down the original source.*

*Thanks to the wonders of Google, it didn't take very long. It appears that* The Tragical History of Romeus and Juliet *had previously been chronicled in 1562 in a long (and frankly rather tedious) poem by a man called Arthur Brooke, and that this poem had been Shakespeare's primary source when he had been writing the play. But even this had not been the original; it transpired that there had been several other (even earlier) versions of the story. A bit more research revealed that the earliest of these accounts was entitled* Historia novellamente ritrovata di due nobili amanti *(A Newly Discovered Story of Two Noble Lovers). This story also told of how Juliet had awoken in the tomb to find Romeo dead beside her, and had, to use her own words, "ended [her] own life then and there." It had first appeared some time around 1530, and was written by someone called – wait for it – Count Luigi Da Porto.*

*Is it too much of a coincidence that this is the same name (according to Lorenzo's manuscript) as that of Romeo and Giulietta's eldest son?*

\*\*\*

…For I will raise her statue in pure gold,
That while Verona by that name is known,
There shall no figure at such rate be set
As that of true and faithful Juliet.

*The statue is not, in fact, "pure gold", but bronze. And it was not raised by Lord Montague, but is a twentieth-century tourist attraction – as is the small courtyard in which it stands, adjacent to the so-called "Casa di Giulietta" on Verona's bustling Via Cappello.*

*The walls of the passageway leading from the street into the courtyard are covered from top to bottom with swirling multicoloured graffiti. The courtyard itself is unpleasantly crowded, and many of the visitors look and sound as though they have travelled halfway round the world for the privilege of being able to stand here and gawp. Most of them have formed a disorderly queue to be photographed with the statue whilst groping her in a totally inappropriate way. For some bizarre reason, this is believed to bring good luck to the groper.*

*Meanwhile, on the tiny balcony high above the courtyard, a girl is standing declaiming something in a language I don't recognise. The only word I can understand is "Romeo," which she repeats three times. Presumably it is her native tongue's equivalent of "Romeo, Romeo, wherefore art thou Romeo?"*

*Sorry, Will. I'm sure this is never what you envisaged, much less what you intended, when you first penned the story of the star-crossed lovers.*

*But the interior of the house is tastefully decorated and pleasantly cool and quiet, and although the attraction is a modern invention, it is not difficult to imagine how the Capuleti family might have lived. A window on the top floor overlooks the balcony and the crowded courtyard, and as I gaze down at the statue of my world-famous namesake, I cannot suppress a small frisson of excitement at the thought that I now know something which nobody else here knows: that **perhaps this is not what really happened**.*

*Returning to the ground floor I fight my way through the crowds and out into the Via Cappello – none too soon, for three more huge groups, each led by a diminutive guide brandishing an enormous brightly-coloured umbrella, are making their way towards the house. Struggling against the tide I finally reach the refreshing space of the Piazza Brà, flanked along one side by the vast Roman Arena. It is the middle of the opera season, and posters outside advertise tonight's performance: Gounod's* Roméo et Juliette.

*I make my way across the square to the Brà gate. Beyond this is the road which leads towards Mantua – the route the fugitives would have taken.*

*A much smaller and more select group has gathered here, to admire the tasteful bronze bust of Shakespeare which sits discreetly in a corner by the huge arched portal. Alongside, in English and Italian, are inscribed the words which Shakespeare gave to Romeo when he was given the news of his banishment:*

There is no world without Verona walls
But purgatory, torture, hell itself,
Hence banishèd is banished from the world,
And world's exile is death.

*Standing here, somehow I feel much closer to the lovers.*

*I can't help feeling what a great shame it was that Lorenzo (or should I call him Sebastiano?) was never able to tell Romeo the truth face to face.*

*And how sad it was that because Romeo never knew the whole story whilst Lorenzo was still alive, they both missed out on so much. But then, when I come to think about it more seriously, I find that somehow I can't ever imagine the two of them having what Star Wars fans would probably call "a Darth Vader moment."*

*And I must admit to being amazed that Lorenzo managed to fight consumption for so long. What on earth could have been in that medicine? Just as with the famous sleeping draught, I don't suppose we'll ever know.*

*As an extra gift for Grandpa, I'd hoped to be able to trace back through the original Venetian church records and try to link up the top end of his family tree with the Luigi Da Porto who wrote the first version of the Romeo & Juliet story. But after going along endless blind alleys and hacking my way through mountains of Italian red tape, I've now, sadly, had to file that one under "Too Difficult."*

*So, just as it has been with Black Bart, so it will be with Romeo and Juliet; it doesn't look as though we'll ever succeed in proving the connection definitely one way or the other. But perhaps it's better that way. It would be a great shame to allow hard facts to get in the way of a good (and much more satisfying) theory.*

*But whichever account of the story is the correct one – no offence, Will, but I think that on the whole (at least in terms of outcome), I prefer Lorenzo's version.*

# THE END

# Fantastic Books
# Great Authors

Meet our authors and discover our exciting range:

- Gripping Thrillers
- Cosy Mysteries
- Romantic Chick-Lit
- Fascinating Historicals
- Exciting Fantasy
- Young Adult and Children's Adventures

Visit us at:
**www.crookedcatbooks.com**

Join us on facebook:
**www.facebook.com/crookedcatpublishing**

Lightning Source UK Ltd.
Milton Keynes UK
UKOW05f0323210114

224966UK00001B/10/P